THE MAN SHE MADE

Sarah Deuchar

Contents

prologue

H ertfordshire, England
  1802

What was this pain?

It felt as though iron rods were puncturing his stomach over and over. He was so tired and so weak. His limbs did not want to perform normal actions. He could not remember the last time he had tasted food. It could have been weeks. His gums hurt and bled. He felt as though he was rotting from the inside out. His mouth was dryer than sand and his lips were cracked and scabbed. His staggered, raspy breathing was only making this worse. He had become so thin that his bones protruded everywhere, and his once thick, curly black hair had begun to thin and fall out.

Cassian Kensington was starving, and was the poorest of poor men. He had not a penny to his name, with nothing but lint in his moth-eaten pockets.

While he was not born into poverty, it had soon found him. Cassian was born the son of a blacksmith and his wife. But an accident had claimed his father's life only three years later, and what little money that had was quickly taken in rent.

Out of utter desperation, and on the brink of starvation, Cassian's poor mother had turned to the entertainment profession. Cast out of their village in shame, Cassian and his mother lived in appalling conditions while his mother entertained strange gentlemen.

"Just you wait here, and you may choose whatever you like for supper tonight."

Cassian remembered her telling him that over and over as she left him in strange rooms, and on strange corners, or alleys, while she went away to do business. He remembered standing on street corners, only a small child, and watching the rich walk by him. They had such fine coats and hats. But they did not see him.

He quickly learned that the rich preferred not to notice the poor.

His poor mother suffered in those conditions. She wasted away, eventually dying from typhoid fever when Cassian was only ten years old.

Cassian had been on his own for twelve years. As a dirty, skinny, young street urchin, work was scarce, and impossible to find. As he grew older, he had hoped to find an apprenticeship, but no master would even consider him when they had older, burlier, stronger boys from families to choose from.

Every so often vicars would take pity on him, and find him odd jobs to do for a penny now and then, but steady work was virtually impossible for him to secure.

Despite his poverty, Cassian had never resorted to thievery. He had seen men in his similar situation hung for stealing, and sentenced to seven years transportation for poaching. No matter how hungry he was, he had never poached, and never stolen, not even a loaf of bread.

Though now, lying half dead on the side of the road as he was, a loaf of bread, stolen or not, would have made him feel like the richest man alive.

He was dying. He could feel it. Cassian's eyelids were heavy as he laid his head down on the ground next to the road. The grassy mounds beside the gravel road were comfortable.

As good a place as any for the death of a man like him. A man who mattered to no-one.

Would anyone find him before the animals made a meal out of him? Would anyone care? Would he have a burial? A grave? Would he be remembered?

Cassian knew his death would not affect a soul on this earth. He would die at the ripe old age of twenty-two without having lived. His position in life having given him the death sentence years ago.

Had he had the strength to cry out in anger, he would have. Cassian had never been given a chance! Not one! He had never been given the opportunity to prove himself, to be able to make a contribution to society.

No woman had ever looked upon him with anything except disgust when he had been in their way. He could never have dreamed to find a woman to love, and one who might love him in return.

Please, he willed in silence, please, I want to live.

In the distance, he faintly heard the sound of hooves on the road. A carriage was coming. Using whatever strength he had left, Cassian lifted his head ever so slightly.

There was a fine carriage travelling along the road towards him. The finest he had ever seen. All those years wandering the streets of London and he had never seen a finer carriage. Four strong horses pulled the carriage, and their hooves thundered against the road. As the carriage drew nearer, he felt the vibration in the earth.

Please, he prayed, I am here. I am alive. Please help me.

But he knew there was no point in hoping. A rich man would never stop to help a poor one. They would not sully their clean hands with the likes of him.

But he heard a voice, a lovely, female voice, cry out, "Stop the carriage!"

The driver immediately pulled on the reins and the horses skidded to a stop.

Cassian squinted up at the carriage as the window in the door dropped down and a face appeared.

An angel. She was an angel! Was he dead? He had to be. An angel was before him. Was this carriage the vessel that was to take him to heaven?

A white gloved hand appeared on the door as she opened it and climbed out gracefully. She wore an exquisite gown, the colour of the sky, and the softness of the fabric touched his bare arm as she knelt down in the dirt beside him. Her brown hair was perfectly pinned and curled, though a rebellious tendril had fallen across her forehead. Her skin was the colour of porcelain, so perfectly smooth and delicate. There was a slight flush to her cheeks and her soft, full lips were parted slightly.

But the angel's eyes were what captivated him. The brown colour reminded him of the extraordinary confection windows he had seen in London, of the chocolate he had always longed to taste. The concern in her eyes was something he had never seen before. Nobody had ever looked upon him with anything but disgust or pity. The angel was kind.

Cassian was grateful God had sent his most beautiful angel to collect him.

"Don' touch 'im, ma'am," grunted the driver, though Cassian barely heard him. "You don' know what crawlers he's carryin'."

"Oh, hush," warned the angel, "can you not see that this poor man needs my help?" The angel placed her gloved hand on the side of his cheek. Cassian willed his eyes to stay open, to see her beautiful face for as long as he could. "Oh, you poor thing. What must have happened to you?" Her face turned to her driver. "Mr Carne, fetch me the water from inside. I have some biscuits, too. Bring them," she instructed.

The driver must have obeyed, as within moments the angel was trying to help him sit up to eat. The angel's arm was around him, supporting him, and he could feel her soft hair on his cheek. She had a sweet scent, something floral that reminded him of spring time.

"Here, drink," she urged, bringing the cool metal of a flask to his lips.

Cassian could not remember the last time he had tasted clean water. He usually drank from whatever pool of water he came across. The water soothed his parched throat, and was welcome relief on his bloodied and chapped lips.

Next the angel was feeding him the most incredible sugared biscuits. They melted in his mouth but his stomach hurt as it received its first food in an age. It hurt to chew, but the nourishment was more important.

"We need to go, ma'am," urged the angel's driver.

"One minute," replied the angel. "He must eat."

"Ma'am, he's just an urchin. Ain't nothin' you can do for 'im. He's half dead already. Just look at 'im!"

Cassian watched as the angel pressed her lips together firmly. "He is not just an urchin, Mr Carne. He is important to somebody." The angel brushed her white glove over his forehead, pushing away some of his matted, curly dark hair, and she smiled her angelic smile. "And I am familiar with the feeling of desperation. What is your name?" she asked him. "I can write to your family if you wish."

With moisture returned to his mouth, he managed to reply, "No family, ma'am, and my name is Cassian. Cassian Kensington."

"I am glad we met, Mr Kensington. My name is -"

"Ma'am, we need to go!" her driver urged more forcefully.

The angel regretfully nodded. "I am afraid Mr Carne is right, Mr Kensington. It is essential for me to reach my destination by sundown." She looked truly regretful. "This," she said, holding up the flask, "is made of silver. You will fetch a fine price for it." She then dug her delicate hand into the pocket of her dress and pulled out a coin purse. "Take this as well," she insisted. She pushed the heavy coin purse into his hand.

Cassian barely had the strength to hold it. "Ma'am, no..." he said weakly.

"Yes," she insisted. "You will take this." She then removed the glove on her right hand. Her hands were so delicate and dainty, and residing on her ring finger was a beautiful jewelled ring. Cassian had never seen anything so valuable up close. "And this," she decided, removing the ring and placing it in the coin purse for safekeeping. "You will take this, too."

"Why?" Cassian struggled to ask.

As the angel slipped her glove back onto her hand, she smiled at him. "I have good intuition about people, Mr Kensington. You are a good man who just needs a little help. You will take this money and you will make something of yourself. I have faith in you."

The angel knew nothing about him. Why would she show him this kindness? He could have been a criminal for all she knew. "How can I ever thank you?" Cassian rasped.

"Thank me by living a better life." She placed her hand on his cheek once more. "I know what it is to be desperate, but yours is a far greater need than mine." The angel got to her feet and brushed the dirt off of her skirt. "There is a village, that way, not a half mile. Rest a little, and when you have your strength, you will find a bed and a meal there."

"May I have your name, ma'am?" He needed to know who to thank in his prayers. This angel deserved eternal blessings or her kindness.

As she climbed back into her carriage, she turned back to look at him once more. "I suppose you may call me Faith." She smiled warmly. "Good luck, Mr Kensington. May we meet again."

The angel, Faith, was taken away in the carriage, and Cassian was left on the side of the road richer than he could have ever imagined.

CHAPTER 1

London, England
1805

"It has been an absolute pleasure, gentlemen," boasted Cassian as he collected his winnings from his weekly card game.

Henry Weatherby groaned as he tossed a number of bank notes onto the table. "You always have the best luck, Kensington."

Cassian chuckled as he collected the money. "I suppose I have just developed a good intuition for people. I can call a bluff."

"Intuition, my arse," swore Geoffrey Hounslow. "Just bloody lucky," he muttered as he too paid what he owed.

"Well, gentleman, my wife expected me home hours ago so I had best be off to face the music," murmured Percy Townsend.

"Townsend, how about you stop fretting about getting in trouble like you are a little schoolgirl and stay for a whiskey. Have a little fun," teased Cassian. Cassian snapped his fingers to summon the servant that was attending their table at the club. The servant appeared instantly and Cassian ordered a bottle of their most expensive ale.

Townsend frowned and looked down at Cassian. "This is gambling, Kensington, not fun. While my wife might be demanding,

I still would rather please her than you." Townsend paid what he owed and left them.

"Can you believe him?" Cassian asked Weatherby and Hounslow.

Weatherby laughed. "You will understand when you marry, Kensington."

"Yes, you are still a baby in comparison to us," added Hounslow.

"Marry? I have no time to marry," rebuffed Cassian.

"No, but plenty of time to fool around while flashing your dashing smile at every giggling young girl you come across." Weatherby raised a disapproving brow. "Perhaps a wife would do you some good. But alas, I must follow Townsend. My wife awaits me, as well."

"Goodnight, Kensington," said Hounslow, "until next week."

Just as his friends had left, the servant returned with the bottle of whiskey. Not wanting the ale to go to waste, he poured himself a generous glass.

Cassian did not know whether Townsend, Weatherby, and Hounslow were really his friends. They were rich men. Cassian was a rich man. Were not rich men supposed to associate with each other, gamble, and complain about their women? Cassian did not have a woman, but he had plenty of money to gamble with.

Cassian was one of the richest men in London. In just under three years, he had made himself a fortune that meant he was the envy of every man in the city, and the desire of every woman.

Cassian had been fortunate in a speculation that had benefitted him nearly a thousand pounds. With that money he had purchased his first factory. Cassian had made his fortune in industry, and was always looking to acquire struggling factories.

He owned seven factories in London, and a dozen more in the north of England. He was responsible for nearly fifteen hundred souls in his factories, which was not a responsibility he took lightly.

Cassian worked hard. He had made something of himself. So when he was not working, he liked to enjoy himself. He indulged on fine clothes, ales, and women. He lived in a luxurious London townhouse and he was quite content.

Cassian finished his whiskey and left the bottle on the table, as well as payment for the servant's services that evening. Perhaps the servants could enjoy the fine ale together. Cassian was suddenly not in the mood to overindulge.

At that moment, a pair of arms wound their way around his waist. The sweet scent of her perfume permeated the air around him. He knew it was Fanny, one of the girls who worked at the club. Fanny was one of the prettiest girls in their employ. Her lovely blonde hair was always perfectly pinned, and she always wore appealing gowns.

"Did you have a nice evening, Mr Kensington?" Fanny whispered.

"I did, thank you," he replied with a smile. He turned around to look at her just as he checked the time on his gold pocket watch. It was nearing midnight. He supposed he ought to return home to bed. "But I have to go home unfortunately." He left her embrace to put in his fine coat.

Fanny sighed impatiently. "But why?" she whined, pouting her full lips.

The sound annoyed him. "I have to work," he replied. "Goodnight, Fanny. I will be back for cards next week." He was due to inspect one of his factories in the morning. His very first factory, actually.

Angel Faith Textiles. It had only seemed right to thank his angel Faith in some way. Perhaps, wherever she was, she might one day walk past the factory and see that it was named for her. Perhaps one day she might even purchase fabric from a dressmaker and see his business name and be reminded.

He owed his life to that woman. He owed everything to her. Wherever she was, he hoped she was alright and he hoped she was proud. He had made something of himself, just as she had asked.

Cassian swiftly left the club, thanking their servant on his way out, and made his way out into the cool London evening. It was nearing the end of October, and there was a real bite to the air.

Cassian's driver, Mr Green, was waiting for him, and opened the door to his carriage promptly. Cassian's carriage was another one of his large purchases. Not an expense was spared on the luxurious interior. Only the best fabrics, panelling, and lighting were installed.

"Home, Mr Kensington?" called Mr Green.

"Yes, home," he replied.

Cassian lived in Kensington. He had selected the area partially as it shared his name, but mostly because of the prestige of the address. He was very proud to own his own home, when only three years earlier he had not owned a pair of shoes.

Cassian's townhouse was large, lavish, and white, and stretched four storeys high. A white set of steps greeted every visitor, and they led up to a navy coloured door. He promptly left his carriage as soon as it had stopped outside his house and he climbed the steps two at a time.

He knew that his household would be in bed, and so he opened the front door himself. Cassian kept a small, but efficient household. His butler, Geoffrey Wade, had essentially educated him on what it was to be rich. He served him, took care of household affairs, and controlled the staff.

Four housemaids took care of the housekeeping, and his cook and kitchen maid kept him eating like a king. He ate something different every night. It was not hard to surprise Cassian as he had very little experience with refined dishes.

His house was filled with all of the things that rich people ought to own. Paintings, sculptures, and varying pieces of furniture that were never really used. He owned a piano that had never been played and his drawing room had never been sat in.

Cassian did not entertain, and he preferred to keep to his study when at home.

Cassian climbed the two flights of stairs up to the third floor. His private quarters, as well as several unused bedrooms, were on the third floor.

Once inside his bedroom, Cassian closed the door, and then proceeded to remove his cravat. He discarded it on the trunk that lay at the end of his bed. He removed the pile of notes that he had won in tonight's card game and quickly counted it.

Sixty pounds.

Such a sum would have made him a rich man three years earlier, but now, sixty pounds felt like pocket change. He placed the money on his bed as he removed his coat, waist jacket, shirt, boots and breeches. He then slipped a nightshirt on over his head and picked up the bank notes again.

Cassian opened the drawer beside his bed and set the notes in there temporarily. He would take them to his study in the morning and record the income. Cassian owned very few personal posses-sions. Of course, he had things, but hardly anything that mattered.

What did matter was in this drawer. His mother's crucifix neck-lace. The first pound he had ever profited. And the little jewelled ring his angel had gifted him three years before.

Cassian reached into the drawer and picked up the ring. He had never had the ring appraised, or looked at by a jeweller, but he knew the stones were real. Three exquisite diamonds sat atop the gold band, sparkling just as much as they had the day his angel had given it to him.

Cassian had never had any inclination to sell it. Not even in the beginning. He had made a promise to himself, and to Faith, three years ago. He would make something of himself, and he would find her. He would show her just what he had done with her money, and he would give the ring back to her.

He put the ring away and climbed into bed. He sighed as he turned down the light in his lamp. His existence was a lonely one, even now. He had friends of a sort, and a household to serve him, and a woman to keep him company now and then, but he was still alone.

Cassian awoke to the sound of his drapes being opened. He squinted and covered his eyes as the sunlight hit his face.

"Good morning, sir," chirped Nancy, one of his housemaids. "Breakfast is served."

"Thank you, Nancy," grumbled Cassian.

Once he had heard his bedroom door close, he threw back the bedclothes and wandered over to his breakfast table. Cassian rarely ate breakfast down in the dining room. He liked to eat quickly before moving on to his study.

Cassian was dedicated to his work, meticulous with his ledgers, and determined to be a success. He had only recently returned from a trip up north to inspect his factories there. He liked to be well informed of the goings on, the workers, the working conditions, everything. He had only just put in an order for half a dozen wheels to be installed in his cotton mills to make it easier on the workers' lungs.

Cassian picked at his boiled egg and took a few sips of tea before he dressed for the day. He had too much to do before he left for Angel Faith Textiles. He was due there at nine, and he wanted to go over the numbers prior to leaving.

Cassian knew that rich men employed valets, but he had not quite got used to that idea yet. He could dress himself, and Wade took care of everything else anyway, so what need did he have? He pulled on a fresh pair of breeches and chose an ivory waist jacket and a dark coat.

Cassian attached his pocket watch and placed it in his pocket, and then pocketed his sixty pounds in winnings, before running his fingers through his untameable, thick, curly black hair.

His hair had grown back, and was as unruly as ever.

Cassian descended the stairs to the second floor and entered his study. His study was a simple room with a large desk covered in books and folders. His books shelves were quite empty, as he was not an exceptionally well read man.

His mother had seen to it that he learned to read, but he had not had the opportunity to ever really read a book. Now, he did not have the time.

Cassian's desk was organised chaos. He knew where everything was and the maids knew not to touch anything. Now that he was returned from the north, he put those ledgers away. He would pull them out again once he received figures from his managers.

He pulled one of the leather bound ledgers from the pile, and ran his fingers over the embossed "AFT" on the cover. This was his first ledger, purchased for his first factory.

Angel Faith Textiles manufactured fabric. He purchased fibres, such as the cotton he manufactured in the north, and his workers converted the fibres into fabric. Once it was a usable material, his workers then dyed or printed the fabric, and it was then sold on in bolts to dressmakers and such at a profit.

Cassian read over the numbers, memorising what they paid for fibres last quarter, and what profit was generated from sales. A tidy sum, indeed. Fifty-six women were employed at Angel Faith Textiles, as well as his manager, Gregory Drew, and a second-in-charge, overseer Henry Towler.

Cassian checked the time on his pocket watch. It was half-past eight. He needed to leave. He closed the ledger and tucked it under his arm and proceeded to make his way downstairs.

He could hear that his household were awake and working. Rooms that were left vacant were being dusted. Silverware that was never used was being polished.

Cassian did not see the appeal in sitting at a dining table meant for sixteen while dining alone. Perhaps ... one day ... if he was not alone.

Wade quickly made his way into the entry foyer to open the door for Cassian. "Can we expect you home for luncheon, sir?" he asked.

Cassian smiled at his faithful butler. He knew he was not the most traditional of masters. "Just supper tonight. Thank you, Wade."

"Good day, sir," farewelled Wade.

His driver, Mr Green, was waiting for him as this was a pre-arranged trip.

"Good morning, sir," greeted Mr Green as he opened the door for Cassian.

"Good morning, Green," replied Cassian as he climbed inside. Mr Green closed the door and Cassian settled down on the comfortable seat.

It was not a terribly long journey to Angel Faith Textiles. They had arrived within thirty minutes but Cassian was running a few minutes late.

He climbed out of the carriage and looked up at his building. The first building he had ever purchased. He smiled with pride. The large sign on the front of the building had a lovely halo, with the words "Angel Faith Textiles" written below it. The halo was purposefully positioned above the word "Faith".

Cassian truly wondered if Faith had ever happened upon a bolt of her own fabric at any time. He remembered exactly what she had been wearing the day they had met. Well, he remembered everything about her. But he knew that she wore fine clothing made from the fabrics that he manufactured. He prayed that she knew this was all because of her.

Cassian climbed the steps up to the factory door and let himself in. He enjoyed the busy rhythm in his factories. Each floor was dedicated to part of the process. The ground floor housed the looms. After going through the looms, the fibres were then transported through each of the rooms in the factories. The fibres were wound, warped, sized, and then woven before the newly manufactured fabric could be dyed and printed.

"Ah, Mr Kensington, you are here," cheered his manager, Gregory Drew as he descended the narrow staircase that led to the upper levels.

"Yes, Mr Drew," replied Cassian. "Apologies if I am late. London traffic."

"Of course," replied Mr Drew. "Not at all."

Mr Drew was slightly shorter than Cassian, and was about a decade older than him. All of Cassian's managerial employees were older than him.

Mr Drew smiled at Cassian, the skin around his grey eyes crinkling. He then extended his hand out to Cassian. "Are you well?"

"Yes, very well, thank you," he replied. "And you? How is your wife?" he asked as he shook Mr Drew's hand.

"Oh, Margaret is fine. Always something to complain about, though," he replied dismissively.

Cassian found that was the usual response he heard from men when he asked after their wives. They complained too much. They nagged. They gave their husbands headaches when they should be grateful to their husbands for providing.

His friends at the club would always complain about their wives. They seemed to have affection for them, but they always complained.

It did not entice Cassian into the institution. He did not want to complain about his wife. It was not a kind way to talk about the woman one had vowed to love.

"Give her my regards," replied Cassian.

"Thank you, sir," replied Mr Drew.

"How goes things?" he asked.

"Shall we go upstairs to my office?" suggested Mr Drew.

Cassian nodded and followed Mr Drew up the narrow staircase. As he was used to the luxurious staircases in his Kensington home, the narrow ones were a little unnerving.

As they moved from floor to floor, Cassian could see the female workers moving the fibres through the varying steps. They all looked very focussed. He wanted to speak to as many women as he could before he left. He prided himself on maintaining good working conditions.

His workers up north in the cotton mills had complained to him about lung illnesses after inhaling too much of the excess cotton.

Upon hearing this, he had immediately put in an order for wheels to be installed in each factory to help with this problem.

Mr Drew's top floor office was quite stuffy, but an open window was helping with the air flow. The office itself was crowded with furniture and papers.

Cassian was not too self-important that he sat behind the master's desk. He sat in one of the little wooden chairs before Mr Drew's desk and opened the ledger.

"Will Mr Towler be joining us?" asked Cassian.

"He is directing the new girl," replied Mr Drew. "He will come up soon, I imagine."

Cassian nodded. "Alright. Quarterly reports," he began.

Cassian and Mr Drew spent a good half hour discussing the income and expenses of Angel Faith Textiles. Sixty women were now employed, to compensate for the demand. Business was good.

Eleven women had left the factory for other jobs, or to get married, and fifteen had been taken on, the latest only the day before. Mr Drew was planning on taking on at least a dozen more in the coming weeks.

Cassian was pleased. Angel Faith Textiles was his favourite. It had to succeed.

"Thank you for all your hard work, Mr Drew. I appreciate it." Cassian closed his ledger, now with updated numbers, and tucked it under his arm.

"Thank you, sir."

"I am going to go and speak to some of the women now, but I will say goodbye before I leave."

Cassian made his way through each of the rooms in the factory, talking to as many of his workers as he could. He was happy to hear that there were not any health complaints about conditions, mainly quiet requests for an increase in wages.

After his discussion with Mr Drew about the state of things, he believed there could be the possibility of an extra shilling a week. But he would not discuss it until all the calculations had been done.

He found his second overseer, Henry Towler, on the ground floor, supervising the women working on the looms. Mr Towler was only a few years older than Cassian, but he had an air of self-importance about him. Cassian had only taken him on after Mr Drew had vouched for him. He was yet to impress Cassian, but he did not have any overwhelming reason to sack the man except for a gut feeling.

"Ah, Mr Kensington. I heard you were due to visit today," greeted Mr Towler.

"How are you?" Cassian asked, forcing a smile.

"Good, good, sir," replied Mr Towler. "Very good this morning. Listen, I have had an idea."

"Go on," said Cassian carefully.

"With all the extra workers being taken on, it is getting hard to keep track of the level of performance. We want to ensure that we have exceptional standards, don't we?"

Cassian pursed his lips.

"Well, I have been thinking about taking on an assistant ... in house," he continued.

Cassian arched an eyebrow. "An assistant?" he repeated. In house? He wanted one of the women to assist him? He did not like the sound of that at all. Just as he was about to reject Mr Towler's request, he continued.

"Yes, the girl we took on yesterday. I see great potential in her. I would like to take her under my wing."

Take her into his bed, more like. "Mr Towler, I do not see the —"

"But the girl is right here. Meet her if you like," insisted Mr Towler. "Odd name, but then, you would like it." He chuckled to himself. "Mrs Rowe!" he shouted.

Of all the women who were looking down at their looms, only one looked up. Cassian's eyes found her immediately.

His heart stopped.

It was her.

CHAPTER 2

His angel stood up from her loom and walked gracefully from her station to stand before Cassian and Mr Towler. She was still an angel. She had not changed a bit. Her face was still the most beautiful face he had ever seen. Her lovely brown hair was pulled into a braid over her shoulder, with the same rebellious little curls framing her face. He remembered her eyes, seeing them from above as he felt death taking him. The kindness in their chocolate depths was unlike anything he had ever seen.

Today they appeared wary. He did not like it. Was she wary of Henry Towler? Did he make her uncomfortable? Did he make the other women feel uncomfortable?

Something told Cassian he would soon have to advertise for a new overseer.

"Mr Kensington, let me introduce you to Mrs Faith Rowe. She joined Angel Faith Textiles just yesterday," Mr Towler introduced. "Mrs Rowe, Mr Kensington, our owner."

Faith smiled briefly before curtseying. There was no recognition in her brown eyes. She did not remember him.

That was actually quite disappointing. Then he focussed on a word he had not properly registered. Mrs.

She was married.

His eyes immediately went down to her left hand, which was intertwined with her right. She was twisting her hands nervously. She wore a wedding band on her left hand. Had she been wearing that when they had met previously? He could not remember. He supposed he was a little preoccupied with dying to notice his saviour's left hand.

What was she doing here? He remembered that she had been wearing clothes of fine silk. Now she wore a dark uniform. She had been travelling in the finest carriage he had ever seen. What happened?

"It is nice to meet you, Mr Kensington," she said politely.

Her voice. Her angelic voice. The voice that had haunted his dreams for years. Why did she not remember him?

"Does your husband approve of you working in my factory, Mrs Rowe?" Cassian asked curiously. He knew it was rude as soon as he spoke the words, but he wanted to know.

He could tell that Faith thought he was being rude as well, but she did her best to hide it. "My husband passed away, Mr Kensington."

The blood drained from his face and Cassian felt like a right cad. That explained why she was working in the factory. Her husband's money must have been lost. Perhaps he was a gambler. Perhaps she never loved him and was happy to be free of him. Before he could apologise, Mr Towler spoke.

"I was just explaining to Mr Kensington that I am in need of an assistant, to help me with the day to day supervision of the factory. I think you are the perfect candidate, Mrs Rowe."

Faith pressed her lips together, the movement capturing Cassian's attention immediately. It took him a moment to observe that Faith appeared uncomfortable with the idea of assisting Mr Towler.

Henry Towler was not the sort of man to treat such a close subordinate with respect, especially not a woman. Cassian needed to sack the man. He was growing more irritating by the minute.

"Mr Towler, if you are not equipped to undertake your own duties, perhaps I should find another to take your place?"

Cassian noticed that Faith's face instantly relaxed. He smiled at her.

Faith furrowed her eyebrows at him, unsure of him. It bewildered him that she did not remember him. How many half-dead men did she come across?

Mr Towler was left speechless. He had not been expecting that reply. "I suppose I should get back ..." he trailed off and left the loom room.

Faith flattened her apron nervously. "Thank you, sir," she murmured.

"Not at all, Mrs Rowe," he replied. "Does he bother you? Please tell me the truth."

His question startled her. Faith sucked in a breath before saying, "He is a man."

What sort of answer was that? Cassian frowned. "I am a man," he countered.

Faith did not reply.

Cassian looked beyond her to the dozen or so ladies that were working at the looms pretending not to listen. "How many of you have been bothered by Mr Towler?" he asked the room.

They all ceased work and looked up at Cassian. Only one spoke. She was an older lady, perhaps forty or so, with her thinning brown hair tucked underneath a cap. "As Mrs Rowe said, Mr Kensington, he is a man."

That was no excuse. He was a man, after all, and he never would have abused his power over a woman. In Cassian's opinion, Mr Towler was not a man. "Excuse me, ladies," he muttered before departing the room.

It angered him to know that Mr Towler had been taking liberties with his workers, but it infuriated him to know that his own angel had been subject to him after only working in the factory for a day.

Faith deserved better. She was an angel.

Cassian marched up the stairs and encountered Mr Towler talking to Mr Drew on the third floor. Mr Towler appeared to be complaining about something. No doubt it being Cassian's refusal to allow him a woman to harass.

Mr Drew could see the anger permeating from Cassian. "Sir, all Henry was asking for was —"

"If you need more men, Mr Drew, then tell me. I will hire two overseers. But I will not have any of my workers harassed by someone in my employ," snapped Cassian. Both men took a step back from him. "You had every intention of taking advantage of Mrs Rowe, did you not?" he seethed.

Mr Towler paled. "I thought her competent," he stammered.

Cassian scoffed. "You thought her pretty," he retorted. The word did not do justice to Faith but that was beside the point. "Mr Towler, I no longer have need of your services. You shall leave the premises immediately with a month's pay." Cassian was being generous. He suddenly remembered the bank notes in his pocket that he had never put away. He fished out the correct amount and tossed the money in Mr Towler's direction. The paper floated to the floor in front of a stunned Drew and Towler. "I shall find a replacement myself," Cassian told Mr Drew.

"Are you going to let him do this?" asked Mr Towler of Drew in disbelief. "I saw it with my own eyes. He wants that girl for himself! He is just trying to get me out of the way!"

Something told Cassian that Mr Drew knew a little more about these allegations then he was letting on. "Henry, you ought to take the money and go. I will be a reference for you," he said firmly.

Mr Towler haughtily gathered up his money and proceeded to stomp down the stairs, swearing and cursing the place as he left.

"You will be the one to go if I ever hear that this happens again," warned Cassian. Little did Mr Drew know, but he had a very precious person in his charge. If anything happened to Faith within these walls then Cassian would have blood.

"I understand, sir," replied Mr Drew seriously. He respectfully bowed his head before continuing up to his office.

Cassian knew that with the departure of Mr Towler, Angel Faith Textiles was now understaffed. He made the decision to remain in the factory for the rest of the day to supervise the workers. As he stood on the landing, overlooking one of the processing rooms, he caught his reflection in the window that looked out onto the London street below.

His appearance had changed a great deal in three years. He had always been a skinny child, then teenager, and then an adult, never having enough to eat. The lack of nutrients had meant grey skin, gaunt features, thinning hair, and constant illness.

It was a miracle he survived. A miracle Faith had found him.

Now he was a tall, healthy looking young man of twenty-five. His hair was no longer thin and patchy. It was thick, black, and curly, and fell to his jawline. His skin was no longer grey. It was clear, and perhaps a little tan from travelling recently. His fine, expensive clothing fit his lean physique well, and his bones no longer protruded anywhere.

He supposed it was perfectly reasonable for Faith not to recognise him, but perhaps she did remember him. It took all his strength not to follow the workers into the dining room once the bell from the midday break rang.

Faith did not know who he was, and he did not want to frighten her. As far as she knew, he was the owner of the factory, and the last thing he wanted to do was to appear like one of the men his workers were used to.

But he wanted to tell her who he was. He wanted to show her what her kindness had achieved. He wanted to prove to her that he had made something of himself, just as she had asked him to.

Cassian watched her over the landing as she walked with the others to eat the midday meal. She looked so small in and amongst the others. He could help her now.

Cassian spent the rest of the day helping where he could. He fixed jammed machinery. He moved materials from floor to floor. He carried the finished bolts of fabric downstairs, ready to be sent to the buyers. And he avoided the loom room at all costs.

At eight o'clock, the bell sounded for end of day. Cassian immediately wondered if his poor driver was still waiting outside for him. He would have to pour the man a drink.

The workers tidied and then left their stations before collecting their coats and hats. Those who walked by him smiled and said their goodbyes. Several expressed enthusiastic thanks. He attributed that to Mr Towler's dismissal. It gave him further affirmation that he had made the right decision.

Cassian farewelled Mr Drew, and informed him that he would place an advertisement for a new overseer in the morning. In the meantime, he would send a servant to help.

Cassian exited the factory and saw that Mr Green was still waiting with his carriage. Perhaps he would buy the man a bottle of whiskey. The street was dark, and was only illuminated by the few flickering street lamps. He could see several of his workers walking home in pairs or groups. He was now annoyed with himself that he did not see which way Faith went.

There was a single figure walking down the street, but he could not be sure it was her. The woman was wrapped in a brown coat, and that was really all he could see.

"Sir, look out!" cried Mr Green.

Cassian turned around just as a glass bottle collided with his temple. The bottle smashed upon impact and he felt several shards of it pierce his skin. The pain only worsened as he was knocked to the ground, and he collided with the hard, cobbled road.

"What you deserve," slurred a familiar voice.

CHAPTER 3

Through the pained haze, Cassian recognised the voice as a drunken Mr Towler. The man had obviously taken his money straight to the tavern.

Cassian cradled his bleeding head, and felt the glass in his skin as his eyes fluttered, unconsciousness wanting to take him. Warm blood was running over his fingers and pooling around him.

"You wretch!" cursed Mr Green.

Cassian could not see properly, but he heard the sound of a man falling to the ground. He could not be sure it was Towler.

He faintly heard footsteps running towards him. "Oh my goodness!" cried another voice, a female voice.

An angelic voice. Cassian smiled dopily. Perhaps he was dying again. His eyes closed and he fell from awareness.

Cassian was suddenly aware that he had a pounding headache. His right temple was throbbing, the pain encompassing his entire head. Instinctively, Cassian lifted a hand to support his temple.

This sudden movement elicited a gasp from someone sitting beside him. He was not alone.

Cassian's eyes opened slowly, and they were immediately assaulted by the light from a lamp situated beside him. It took a few moments for his eyes to adjust before he could take in where he was.

He was in a room, one he had never seen before. It was dark, but he could see that it was a small flat, with a kitchen, sitting, and dining room all crammed into the tiny space. He was laying in the only bed.

He noticed Mr Green sitting at the little dining table, a bowl of something in front of him. He turned his head in the direction that the gasp had come from.

Cassian stared at her for a few moments, waiting for her to disappear. But she did not. Faith was not a hallucination. She was sitting beside his bed on a little stool, wearing the same concerned expression that she had three years earlier.

Faith's lips parted, but no words escaped. Her brown eyes glistened.

"Ouch," Cassian whispered.

Faith exhaled, her breath staggered. "Oh, Mr Kensington. Are you alright? I am so sorry. This was my fault."

Cassian frowned. The muscle movement painted him, as it felt as though he was pulling something. He wondered if he had stiches in his head.

Her voice had alerted Mr Green, who had risen from his seat. Cassian's driver was not standing at the foot of the bed.

"It was not you who struck me, Mrs Rowe," Cassian mumbled. His eyes flicked to Mr Green. His driver did not appear to have a scratch. "What happened to him?"

"Arrested," he replied. "An officer heard the noise and took the assailant to prison for the night. Intoxication and assault. I am sure they will contact you, sir."

Cassian nodded, immediately regretting the motion. It hurt. His eyes returned to Faith. She still appeared to feel incredibly guilty.

She pressed her hands together and held them to her lips. Why was she blaming herself? She was not the one who had hit him with a bottle. Henry Towler was spending the night in prison because he was the one who was guilty.

"Mr Kensington, please forgive me," Faith whispered. "If I had not behaved so ... if I had never said a word ... oh, if only I had accepted Mr Towler's position then this would not have happened."

"Towler's actions were his own," Cassian said firmly, finding his voice. "Do you know what would have happened if you had accepted that position?" Cassian hated to think. He hated to think of such a good person in any danger. He hated that his other workers had been at Towler's mercy for years. How could he have not known?

"But then you would be alright," Faith insisted. "You would not have been hurt."

What twisted logic. It was almost stupid to be that selfless.

"Better me than you," Cassian replied.

Faith pursed her lips and her eyes widened.

"Just because a man is your superior, it does not give him the right to take liberties," said Cassian. "A woman should be able to say no to a man and not fear retaliation. This is something I firmly believe." He had only been young when his mother had died, but he was not oblivious as to what she was doing. A hazard of having to grow up early. His mother had returned to him on countless occasions bloodied and bruised after refusing service.

Faith was silent. Cassian watched her as a single tear rolled down her cheek. It made Cassian wonder about her. He did not know her, not really. But he hoped that his logic would help her to have higher standards for the behaviour of men.

"What time is it, Green?" Cassian asked.

"A little after three, sir," replied Mr Green.

Cassian had been unconscious for seven hours, and poor Faith was due back at the factory for work in five hours. He knew they ought to leave, but it hurt his head to move.

"Help me up, Green," Cassian instructed, raising his right arm.

Mr Green immediately started around the bed just as Faith cried, "No, what are you doing?"

"I have imposed upon you long enough, Mrs Rowe," Cassian groaned, just as Mr Green pulled him up into a seated position. "I owe you a great debt." Faith was unaware just how great a debt that was.

"Nonsense," she snapped, finding her voice. "You are concussed, sir!"

It was strange to hear his angel call him sir. But it was not appropriate to ask her to call him Cassian in front of another man. Cassian then realised that Faith had taken a great risk bringing two men into her home without another woman present. He supposed they were lucky that it was the middle of the night.

"You lay right back down." Faith placed her hands on his chest and pushed Cassian back down again. She was over him again, looking down at him as she had three years earlier. He stared up at her, daring not to breathe.

She was still so beautiful. He had not imagined that. As she stared down at him, her eyebrows furrowed a little. There was not recognition in her eyes, but slight confusion.

Mr Green cleared his throat.

Faith stood up straight ever so quickly, realising that her hands were still on Cassian's chest. "Right, Mr Kensington, you will stay put. Mr Green, you may have the settee, and Lucy and I will sleep in the armchair."

Lucy? Had Cassian heard right? Was there another who lived here? Did Faith have a cat?

Cassian had not realised that he had said Lucy's name aloud, his tone indicating a question.

"My daughter," Faith explained, walking over to the settee.

She has a child.

Faith was a mother.

The light was dim by the settee, but he watched as Faith lifted a small figure into her arms. Cassian was frozen as he saw his angel transform into a mother. He could not see the child, but he watched as Faith cradled her, rocking her gently. She hummed a sweet tune and settled into the armchair.

If anything, it made her more beautiful.

"You heard the lady, Mr Green," Cassian said finally. His driver nodded and walked over to the settee to settle down. Had Cassian been able to move, he would have gladly slept in the armchair. But for now, he had a wonderful view of his angel, and her little baby.

Cassian awoke to the sensation of being poked.

He squinted. The light of the early morning had crept into the little flat, but the room was still relatively dim.

What he could see clearly, however, were Faith's eyes. It took a minute to realise that those chocolate brown eyes were on the face of another. She was young, but not a baby. Cassian had not known many children, so he was not sure of her age.

She was a very cute child, though. Her eyes, brown like her mother's, were beautiful, and were framed by the longest possible eyelashes. Her brown hair was impossibly curly. The tight brown spirals framed her face, and were in disarray after sleep. Her cheeks were round and flushed, and her little mouth was parted out of curiosity.

"Who are you?" Lucy whispered in a sweet, youthful voice.

Cassian craned his neck up, the action not hurting as much as it had the night before.

Mr Green was still fast asleep on the settee. He was much too long for the little sofa and his legs hung over the end of it.

He smiled slightly when he saw Faith. She, too, was still fast asleep, curled up on the armchair.

"My name is Cassian," he whispered back. "What is your name?" he asked Lucy.

Lucy, who had been sitting beside him on the bed, climbed onto Cassian's stomach and crossed her legs. She was not heavy, but it was still awkward to have dead weight on his stomach. "My name is Lucy," she replied.

Lucy looked so much like Faith. She would grow up to be beautiful. She did not appear to have much of anyone else in her. He could not help but wonder about Lucy's father ... and Faith's husband.

Cassian spied his coat hanging by the door, his waist jacket on the floor below it. It must have fallen off the hook during the night. "Lucy, do you see that piece of clothing on the floor over there?" he asked.

Lucy turned her head, her curls bouncing. She nodded.

"In the pocket is my watch. It is a little golden watch. Would you fetch it for me?" he asked.

Lucy climbed off of Cassian and obediently went to search the pockets of his waist coat. Cassian felt relief as soon as she was gone. He took a deep breath. He sat up in the bed slowly, every inch of him sore and stiff. The mattress was not at all comfortable, though he would say nothing.

His head did feel significantly less painful. The surrounding area was still painful, but his headache was gone.

Lucy promptly returned with his pocket watch.

"Thank you," Cassian said gratefully. It was twenty minutes past seven. The factory was due to resume operations in forty minutes.

Cassian knew that had he not interrupted Faith's evening, she would have already been awake.

But seeing her, curled up as she was, he did not have the heart to wake her.

He did need to send a servant to help Mr Drew with daily operations, which meant that he needed to return home.

Lucy stood to the side of the bed, staring at him. Why was she looking at him like that?

Cassian frowned at her. Lucy returned his expression. Even though she was frowning, she was still very cute. Cassian cocked his head to the side, and Lucy copied him once more.

Lucy was just curious about the stranger in her house.

Cassian chuckled lightly and smiled at her. Lucy returned his smile, showing him every one of her baby teeth.

There was a sudden loud knock at the door.

Faith had jumped so much that she had practically fallen out of the armchair, something that Lucy found highly amusing. Faith scrambled to her feet and rubbed her face. She looked so tired. She had not had enough sleep. "What time is it?" she gasped.

"Nearly half past seven," replied Cassian. "Are you expecting someone?"

Faith was running around her flat frantically, and achieving nothing.

Mr Green had since awoken, and was now sitting up on the settee.

"Lucy, that will be Mrs Berwick!" cried Faith. "Hurry and gather whatever you want to take with you for today." Faith paused in front of the bed and chewed on her bottom lip. "I cannot explain you," she whispered. "I have to hide you. You know what people will say. We will be evicted."

"Who is Mrs Berwick?" Cassian asked, just as a crumpled dress was thrown at his face. Faith had begun to throw laundry on the bed to disguise him as a pile of clothing.

"I pay her to care for Lucy while I am working," explained Faith as she fixed the clothing on the bed to hide Cassian. "Mr Green, please get down behind the settee!" she hissed frantically. "Oh, Lord, we will be evicted," she worried under her breath.

Perhaps it was the concussion talking, but Cassian did not think it fair that anyone should be evicted for caring for an ill man, no matter their sex. Cassian understood there were certain propriety expectations, but it would not be right.

Even then, it had been him that had kept Faith up half the night. She had cared for him again, at great personal risk. Cassian could start to repay her right at that minute.

He pushed the laundry off of his face and caught her just as she was approaching the door. "Tell her to go," he hissed. "Tell her you do not need her to watch Lucy today."

Faith spun on her heel and gaped at him. "What are you talking about?"

"Tell her to go," he reiterated. "Trust me," he implored. She had no reason to, really. Cassian was a stranger to her. Merely her employer. Little did she know that he would do everything in his power to take care of her.

And Lucy. He would take care of her, too.

Faith nodded, and motioned for him to hide again. Cassian laid back down and covered himself with the laundry.

"Good morning, Mrs Berwick," Faith sung in a falsely cheerful tone.

"Is everything alright, Mrs Rowe? I thought I heard voices," said Mrs Berwick suspiciously.

"Oh, no, it is just Lucy and I. We like to have ... loud conversa-
tions."

"Of course," said Mrs Berwick flatly. "Is Lucy ready?"

"Oh, um, no, not today. I appreciate you coming to collect her,
but I am not working at the factory today. I am ... uh ... ill." Faith
promptly coughed. "A cough, you see. I would not want Lucy to
endanger your children."

Cassian stifled a laugh.

"You are going to forgo a day's wages because of a cough?"
repeated Mrs Berwick.

"So it seems," replied Faith. Her tone changed, and she sounded
worried. Worried about money, most likely.

Cassian would never let her struggle financially. Not now he was
in the position to repay her.

"Feel better, Mrs Rowe," Mrs Berwick said half-heartedly.

"Thank you," replied Faith as she closed the door.

Cassian threw the laundry off of him and Mr Green rose from
behind the settee. Lucy stood by her mother, clutching the arm
of a cloth doll.

"She did not believe me," murmured Faith.

Cassian grinned. "You were not convincing."

Faith glared at him. "This is not a joke, Mr Kensington," she
snapped. "It is rare that rooms will be rented to women without
husbands, especially those with children. They do not care a bit
if you are widowed or not."

Cassian controlled his amusement. It was not funny. She was
panicking. She had a child to provide for, and a dead husband that
had left her with nothing. Cassian could understand this. His own
mother had been in the same situation. Faith was doing well.

"Mrs Rowe, please. I will ensure that you and Lucy will always
have a safe home," Cassian promised. "Green, will you please fetch

the carriage?" It suddenly occurred to Cassian that he was unsure as to what had happened to the carriage or the horses the night before, but Green would know

"Yes, sir," said Mr Green.

"Be careful!" exclaimed Faith. "Do not be seen!"

"Yes, ma'am," replied Mr Green. He discreetly slipped out of Faith's flat and closed the door behind him.

Faith's attention returned to Cassian. "How can you promise such things, Mr Kensington?"

"Because I was given a chance," he replied. "I need to send a servant to the factory this morning to help Mr Drew now that I have sacked Mr Towler, so I need to return to my home. If you would like, you and Lucy can come with me." Cassian paused. Faith was still staring at him. Her head cocked to the side slightly. Her expression was identical to that of Lucy's earlier. He resisted laughing. "I will employ you in my household. I have a small staff who would be thankful for the help. I will pay you ten pounds annually, as well as room and board, everything." That was more than any other housemaid salary he was aware of. But he owed Faith much more than that. "You will not need to pay anyone to care for Lucy. There are always people around my house. I am there a lot." He could watch Lucy for a little while here and there. How hard could it be?

There was at least two minutes of silence before Faith spoke. "Ten pounds ... and board ... and food ... and Lucy." She exhaled as a large smile spread across her face. "But why would you help me?" Faith asked in disbelief.

"Because you once did the same for me."

CHAPTER 4

Faith furrowed her eyebrows. "I beg your pardon?"

Cassian chuckled softly. "Don't you know me, Faith?"

Faith shook her head slowly. Cassian noticed her grip tightening on Lucy's hand. She was nervous. "Should I?" she asked quietly.

Even though his face was not as gaunt as it once was, Cassian still tucked his wayward black curls behind his ears so she could better see his face. "Do you not remember the half-dead boy you once met on the side of the road?"

Faith's shoulders immediately relaxed as her mouth opened in shock. He could see it in her eyes. She remembered. She may not have recognised him but she did remember him. Faith covered her mouth with her hand as she gasped.

Lucy tugged on the skirt of Faith's dress. "Mama?" she questioned.

Faith did not seem to even hear her. Her brown eyes were appraising him, looking over his entire person in utter shock. He had certainly changed. When last they met he had not owned a pair of boots.

"Yes, I remember you, Cassian," she finally said.

Cassian smiled. She remembered his name.

Faith released Lucy's hand and left her holding her doll. She walked slowly towards him, still searching him with her eyes. She stopped not even a foot from him. She looked up into his eyes and cocked her head once more, a smile teasing her lips.

Cassian could not look away. Her stare was captivating.

"I can see you now," she whispered. She was so close that he could feel her breath on his throat. Goose pimples quickly covered his body and he shivered.

Cassian had wanted to reunite with his angel for so long. He had dreamed of her countless nights. He had seen her in crowds dozens of times, only to realise it was another. Her voice had haunted him.

Before Faith had found him, he could count on one hand the number of souls he had spoken to. He had been a poor, street urchin, worthy of nothing and no-one. People avoided him and ignored him. His death would not have affected anyone. One less urchin that polluted the street.

Cassian's existence had been meaningless until he had met Faith.

Faith had stopped. She had given up everything to help a stranger. She had been travelling as a rich woman and was now living in a tiny flat. Perhaps she had given Cassian everything.

"You saved my life, Faith," he said softly, "and I have been waiting three years to thank you."

Faith's eyes became glassy and he watched a tear travel down her cheek. "You cannot know how often I wondered about you. I felt such guilt for not taking you back into the village, or to a doctor. But you must understand, I could not, there was something that I desperately needed to do on that day."

Cassian recalled her driver urging her away from the man with possible "crawlers". They were anxious to be somewhere. He wondered where. But she did not need to feel guilty. "I was dying," he emphasised. "I felt myself dying. Had you not stopped I would have been dead within the hour, I know it. You saved my life. You were an angel," he said sincerely. "Are an angel," he corrected.

"Angel," she repeated. "Angel Faith ... is that supposed to be me?" she asked.

"An offering to the woman responsible for my success," replied Cassian, "and a thank you. Faith, I want you to know that I made something of myself, just as you asked. I am a success because of you."

Faith smiled peacefully and stepped backward. Cassian tried not to frown. He enjoyed their closeness. "I can see that you are a success. Well done."

Much to Cassian's disappointment, Faith's voice was quite flat as she congratulated him. Perhaps she was unaware of just how successful he was. She did not know of the other factories. She had not seen his house, his carriage, or any of his fine things.

"And so you must allow me to repay you," he then insisted.

Faith's eyes widened. "Oh, no!" she exclaimed. "What I gave you ... it was an investment, and the mere fact that you are well is enough of a dividend for me. I ... I want to earn my money. I will not accept money that I have not worked for."

As much as Cassian wanted to put the pile of banknotes that were still in his coat pocket into Faith's hands, he respected her for her determination to earn an honest living. She was providing for a child without a husband.

"If your offer is still valid, I will accept your ten pounds and I will work in your household. I would be glad to." Faith knitted her hands together and exhaled.

Cassian grinned. Firstly, he was immensely happy to have the opportunity to look after Faith and Lucy. It was clear that her husband had been unable to in the event of his death. And secondly, he was excited to show Faith his house. When she saw just what her investment in him had reaped, she would know that he had made something of himself.

"Happy to have you on board, Faith," Cassian said gladly.

"It is I who now needs to thank you, Mr Kensington."

"I think we are acquainted well enough for you to know me as Cassian," Cassian insisted. He liked hearing his name in her angelic voice.

"You are my master now, Mr Kensington. That would not be appropriate," countered Faith. She turned her back on him just as Cassian frowned. Faith took hold of Lucy's hand again and started to look around her flat. "We do not have much, but I do need time to pack my possessions."

"I will send a servant to pack your things for you," Cassian promised. "We really ought to get going."

Faith and Lucy left the flat first. Cassian waited thirty seconds before following them downstairs, so as not to appear like they were travelling together. Not that it mattered now that Faith was no longer living there, maintaining a good name was still important to her.

Mr Green was waiting a little ways down the street for them. He had the door of the carriage open, waiting for them.

"Mrs Rowe and Lucy are coming with me. Mrs Rowe has accepted a position in my household," Cassian informed him.

"Very good, sir. Congratulations, Mrs Rowe."

"Thank you," said Faith sincerely.

Cassian offered his hand to Faith as she climbed into his carriage. The minute she placed her small hand in his, and gripped it for stability, he felt a flutter in his stomach. He was excited about her. As soon as Faith was safely inside, he placed his hands underneath Lucy's arms and lifted her up. He placed her inside and she climbed on the padded seat beside her mother.

Cassian then closed the door behind him and sat down opposite Faith and Lucy. He placed his hands on the luxurious fabric of the seat and smiled proudly. "This carriage was one of the first larger purchases I made after becoming successful," he told her. "I designed it myself. What with all the travelling I do, I thought it prudent to ensure that my carriage was safe as well as comfortable."

"I see," she murmured.

Cassian pursed his lips. "It is velvet, the fabric," he continued impatiently. "Italian. The very best."

Faith ran her index finger over the area next to her, leaving a trail in the fabric. "And we are sitting on it," she replied quietly.

Did she not like velvet? Cassian supposed it could become rather warm in summertime but it was nearing winter.

"What happened to you after I left?" Faith suddenly asked. "What did you do?"

Cassian thought back to the moments after he had watched Faith's carriage drive away. He was still dangerously malnourished, but he had hope inside him. In some respects, it was greater than food. "I found the strength to get to the nearby village," he explained. "I do not know how I got there. I could barely stand, I was so weak. But I did. I found a bed and a meal, and an inn that would serve me despite my appearance." He had not looked like the sort of man to have a purse full of money.

Faith was absently playing with one of Lucy's tight curls as she listened. Faith pulled the curl lightly before allowing it to spring back into place.

"I stayed there for a while. I regained my strength. I bought my first pair of boots and I made my way to London," he recalled, "where I made something of myself," he added.

"I am interested to see," Faith replied.

Cassian would show her everything. She would see. He had made something of himself. Her kindness had been bestowed on the right person.

"I live in Kensington," he told Faith as the carriage travelled further and further away from her flat.

"Near the palace?"

"But a stone's throw away."

Faith did not reply. She simply looked out the window.

Living near the palace should be exciting. She would get a glimpse of one of the royals if she was lucky.

Cassian decided that Faith's quiet demeanour was as a result of nerves. She was travelling to a new job at a strange house. She would be working with people she did not know.

When they finally arrived at his house, Cassian was anxious to see Faith's reaction. He was not disappointed. Her eyes widened as she took in the sheer size of the white townhouse. She craned her neck to see up to the top of the fourth floor. "Is not that a big house, Lucy?" she murmured to Lucy.

Lucy scrambled to look out the window, and mirrored her reaction to that of her mother's.

"Come," Cassian said proudly. "Allow me to give you a tour."

Cassian helped Faith and Lucy down from the carriage. He then told Mr Green that he had earned a day's rest.

They climbed the stairs up to the navy door, which was promptly opened by Wade.

"Sir, are you alright?" his butler asked, whilst subtly spying Faith and Lucy with questioning eyes. "We expected you yesterday evening."

"Yes, thank you, Wade. I was otherwise engaged," he replied, gesturing to his bandage. "My I introduce Mrs Faith Rowe, and her daughter, Miss Lucy?" Cassian gestured to Faith and Lucy. "Ladies, this is Mr Geoffrey Wade, my butler. I have decided to employ Mrs Rowe as a housemaid."

"It is a pleasure to meet you, Mr Wade," greeted Faith politely.

"Welcome, Mrs Rowe, Miss Rowe," Wade replied stiffly.

Cassian suspected that Wade felt put out not being included in the employment decision. "I have a few things that need organising very quickly, Wade," Cassian changed the subject.

"Yes, sir?"

"I need you to send something, whoever you can spare, to Angel Faith Textiles this morning. I sacked my overseer and I need to advertise for a new one," he instructed.

"Of course, sir."

"I will also need you to send someone to fetch Mrs Rowe's things from her flat. She lives ..." It suddenly occurred to Cassian that he had been unconscious when he was brought to Faith's home. "What was your address, Mrs Rowe?"

Faith gave Wade her address and Wade promised to have her possessions collected by the end of the day.

Lastly, he instructed his butler to alert him immediately if detectives arrived. He was unsure of when the police would want to speak to him, but he imagined it would be soon.

Wade was clearly uneasy at the fact that Faith had a child, but nonetheless he offered to take them both upstairs to show them to a room.

"I will do that, Wade. Not to worry," Cassian selfishly volun-teered. He wanted to give them both a tour.

CHAPTER 5

"Are you certain it is alright for us to be here, Mr Kensington?" asked Faith nervously as soon as Wade was gone.

Cassian wished she would not call him that. But he knew that as she was now part of his household that she was only being proper. "It is my house, Faith," he assured her.

"I know it is not normal for a housemaid to have a child," she stressed. "When women marry they leave employment, I know that. People might think I am an unwed mother."

"You are a widow, Faith," Cassian said softly. How could her husband not have left provisions for his wife and child? When Cassian married, if he ever married, then he would ensure that those he loved would be provided for upon his death. "If anyone has a problem with Lucy then they can answer directly to me."

He saw the relief upon Faith's face, just as her grip of Lucy's hand tightened. She smiled up at him, and he was glad to have brought her reassurance. Cassian hoped that there would be no conflict regarding Lucy. She seemed more like an inquisitive child, rather than a naughty one, anyway.

"Lucy will behave, I promise," Faith said vehemently.

"Good." Cassian smiled. "Would you like a tour?"

Faith's eyes immediately flitted around the foyer. She looked a little intimidated. That was not what Cassian wanted her to feel. He wanted her to be impressed. He wanted to show her that her generosity had not been for nothing.

"Come," he said encouragingly, selecting the drawing room first. Cassian opened the door into his drawing room. He never used the room, but it was decorated finely.

Expensive sofas, lush rugs, and historic timber furniture were expertly placed about the room. In pride of place was his stunning pianoforte. Cassian loved the music, but could not play himself.

It was remarkable, really, that Cassian had gone from death's door to enormous wealth in only three years. His home, and his things, ought to show Faith that she had invested in a clever man.

"This is the drawing room," said Cassian. "I hardly ever sit in here. But the maids keep it beautifully tidy. You will enjoy it more than I," he joked, but Faith did not respond.

Faith's attention was on a painting that hung on the wall. It was a portrait of a family. A mother, father, two sons, and a dog. Painted by a famous artist, he had been told, and purchased for a bargain.

"Who are these people?" she asked. Faith had let go of Lucy, who was now kneeling on the rug tracing the patterns with her finger.

Cassian suddenly felt very foolish, now realising that he had hung a painting of a family that he did not know. "It's a Jourdain," he murmured. "It will only increase in value."

Faith simply smiled. "I used to do that, too."

"What?" Cassian frowned.

"Collect pictures of people. It helps."

"I do not collect pictures of people," he rebuffed. "It is a Jourdain. It is expensive." He pursed his lips. "Helps with what?"

Faith sighed and looked back to the painting. "Loneliness."

Before Cassian could ask her what she meant, Faith had moved on to the pianoforte.

He looked back at the painting and wondered if Faith was right. He had the family in the drawing room. A general in the upstairs hallway. A mother and daughter in the library. Sisters in the dining room. Was he collecting pictures of people? Those were the paintings that he liked.

Cassian liked knowing that there were other faces in his house other than his own. He had not given them names, or anything else that would classify him as a lunatic, but he did wonder about the real people from time to time.

How had Faith guessed that within seconds of viewing the painting? Was he that transparent?

But Faith had admitted to doing the same thing in the past. Why had she been lonely?

Cassian was pulled back into reality when Faith ran her fingers over the ivory keys. The sound was awful. It was terribly out of tune.

"When was the last time you tuned your instrument?" she asked, pulling her hand away from the keys.

"Seeing as it has not once been touched, I would say never." He forgot that pianos needed tuning. They were not simply there to look at.

"Not once? Does not Mrs Kensington play?" Faith asked casually.

Had she not already noticed his pathetic collection of companions that hung on is wall? "I am not married."

Faith smiled. "If you have the tools, I can tune this for you. I used to look after my own pianoforte once."

Cassian truly wondered what must have happened to her husband's finances. To have lived so finely, and to fall to such poverty was truly confusing. "I would appreciate it." And he would pay her for it, no matter how she protested. "Shall we continue?"

Faith nodded. "Come along, Lucy," she said, extending her hand.

Cassian led them into his dining room, another room that he rarely used. His long dining table was the feature of the room, and one of these days, he was going to use it.

"What a lovely table," Faith complimented.

"It cost me thirty pounds," explained Cassian. "I overpaid most definitely, but just listen to that," he knocked on the table, enjoying the sound, "solid oak."

"Oh," was all Faith said in response.

Cassian frowned. "I wish I used it more." He just did not enjoy dining alone.

Faith's eyes widened. "You paid thirty pounds for a table you do not even use?" She quickly clamped her mouth shut. "I apologise. That is none of my business."

On the contrary, it was. It was her business to see that he had used her money to make himself a success. But when she put it like that, it was a little ridiculous to have such an expensive table sitting idly when he did not use it.

"I will make an effort to eat in here more often."

Cassian continued to show Faith and Lucy around his house. He pointed out his favourite pieces, and made sure to inform Faith of how he came across them, and how much he paid for them. He thought it important for Faith to know that he had not wasted her kindness.

But her responses became fewer and far between. She stayed silent, not giving him any clue as to what she was thinking. She certainly was not as impressed as he was hoping she would be, and he had no idea why.

When they finally reached the fourth floor, and the room where she and Lucy would be sleeping, Cassian had had enough.

"Faith, what is the matter with you?" he asked suddenly.

"What do you mean?" she asked dismissively.

"You have not said a word this whole time. I have been showing you my house and you have been silent."

Faith's eyes narrowed. "What do you want from me?"

Cassian huffed. "I want you to be impressed," he said flatly.

"Why?" Faith asked, sounding confused.

Cassian suddenly had a thought. He had spent the whole morning showing her every part of his success. Their circumstances had changed so. They were entirely reversed. Faith and Lucy had been living in a tiny room after having been rich once.

"Are you jealous?" he asked accusingly, immediately regretting it. But his stupid mouth would not stop. "Are you jealous because our circumstances are reversed?"

Faith's eyes flared. "Jealous?" she repeated. "Of what?"

Cassian could not stop. "Of my things. Of my success," he continued.

Faith held Lucy in front of her, playing with her curls as she spoke. Her tone was calm, despite Cassian's thoughtless insult. "Your things do not define you."

"I know that."

Faith shook her head. "I do not think that you do. You have spent the best part of the morning telling me the price of everything you own. You are proud of them, and that is wonderful, but you speak of them as though they define you. You and I differ immensely in what we value, I think. I have a healthy child. I have my health. We are safe. We are well. Those are the things that I value, Mr Kensington."

Having a nice dining table did not define him. Having a nice piano did not define him. His success defined him. And he had fine things because of his success. "I only want to impress you," he said sincerely.

"You do not need to impress me."

"I need to show you that I have made something of myself." Cassian sighed and leant against the wall.

"Is that what all this is about?"

Cassian stared at her. "Of course. It was what you asked of me."

"Is this our bedroom?"

Cassian nodded.

Faith opened the door to her and Lucy's bedroom. "Go and get into bed Lucy. I shall be in to kiss you in a minute." Lucy obeyed her mother and Faith shut the door. "She needs to have a sleep," she explained. "Do you think that you have made something of yourself, Mr Kensington?"

"Yes." Was it not obvious? They were standing in the product of his success. "I made my fortune. I built my business."

Faith knitted her fingers together and stood before him. "If you think that by having wealth you have made something of yourself then you are mistaken. You have made your fortune, but what have you done with it? Who has benefitted from it but you? What sort of man are you?"

Cassian was speechless. And then he was overwhelmingly dis-appointed. He had spent the last three years building his business, and making his fortune, in an attempt to make something of himself, just as Faith had asked. He had done that, or so he had believed.

And now it was all for nothing.

"No matter our past, my opinion of you does not matter. I am grateful to you. You have helped Lucy and me immeasurably."

But her opinion did matter to him. And to not have her approval was honestly heartbreaking. Cassian had never felt like such a failure before.

"Our circumstances have reversed, you are right. But I feel I have more with nothing, then I ever did with everything," she said softly.

Cassian could not understand it. When he had nothing, he was dying. He was starving to death. Faith could never understand what that was like. He would never go back to that. "I cannot go back to having nothing, Faith. I was dying."

"I do not mean it literally, if only you knew ... oh, forget I said anything." Faith covered her face with her hands. "I am not the person to give advice on what it is right or wrong. I am sorry."

What did that mean? He had always thought of Faith as an angel. He had held her to a higher standard of being, really. She had been perfect in his mind. But here she was, in reality, and perhaps she was not as perfect as he had imagined. But who was?

Faith had pointed out, as clear as day, that he was not perfect. Neither was she. Cassian was beginning tounderstand that there was a lot more to Faith Rowe than met the eye.

"I had better make sure Lucy is sleeping. We all had a long night."

"Yes, you should rest, too," Cassian said quietly.

Faith smiled at him sadly and disappeared behind her door.

"There you are, sir," panted Wade.

Cassian turned his head toward his butler.

"The detectives are here, sir."

"Thank you, Wade. I shall be right down."

Faith wanted to know what sort of man he was. He was the sort of man to look after his workers and his household. With one last look at Faith's door, Cassian made his way downstairs.

CHAPTER 6

The metropolitan police had departed Cassian's home. Cassian had given his statement, but had emphasised that he did
not want Henry Towler's life to be ruined. While his behaviour
and actions were deplorable, Cassian did not believe that the
typhus filled prisons were a just punishment.

He had instead urged for penal labour as an alternative.

Cassian sat back in his desk chair and placed his hands on his
stomach. He had just spared a man who had done him wrong
certain imprisonment. Did that not make him a good man?

And just because he enjoyed being able to purchase fine things,
that did not make him a bad person.

Cassian had dreamed of finding his angel for years. He had long
imagined the day that he would find her, and he would show her
what her generosity had brought about.

And that dream had come to fruition, and it was nothing like he
had imagined. Faith was not proud of him, and she had questioned
the sort of man he was instead.

Cassian did not see much of Faith during her first week in his
home. He saw her infrequently, and when he did, she had her

head down, and a serious expression upon her fair face as she carried a broom or a mop off to her next chore.

The following Tuesday morning, Cassian was reviewing a report he had been sent from his factory in Yorkshire. The manager had compiled a detailed list of profits and expenses, as well as an updated employee list.

Cassian's eyes were still quite tired. The figures were hazy as it was still quite early in the morning. But he had not slept well, and so he had decided to get up and be productive.

He was suddenly startled by the door to his study opening abruptly. Cassian's head snapped up to see Faith standing in the doorway, a cloth in one hand, and a duster in the other.

Faith looked especially beautiful this morning, owing to a healthy flush in her cheeks. Her hair was tucked underneath a white cap, however a few stray curls hung either side of her face. She wore the plain maid's uniform, however, Cassian appreciated how the apron fixed around her waist emphasised her fine figure.

She was truly an angel. Only angels were that beautiful.

"Oh, I am sorry to disturb you!" she cried bashfully. "They told me you were still in bed so it was alright to come in here."

It was the first time they had spoken in nearly a week. Cassian had not realised how accustomed he was already to hearing her voice. He missed it. "It is quite alright. I got up early," he assured her. "Please, do not let me disturb you."

"No, it is I who is disturbing you, sir. I will leave you be."

Cassian did not want Faith to address him so formally, but she was the one who was insisting. "No, please. I am half asleep anyway. I have ready the same line twenty times already."

Faith laughed lightly. Cassian grinned in response. He had made her laugh.

Faith placed the cleaning instruments down and closed his study door. She took a deep breath, suddenly very serious. "Mr Kensington, I have been meaning to seek an audience with you. Do you mind?"

Cassian frowned as he motioned Faith forward. She did not need to ask.

Faith walked over gracefully and stood before his desk. "I wanted to apologise to you."

Apologise? Cassian suddenly felt very annoyed with himself for not standing as she had entered the room. How rude of him. She was a lady. Cassian immediately stood up from his chair and walked around his desk. He was now standing some three feet from Faith. "Apologise for what?"

Faith appeared to be internally chastising herself. "For being so judgemental last week. It was not my place. I was terribly rude when you were being so kind to Lucy and me."

"You were not rude. You had an opinion." Her opinion on his possessions had irritated him, but it had not offended him. What had hurt was her questioning of his character. Did she still mean that?

"You are a good man. I can see that," Faith continued. "I know you are good. Your servants speak very highly of you. They respect you. As do your workers."

Was that his question answered?

"May I?" she asked, gesturing to the chairs before his desk. Cassian nodded, and they both sat down beside each other. Faith knitted her hands together and said, "I have a terrible habit of not being able to hold my tongue."

"One might attribute that to you being honest," replied Cassian.

Faith smiled gratefully. "It is not my business what you choose to do with your money, Mr Kensington. I only gave you a purse full of coins. You were the one who earned ... this!" she said, gesturing to the walls around them.

Cassian had worked hard to run his successful business. "I do not want you to doubt my character," he said softly.

Faith's brown eyes softened. "And I do not. That was cruel of me to question what sort of man you were. I barely know you. How could I say such a thing? I need to learn to hold my tongue," she scolded herself.

Cassian was glad that she suddenly seemed to have a good opinion of him. It was ... it truly was very important to him that she held him in high regard.

"You and I were born to very different worlds, I think."

That was likely true. "Where were you born?" he asked curiously. He now realised that he did not know very much about Faith Rowe. He really did not know anything at all.

"Gloucestershire," Faith replied. "I was born to very wealthy parents. My father, he owned the bank in our village. And six others."

Cassian was not at all surprised that Faith had been born to privilege.

"I suppose that is where my attitude about things comes from," she confessed. "My father would buy horses and art and my mother had a new dress every other week. Their things gave them status. Their things made them better than other people." Faith chewed on her bottom lip for a moment, before admitting, "The terrible thing is, I believe I was like that for a while, too."

Cassian had not been expecting to hear that.

"I learned the true definition of value the hard way, Mr Kensington." Faith's brown eyes became very glassy all of a sudden. "I paid a very high price for it." Faith's voice cracked and he could see that she was fighting back tears.

What had happened to her? What price had she paid?

Would it be inappropriate to put an arm around her? He did not know the proper way to behave! Cassian hurriedly pulled a clean handkerchief from his pocked and handed it to her.

Faith accepted it with a sad smile. She immediately wiped her eyes. "Oh, I am sorry. This is terribly embarrassing."

"There is no need to be," Cassian assured her worriedly. "What happened, if I may ask?" He immediately wished he had not asked the question. It was none of his business!

Faith did not speak for at least a minute. Cassian was certain she would get up and leave. All he want to do was wrap his arms around her and hold her tightly. She was his angel. He had a duty to protect her now. And she was hurting, and he did not know why.

Faith squeezed his handkerchief tightly before looking up to meet his eyes. "I had another baby before Lucy," she told him, her voice so quiet that he had almost missed what she had said.

But he had not. Faith had been mother to another baby. It was clear what had happened to the poor mite. Faith only had one child with her.

The loss of a child was the highest price to pay.

"A son," she continued. One of her hands rested on her stomach. Cassian was unsure if she was even aware of the action. "My son." Her lip trembled. She held out her hand and made a cup. "He fit in my hand. He was so little." Faith's hand was shaking.

Protocol be damned, he thought, as he seized her hand in his. He held her hand tightly in his, soothingly rubbing the back of her hand with his thumb.

Faith wiped her eyes again with the handkerchief.

Cassian stared at her, not knowing what the right thing to say was. How could he have been taking Faith around his home, boasting about his expensive pianoforte, when she had suffered so?

"You are an angel," Cassian said instinctively. "I do not know how you are still standing."

Faith laughed through her tears. "Oh, I do not know about that. But I do know why I am still standing." She smiled knowingly. "The little girl upstairs gives me my wings. And my little boy in heaven is looking after us both."

Cassian squeezed her hand. "Faith, I am truly sorry for your pain. Losing your son and your husband, I cannot imagine." Cassian wondered what had claimed her husband. He would not ask. He would not have Faith reliving two tragedies.

Faith smiled gratefully. "My judgemental opinion comes from a good place. It really does," she said sincerely. "So long as Lucy is healthy and we are safe, nothing else matters."

Cassian appreciated that. He really did. He understood that her child mattered to her more than any material possession. But Cassian had never really had someone to love like that. Someone to value over a possession. "I have never really had anybody, you see. What I valued growing up was possessions. What little money I could earn. What little food I had. The rare pile of hay I found to sleep on. Those were the things I valued."

"And there is a difference. Those things are essential. I just did not want you to value material things over what is truly important. People."

"I do not have any people," Cassian replied simply. "The paintings," he reminded her. "I collect faces, remember."

Faith was the one who was squeezing his hand now. It felt ... secure. "You will have people one day. You will have a wife one day, and children perhaps. They will be lucky to have you."

He felt lucky to have her confidence. He had never come close to courting, let alone marriage.

"But you must have had family once. Parents?" Faith inquired. "Brothers and sisters?"

"No siblings," Cassian replied, shaking his head.

"Me either," said Faith.

"I did have parents, though. A mother, a father, a home."

"Then what happened?" she asked curiously. "How did you become ..." she trailed off.

"A skinny, little street urchin?" he guessed, finishing her sentence.

Faith blushed. "More or less."

Cassian slouched in his chair. "I do not remember my father," he confessed. "He died when I was three. He was a blacksmith, and there was some sort of accident. My mother would never tell me what. But it took his life."

Faith silently listened.

"My mother tried her best." Cassian had very fond memories of his mother. He knew that she had made impossible sacrifices. "But my parents did not have much in the way of savings, and what little money we had quickly ran out." He sighed. "I was hungry. That is what I remember for much of my childhood. I remember being hungry all the time." Cassian was certain that he had whined to his poor mother about his hunger. He wished he had kept his mouth shut. "She was desperate. She had to have been. We were starving and she needed to feed us. She could not afford to take us to London where people might have been more willing to take on a widow." Cassian noticed Faith's shoulders tense a little. "And so she did the only thing she could. She ... she became a ... prostitute." Cassian pressed his lips together. He had never actually said that word out loud. Did he carry shame about what his mother had done? Cassian did not think so. But he knew others would. He searched Faith's face for a reaction. "I remember her wasting away really. She died when I was ten. I have been on my own ever since."

She was not shocked. She did not appear disgusted. She only smiled serenely. "What was her name?" Faith asked softly.

Cassian breathed a sigh of relief. "Emma," he replied. "Her name was Emma." Emma Kensington had been his mother, and he loved her.

"She loved you," Faith promised him. "Mothers will do anything to keep their children happy and safe. Believe me."

Cassian did believe her. "I have never told anyone about her before," he admitted.

"I have never told anyone about my son before," Faith counter confessed.

Cassian furrowed his eyebrows. "Not even your husband?"

Faith shook her head. "No ... he probably thought I was just tubby," she said flippantly. "I was nearing my fifth month. I was not yet ready to tell him. And I was too late in the end."

Tubby? How could a man not know when his own wife was pregnant? Cassian wondered what sort of marriage Faith and her husband had once had. She did not speak of him. She did not seem to mourn him. At least, not on the same level as her dear son. Perhaps she had been betrothed to someone rich. Her parents were rich. They must have wanted to expand their holdings through their son-in-law, especially if Faith was an only child.

After all, Faith had told him that she had once collected faces too. She had been lonely at some point.

Why did this nasty thought make him happy? It was wrong to hope that Faith had not been married in a love match. Either way, the man was dead. It was wrong to think ill of the dead.

"I ought to dust your study, Mr Kensington," Faith said suddenly. "I really should be finished by now."

Cassian rose from his chair. He did not like the idea of Faith cleaning around him while he sat looking at numbers. "Can I help?" he asked.

Faith's eyes widened. "Really?"

"Put me to work," he encouraged.

Faith grinned as she handed him a cloth.

Together, they dusted and wiped down every surface in Cassian's study. They continued to chat as they worked, and Cassian marvelled at how easy it was to engage in conversation with Faith when he was not trying so hard to impress her.

Faith did not need to be impressed. She was interested in what he had to say anyway. Just as he was interested in what she had to say. She claimed to have an issue with holding her tongue, but he enjoyed her honesty. He had never before spoken to a woman who spoke the truth like she did.

Cassian had never before had a person to care about. He had spent his life on his own. But he sensed things were changing.

As he watched Faith leave, throwing one final beautiful smile over her shoulder at him, Cassian knew that he had made a friend.

CHAPTER 7

"You are awfully chipper this evening, Kensington," murmured Hounslow.

Cassian smirked. "I am always chipper when I am taking your money," he retorted.

Weatherby swore under his breath as he folded. "So bloody lucky. Just once I would like some of your luck, Kensington."

Cassian knew his skill at cards was not luck. In order for him to survive his childhood, Cassian had to learn how to tell if a man was trustworthy. Now the skill helped him to win a very tidy sum every Tuesday evening.

"I need to stop playing with you, Kensington. You will clean me out," complained Townsend. "Then again," he said thoughtfully, "it would give my wife less to spend."

Both Weatherby and Hounslow laughed. Cassian put on a false smile.

"But seriously, Kensington, where has this mood come from?" persisted Hounslow.

All three gentleman, who were now between hands, stared at Cassian waiting for him to answer.

Cassian nonchalantly took a swig of his whiskey. "I suppose I am in a good mood because I made a friend today," he replied honestly.

His conversation with Faith had truly put him in a wonderful mood. Gone was the awkwardness that had lingered between them in the week that she had been in his home, and they could now move forward in friendship.

"A friend?" repeated Townsend. "That is it?"

"She is a very special friend," insisted Cassian. His club friends did not know the circumstances of Cassian's self-made fortune. All they knew was that he had not always been rich.

"Oh, she?" Weatherby said teasingly. "Correct me if I am wrong, gentlemen, but did not Kensington sit here last week claiming that he did not have any time for a woman?"

"Yes, sir, you are right," Hounslow chimed in. "Tell us, Kensington, who is she?"

Much to Cassian's humiliation, he could feel blood rushing to his cheeks. He only hoped the dim candlelight in the room hid his embarrassment.

Faith was a very special person to Cassian for reasons that would always remain between them. He was not about to talk about Faith's business with his club friends. It did not seem right to discuss someone as lovely as Faith in and amongst the company of tipsy gentlemen and scantily clad women.

To end the conversation, Cassian decided to say, "She is a maid in my household."

All three men fell silent.

"A maid?" Hounslow furrowed his brow. "You are friends with a maid?"

"Yes," snapped Cassian.

"But ... she is a servant." Townsend tossed back the rest of his whiskey. "Maids are only good for two things, Kensington. Cleaning and bedding." He spoke as if he stated fact.

Cassian recoiled at his words.

How many maids had the man bedded? Was his wife privy to this knowledge?

And what did her occupation matter? Cassian instantly knew that was a stupid question. Servants were poor. Servants were inferior. Servants were there to serve.

But Cassian did not think that way. He did not behave that way. Did he? For the first time in several dozen Tuesdays, Cassian looked up from the table and noticed his surroundings.

There were half a dozen other tables that filled the large, expensively decorated room. Impossibly rich men sat at each, sipping fine liquor and puffing on pipes, giving the room a smoky haze. Women were draping themselves over the drunkest of men.

He noticed Fanny, the prostitute that had propositioned him only last week. He knew her well, or at least, he recognised her each week, and spoke to her fleetingly. But he did not know her. Was she desperate? Did she have a child? What had brought her to this? Why was she draping her lovely figure over a drunk banker who had a wife at home?

Servants stood around the perimeter of the room as well. The men were quick to scurry over to a table as soon as fingers were snapped or a rude grunt was shouted in their direction.

"What makes you better than them?" Cassian asked all three.

"Alright, you are cut off," announced Weatherby, who took the whiskey bottle out of Cassian's reach.

Cassian had not had more than a finger. "I am not drunk," he snapped, glaring at Weatherby.

"Kensington, it is a fact of life. High do not mix with low," Townsend explained calmly. "There is a reason some people are rich and some people are not. Some people are meant to socialise in ballrooms, and some people are meant to clean them. There is nothing wrong with that."

Cassian could not comprehend the stupidity that was coming out of their mouths. "There is nothing wrong with being a servant. They are people trying to earn an honest living, and they deserve our respect."

"Kensington, we have all been there. I guarantee you every man in this room has fancied a housemaid in his lifetime. Just get it over with," murmured Hounslow. "The sooner you get it out of your system, the better."

Cassian's admiration for Faith went much deeper than merely fancying her. Of course he thought she was pretty. Pretty did not really do her justice. She was beautiful, impossibly so. But her character, her strength, and her selflessness, astounded him. Cassian thought that she was an angel. He always had. An imperfectly perfect angel.

It made him sick to his stomach that Faith was even associated with this conversation.

Cassian stood up from the table abruptly and gathered up his winnings in his fist. The speed in which he stood had caused his chair to topple over backwards. A servant had quickly rushed over to right it for him, but Cassian held up his hand. He righted the chair himself, and then proceeded to hand the man a pound, which was more than likely a month's salary for him.

The servant's tired grey eyes widened as he stared at the money in his hands.

"Thank you, sir," he spluttered gratefully.

Cassian smiled before turning to his table. "Good evening," he wished insincerely.

"Until next Tuesday, Kensington," muttered Weatherby.

Cassian turned his back on the table while uttering, "Not bloody likely," under his breath.

Cassian was immediately faced with the image of Fanny propositioning herself. Her dress was terribly inappropriate, and she was far too young and pretty to be wearing something like that. Her gown was red, and was covered in little white embroidered flowers. The work on the dress was to be admired, but one noticed Fanny's scandalously low bodice before they noticed her gown. Cassian attempted to avert his eyes.

He thought of his mother, his poor, desperate mother, who had once stood in places like this propositioning men, all for the love of her son.

Cassian huffed, marched over to Fanny, and seized her by her upper arm. Fanny gasped in surprise, and the drunkard she was sitting on complained about her sudden absence, but Cassian did not care. He dragged Fanny towards the entryway into the card room.

As subtly as he could, he placed his winnings in Fanny's hand. Fanny's large, blue eyes widened. Her full lips, which were stained red, opened, and she gasped. "What are you doing?" she asked.

Fanny's whiny voice had always annoyed him, but now it was clear it was put on. She sounded relatively normal.

"Go home," he instructed. "Go and get something to eat, and go to bed. You do not need to be here tonight."

Fanny closed her hand around the small pile of bank notes. A smile spread across her face as her eyes filled with tears. "You cannot know what this means," she whispered as she stood up on her toes and kissed his cheek. Fanny scampered off towards a door that only the servants used.

Cassian felt a deep sense of satisfaction. Was this how Faith had felt when she had helped him?

Not an hour later, Cassian had arrived home, and was lying in bed, his mind going over the events of the day.

What had transpired at the club sickened him. It sickened him to know that society fostered such disrespect for one's inferiors.

According to society laws, Fanny was dirt, nothing more than a common whore. But her reaction to receiving the money told him that it meant something. She mattered to someone, or someone mattered to her.

And according to society laws, Faith was below him. But Cassian knew she was superior to him in every way possible.

Faith had endured the loss of a child. The image of her holding out her hand as she described the size of her son would haunt him forever, Cassian was certain. Faith had survived that. She had survived the death of her husband. She had survived the transition into poverty.

And yet, she had found it in her heart to save a dying man, someone who was so obviously beneath her.

Every single one of those gentlemen in that room could stand to learn something from Faith.

Cassian had several errands to run the next day. He needed to go to the bank regarding his purchases of several wheels for his factories up north. He needed to visit his tailor. And he was completing the purchase of a new piece of art.

Faith would love it. It was another face to add to his collection. He wondered if she would like to see it with him.

That idea appealed to him. His day would be remarkably less boring if he had company. And perhaps, if they were alone, Faith would talk to him a bit more.

Of course, he would need an excuse to take Faith away from her duties for the day. Cassian would think of something.

Cassian barely touched his breakfast, took a few sips of tea, before he threw on his clothes for the day. He practically fell down the stairs, taking them three at a time, before he came to the foyer.

In the week that he had been awkwardly avoiding Faith, Cassian had memorised where she would be during the day. Each morning, she and Hattie, another housemaid, polished the already pristine and unused silverware in the dining room.

Cassian opened the dining room door without thinking to knock, surprising the women. Both were sitting at the dining table, polishing cloths in hand, with his entire collection before them. Cassian knew they were not supposed to sit at his table. It was a silly rule of Wade's, but he honestly did not mind.

Both Faith and Hattie were quick to stand up, though.

"Be calm, ladies," said Cassian. "Faith, I was wondering if I might borrow you for the day."

Faith's brows immediately furrowed. "Me?"

"Yes, I have need of a woman's opinion," he lied, for the benefit of Hattie. Where was he going with this? "I am buying a gift. I need a woman's eye." Hmm, believable.

Faith seemed to believe him as her frown deepened and her brown eyes narrowed. "Oh, is there to be a lady visitor?" she asked tensely.

It immensely amused Cassian that Faith felt threatened by his imaginary lover. It also flattered him that she knew that their relationship was more than master and servant. They were friends, and that was very important to him.

"Perhaps," he said, just to vex her. It did just that. He noticed Faith's grip on the polishing cloth tighten. "Hattie, will you please tell Wade that I have relieved Faith of her responsibilities for the day?" he asked.

"Yes, sir," replied Hattie, nodding.

"I cannot leave," Faith insisted. "Lucy..."

"We will watch her," Hattie offered. "She is still in bed, is she not? When she wakes, I shall take her down to the laundry with me. She can play while I fold."

Faith's eyes softened at Hattie's offer, but she still looked a little hesitant.

"Get your cloak," Cassian urged.

Faith did as she was told, albeit reluctantly. She returned wearing her cloak. She was no longer wearing her white cap. Cassian enjoyed being able to properly see her lovely brown hair. She looked at him with wary eyes and Cassian knew he was going to be in trouble for vexing her.

Mr Green was waiting outside Cassian's house, leaning against the carriage as he read the newspaper. As soon as he saw Cassian and Faith he folded the newspaper and tucked it under his arm.

"Good morning, sir," he greeted. "Good morning, Mrs Rowe."

Faith offered Mr Green a kind smile. "Good morning."

"Good morning, Green. The bank first today," he instructed.

"Yes, sir."

Mr Green opened the door for him, just as Faith was doing her best to climb up into the driver's seat. Her skirts made it impossible. She needed help.

"What are you doing?" Cassian asked her.

Faith's head snapped to him. "Trying to climb up gracefully," she huffed. She was still annoyed at him.

"Just a moment, Mrs Rowe. I shall help you," offered Mr Green.

"No, you will ride inside with me," insisted Cassian. "How am I supposed to talk to you if you are sitting up there?"

Faith abandoned her efforts to climb up into the driver's seat and moved before him. "We are not travelling as companions, Mr Kensington. Servants do not share carriages with their masters."

Cassian had half a mind to purchase another carriage specifically for his servants to use after what he had experienced the night before. "You have ridden with me before," he said softly.

Faith's cheeks reddened. "That was different. I was not officially in your employ then, and I had Lucy with me."

Cassian relieved Mr Green of the door and he held it open for her. "In," he urged, motioning her inside.

Faith hesitated for a moment before ultimately giving in and climbing inside the carriage.

Cassian followed her inside and sat down opposite her. Faith's hands were knitted in her lap. He felt a tension in the air, and he immediately wanted to ease it.

"I would like for you to be my companion for the day," he said sincerely.

Confusion filled Faith's face. "I beg your pardon?"

"Faith, are we friends?"

Faith pursed her lips. "We ought not to be," she replied.

"But are we?" he pressed. Words could not be exchanged like they had been the day before without friendship blossoming.

Faith nodded. "Yes."

"Good." Cassian smiled. "Then we are going to do some inordinately dull errands together whilst enjoying each other's company."

"Are you not buying a gift for a woman?"

"Only if you would like one."

Faith laughed and relaxed into her seat, a look of peacefulness filling her face. Cassian wanted to tell her how beautiful she was, but before he spoke, he noticed something about her that he had not seen before.

As her head had turned to look out the window, her fringe had moved away from directly covering her hairline. Along Faith's hairline was a long, pink scar. It was healed, and it looked like it was a few years old, but where had she got that?

CHAPTER 8

The carriage came to a stop outside Cassian's bank. He suddenly wished he did not have a list of banal errands to run. He really wanted to ask Faith about the scar on her hairline.

A dozen different scenarios had crossed his mind since he had noticed it. All of them worse than the last. But was it not rude to comment on a woman's appearance in a negative way?

"What business do you have here?" asked Faith as she looked up at the bank from the window.

"I just need to authorise payment to a wheel manufacturer," replied Cassian. "I have ordered half a dozen of them for my factories in the north."

"What do they do?" asked Faith.

"They help to blow away the excess cotton so that the workers do not inhale it. It is a health risk, you see. Cotton clogs the lungs." And even though these wheels were costing him a fortune, life was far more precious.

Faith smiled. "Take as long as you need."

"Do you want to come inside?" Cassian asked. What a glorious outing it would be. A trip to the bank. He groaned internally.

Faith pursed her lips. "Oh, are women allowed in there?"

Cassian actually did not know. Had he seen women inside the bank before? Surely some of them accompanied their husbands. Either way, Cassian knew he was an important customer to the bank. If he wanted to bring Faith inside with him, he would.

"Come on," he urged.

Mr Green opened the door and Cassian climbed out. He then held his hand out for Faith. She placed her small hand in his and stepped down onto the street. As Cassian started up the steps, he noticed that Faith was not walking beside him. She had allowed him to move five steps ahead of her before following.

"What are you doing?" he asked, stopping midway up the stairs.

Faith looked up at him and frowned. "Walking."

"Behind me?"

Faith pressed her lips firmly together and gave him a knowing look. "Whether you like it or not, servants do not walk beside their masters. They walk behind them. I cannot walk into that building as your equal."

"Do you expect me to talk to you over my shoulder all day?" he challenged. "I shall get a neck ache."

They caught the eyes of several curious strangers walking the streets of London. Men wearing their best coats and hats paused on the bank steps briefly to watch him speak to a woman dressed like a servant.

"You are being difficult, Mr Kensington," Faith murmured, wary of onlookers.

Cassian was not about to give in. "Take my arm," he insisted, offering it to her.

Faith stared at him, her brown eyes flicking between his face and his outstretched arm. She was searching his face to see if he was being sincere. How could he not be?

After a few moments of indecision, Faith gave in. She hurried up the steps and slipped her arm through his. She fit comfortably, and he felt oddly proud to be walking with her like he was.

Cassian found himself enjoyed the stares of others. Were they jealous of the beauty that was on his arm? She was not his, but they did not know that. Little did they all know that there was much more to Faith than just her beauty. Only few were privy to that knowledge. He was one of the lucky few.

Cassian's business inside the bank took just over half an hour. The manager did not challenge the fact that Faith was with him, though his judgemental sneer was enough to let Cassian know that he did not think much of Faith.

It honestly made Cassian want to take his business elsewhere. He would look into it.

Cassian decided to skip seeing his tailor and instead took Faith directly to see the painting he was thinking about buying. They journeyed to the home of an old widow, Mrs Forster. The painting had belonged to her husband, and she was now selling his possessions to pay off debts.

It was really none of his business but the Forster scandal had been front page news for a few weeks in the summer.

Cassian watched Faith as they travelled towards Mrs Forster's London home. She really was angelically beautiful. Cassian knew that he would be lying if he said he were not attracted to her. It was hard not to be.

Any man could see how fair she was. Cassian appreciate her beauty. But he appreciated her heart more, and he meant that sincerely. The gentlemen at the club could mock him all they wanted, but Faith was the sort of good that he wanted to immerse himself in.

Who else but an angel would give a fortune away to an urchin she did not know?

But there were so many questions surrounding Faith.

If he was being honest, Cassian really did not know much about Faith. Cassian was sure he knew more about Faith than most. After all, she had told him about her son, but there was so much more to her. There had to be.

One day, he hoped, she would trust him enough to tell him everything.

Her fringe had fallen aside again as she looked out the window, exposing that pink scar once more.

"What happened to your head?" asked Cassian. It took him a moment to realise he had actually asked the question out loud.

Faith's eyes immediately widened and she slapped her hand over the scar. Faith fluffed her fringe so that it covered her hairline scar properly. "Nasty accident," she murmured. "A few years ago I tripped. Hit my head on a table."

Cassian wondered why she had just lied to him. He could see it in her eyes. She was waiting for him to call her on her lie. But he did not confront her. Faith could tell him the truth when she was ready to.

But that only made the scenarios in his head that much worse.

Mrs Forster was not in. Cassian and Faith was shown to the drawing room by a servant and they were left alone. The drawing room was quite empty. Quite a few pieces had been sold. All that was left was a few settees, a mantel clock, and two paintings on the adjacent walls.

One was of a landscape. The other, the one Cassian was interested in, was a portrait of a woman.

The raven haired woman was sitting by a window, looking over her shoulder at a closed door. She looked ... sad. But that was what

Cassian liked about the painting. Her face told a story. She was a real person. Someone else to add to his collection.

"Who do you suppose she is?" asked Faith. She, too, was standing beside him while looking up at the painting.

"I would like to hear your thoughts," Cassian countered.

Faith exhaled and cocked her head thoughtfully. "I imagine she spends most of her time by that window," she mused. "She looks like she is waiting for someone."

"A man?"

"Perhaps. But he is not coming. He never comes."

"How do you know?"

"Look at her face." Faith sighed. "She looks so sad."

Cassian had never encountered anyone who imagined up personalities for paintings just like he did. "Is she waiting on her lover?"

"No," Faith said firmly. "Look out the window. She is very high up. She is waiting on a rescuer."

Cassian smiled. Faith was imagining a fairy tale. "But he is not coming," Cassian continued. "What is she to do?"

"Rescue herself," Faith said firmly. "She will rescue herself."

"And how does she do that?"

Faith shrugged her shoulders. "I am sure she is still trying to work it out. But women cannot always rely upon knights on white horses. They only exist in stories, you know."

Cassian could read between the lines. Faith was talking about herself in the most cryptic way possible. She was trying to rescue herself. She was trying to pull herself out of the mess that her husband had left her in.

"Well, I pray she does not give up hope," Cassian murmured.

"Oh, she hasn't. She is still by the window. Less frequently now, I imagine, but she still waits. She has ..." Faith smiled bashfully, "faith."

"Mr Kensington, I did not know you were arriving this early!" cried Mrs Forster, who had just entered the drawing room. Mrs Forster was in her late fifties, and the financial stress she had been under these last few months had taken its toll on her. She really looked her age.

Cassian had never been personally acquainted with Mr and Mrs Forster, but they were known to have lived an affluent lifestyle.

"Sorry to intrude. A servant showed us in," replied Cassian.

"Not at all, not at all," replied Mrs Forster. "What do you think of the painting?" she asked.

Before Cassian could answer, Faith asked, "Who is she?"

"Oh, my late sister-in-law. Horrid woman. The sourpuss was painted as a gift for my husband's thirtieth birthday."

Cassian and Faith both looked at each other and laughed. They could not have been more wrong about the woman's story, but Cassian liked theirs better anyway. "I shall take it, Mrs Forster. Thank you very much."

Cassian paid Mrs Forster discreetly as a servant helped to carry the painting out to his waiting carriage. The Forsters lived near Hyde Park. Cassian lived on the other side of the park in Kensington.

It would be just shy of a two mile walk back to his home, give or take a few meandering trails in the park. "Please take the painting home," he told Mr Green. "Faith and I will walk from here."

"Yes, sir," replied Mr Green, as Faith peered at Cassian curiously.

Cassian was not ready for their day to be over.

The November air had a real bite to it. He was warm enough in his overcoat. He only hoped that Faith was warm enough underneath her cloak.

"You really do not have a care for social hierarchy, do you?" Faith murmured just as soon as his carriage moved away.

Cassian offered his arm to Faith, and this time she did not protest. They started towards Hyde Park. "Neither do you," he countered.

Faith furrowed her eyebrows. "What do you mean?"

"A proper lady would never have stopped her carriage to help a grubby street urchin," he replied.

"You are assuming that I am a proper lady," she murmured.

"Come now," Cassian said firmly. "We both know you were, are, a proper lady."

With the clouds as low as they were, the park appeared quite grey and dreary. The deciduous trees had all lost their foliage and their surroundings were quite bleak. But Cassian's focus was solely on the nervous brown eyes of his companion.

"Won't you tell me?" Cassian fought the urge to caress her cheek comfortingly. It would probably startle her more than anything.

Faith clamped her lips shut.

"Surely you must know that anything you tell me will stay between us. I owe you my life, Faith. You can trust me."

"I do know that," whispered Faith.

"What happened to you?" he pressed. "Let me help you."

Faith offered him a touched smile. "You already have helped me," she insisted. "Lucy and I have a home because of you." Faith's grip tightened on Cassian's arm ever so slightly. "I am just like that woman, Mrs Forster," Faith began. "I was married to a very rich man and I lived an extravagant lifestyle. But when he died, it was all gone. I was forced to make the decision to come to London so that I could provide for my child when she came."

Had Faith been pregnant when she had found him? Cassian's memories of that day centred on the angel that had found him. He had not really noticed if her dress was at all tight.

"If you wanted to provide for your child, why would you give everything to me?"

"You cannot know what I saw in your eyes on that day. Your needs were greater than mine," Faith said firmly.

Cassian suddenly felt immensely guilty. His desperate, hungry eyes had taken funds away from Lucy. How was that right?

"I am glad I made the decisions I did. You cannot know how glad I am. The decisions I made brought Lucy and me into your home. We are safe and healthy. What more could a mother want for her child?" Faith's eyes turned away from him. She looked out on the path they were walking. "Where are you going to hang Mrs Forster's vile sister-in-law?" she asked, changing the subject.

Cassian knew Faith was still only telling him pieces of her story.

He knew she was a rich man's widow. Who was this man? He knew she had lost a son and never told anyone. He knew she had left her home, in God knows where, to come to London to find work. Along the way, it seemed, she had found a half dead Cassian on the side of the road.

Cassian probably knew more about this woman that anyone, and yet he still felt as though she was a mystery, hiding pieces of herself. But why?

Cassian knew one more thing.

He knew he was destined to fall in love with this woman. It was only a matter of time.

CHAPTER 9

Faith found Lucy in the laundry room with Hattie just before tea time. Lucy was sitting on top of a pile of freshly laundered sheets playing with her doll, while Hattie folded linen.

"Hello," cooed Faith as she leant down to lift Lucy into her arms. Lucy nuzzled the crook of Faith's neck and her hair tickled Faith's nose. It was one of her favourite feelings in the world.

"We were wondering when you would return," remarked Hattie. "Did you find one then?"

"One what?"

"A gift ..." replied Hattie slowly. "Mr Kensington wanted you to help him find a gift, did he not?"

Faith suddenly remembered the false pretences in which Cassian had asked her out. She had initially believed him. She had thought that he wanted her help in picking out a present for a woman. And if she was being honest, she was glad that it was not the truth. It was selfish of her to think so, but it was the truth.

"Oh, yes," she replied. "He bought a painting." Even if it was of Mrs Forster's vile sister-in-law, Faith liked the story they had imagined up. It really had not taken much for her to imagine up that story.

"A painting?" repeated Hattie, abandoning her laundry. "That is not awfully romantic. Why did he not pick out a nice bauble? That is what I would want from an admirer."

Faith shrugged her shoulders as she peered down at Lucy. "Paintings can be romantic too," she said, especially when people buy them together. Faith pushed away the thought. "Thank you for minding her," Faith said appreciatively, changing the subject. "Was she good?"

"As good as gold," promised Hattie. "We washed the linens together, didn't you Lucy?" Hattie smiled at Faith's toddler. "Then when I went upstairs to change the beds, Lucy went with Mrs Denham and helped make this evening's pudding. You helped stir, didn't you Lucy?"

Faith beamed with pride, but also with gratefulness at the acceptance of her new friends in the household. They all had accepted Lucy so easily. It truly touched her heart. Even Mr Wade had warmed to Lucy. Lucy had a sweet way of wrapping people around her little finger. "Did you help stir, Lucy?"

Lucy bashfully hid her face as she nodded.

"Come on," Hattie urged. "Supper will be served any minute."

Faith was absent from the conversation around the table as she cut up Lucy's mutton into small pieces for her. None of the conversation was really aimed towards her when Lucy was around. The ladies all cooed at Lucy, who bashfully enjoyed the attention, and the men were talking about the latest parliament scandal.

Faith could not quite understand how her trust in Cassian had developed over the past week or so. The man managed to extract information from her that no one else ever had. Not that she made it difficult. She freely told him things, but why?

There was something about him. She had sensed it three years ago, and she felt it now. Cassian Kensington was different, and that made her nervous.

There was an innocence about Cassian. He had not grown up around the poison that the rich fed themselves. He was not raised to think that he was above anyone. If anything, he probably still felt as though he was equal to the lowliest street urchin in London.

Cassian seemed to enjoy the privileges that came with bring rich, without having the selfish, entitled, pretentious attitude that seemed to accompany most men.

Despite the horrific way in which Cassian had grown up, there was not a cold, cruel, resentful bone in his body. Faith could see that Cassian only had love to give. She could see that in the way that he collected paintings. He was lonely. Today was not the first time that she had imagined up a story for a nameless face in a painting.

She had once created a story for every face in her house.

Cassian was good.

Faith knew that she had made the right decision three years ago. She could have given that man a few coins and moved on, but no, she knew she had to give him more. Something inside her had told her on that day to have faith in him.

And after all this time, her faith was repaying her.

Faith had ... a friend. She had not had many of those over the years. Ever. Faith had lived a very lonely existence. Even though she did not have two shillings to rub together, she felt as though she was finally coming up for air.

Things would be alright. Faith exhaled, a small smiled forming on her face. For the first time in three years, Faith was confident that everything would be alright.

Cassian was her friend. It defied all conventions for a man and a woman to be friends, but they were not conventional people.

Cassian was a man raised from the gutter to be a rich man, and Faith was ... well, she was something else.

Faith needed to be honest with Cassian. He deserved it.

"You aren't hungry, Faith?"

Hattie's question broke Faith's daydream. Faith looked down at her untouched meal. "Oh, I am. I was just thinking."

"Happy thoughts, I hope."

"Yes," replied Faith. "Happy thoughts."

Once supper was over, Mr Wade took Cassian's meal upstairs while the evening chores were completed. Faith quickly took Lucy up to bed and tucked her in before running back down to help.

At ten o'clock, it was time for bed. Faith closed the door softly so as not to wake Lucy, but she failed. Lucy sat up lethargically in her little bed, her curly hair sticking up in all directions.

"Mama?" she croaked sleepily.

"Shh," hushed Faith. "It is late, Lucy. I am sorry to wake you." Faith crossed the room and knelt down beside her daughter's bed. She brushed Lucy's hair out of her brown eyes and stroked her forehead. Lucy's forehead was so smooth. There were no lines, but of course there would not be on a two and a half year old child. Lucy had known no worry, no cruelty, and no sadness. Faith would endeavour to keep it that way.

Lucy would have the most beautiful life. Faith would move heaven and earth to ensure that she had the life that was so cruelly denied her brother.

Lucy's eyes fluttered and she fell quickly back to sleep. Faith smiled and kissed her daughter before changing and climbing into bed herself.

As Faith laid her head down on the pillow, she looked over at her sleeping daughter. Lucy was perfect. "I will give you a beautiful life," Faith whispered through the darkness.

Faith knew that Cassian would help to ensure that if she asked. A small part of her wanted to ask, but she could not. It would feel like retreating, relying on a life that she had left behind.

But she did need to be honest with Cassian. She needed to tell him the truth. He called her an angel, but he did not even know the reason she was on that road on that day.

He did not even know her real name.

Stay silent.

Be quiet.

Do not move.

Maybe he will just ignore you.

"Mmm, this wine is excellent." Her husband made a pleasurable noise as he enjoyed on whatever wine the butler had selected for them that night.

She would not know. She had not taken a sip. Perhaps she should. It would make whatever happened later not so painful.

"Delicious," agreed her husband's brother, John.

"It is divine with the pork," added her sister-in-law, Ruth.

She listened to the sounds of cutlery on china. Slowly, she brought her shaking hands to her own silverware and began to cut a slice of her own meat. It took all the strength she had to swallow. She was so tense her jaw could barely move. Underneath her powder, her ashen, lifeless skin was purple.

The unsteadiness of her hands created a rattling noise against her plate, one that drew attention from the whole table. She clamped her eyes shut, daring not to look at him. Anything, any-thing, she did drew his ire.

"Are you cold, Anne?"

Her eyes flashed open at the sound of her name. She mustered whatever courage she had to meet his cool, grey eyes. "No," she stammered.

George placed his silverware down gently, lifted his napkin to his mouth, and then exhaled calmly.

"Oh, well if you are not cold, then why would you interrupt our lovely dinner with your childish racket?" George asked icily.

She wanted to run, but she knew if she did, things would be so much worse.

John and Ruth just sat there, watching. They knew exactly how George was. Everyone knew exactly how George was. Her own parents knew exactly what George was like, but nobody would help her.

Nobody could help her.

She was wed to the devil.

"Maybe I am a little cold," she whispered, only trying to delay what was coming.

"Do you see?" George exclaimed to his brother. "Do you see the liar that she is? I am at my wit's end. She is a disobedient, lying, barren little bitch."

She winced at the words. Barren. She was not barren. But George had seen to it that there was no child. How she wished she had died on that day, too.

"I am going to go and check on Olivia," murmured Ruth. "You know how she likes to read when she should be sleeping." Ruth hurried cowardly out of the dining room to go and check on her eight year old daughter, Olivia.

George had boiled into such a rage, a rage over cutlery noise, and he threw back his chair. It fell over backwards with a loud crash. His boots thundered against the floor as he marched towards her.

All she could do was close her eyes and prepare herself. A single tear rolled down her cheek. She felt him grab a fist full of her hair and he pulled her to her feet. She gasped in pain and her hands went to her head. No sooner had she grabbed at her hair, George had slapped her to the ground.

His strong, hard hand collided with her cheek, and she fell, slamming her temple against the table before crumpling to the ground.

A sharp pain, localised on her temple, suddenly consumed her. Nothing else hurt in that moment but her head. She felt the familiar, warm sensation of blood seeping from the fresh wound.

"Fancy a whiskey, John?" George asked his brother casually. "I need something stiffer to wash down the wine."

"Why not?"

They both left the dining room, leaving her there bleeding on the floor.

All she could do was cry. Cry for help that she knew would never come. Nobody would help her. Nobody was coming to rescue her. She was going to die just like her son, at the hands of a monster.

Faith woke up with a start. Her heart was pounding in her chest and she was covered in a layer of sweat. Faith buried her face in her hands and cried soundless sobs.

It was not odd for her to have nightmares.

She had them often. But that one was a bad one. Faith touched the scar on her forehead, the one Cassian had asked about earlier. Perhaps that was what had brought on the nightmare.

This fear she had in the back of her mind made her feel so powerless. Fear was crippling. No matter how far she progressed in her life, the fear was always there to put her back in her place.

Faith took a deep breath and did her best to control her heartbeat. She threw back the bedclothes and went over to her basin to wash her face free from sweat.

That life was behind her. As far as anyone was concerned, Anne Pendleton was dead.

CHAPTER 10

"The post, sir," murmured Mr Wade, "and today's newspaper."

Cassian could not help but laugh when he looked up at his butler. Mr Wade was holding a silver tray with the daily correspondence in one hand, and little Lucy Rowe in the other. Faith's toddler was sitting contently on his butler's hip.

Considering Mr Wade had been so reluctant to take on a housemaid with a child, he certainly had acclimated himself. In fact, he seemed oblivious to the fact that his behaviour was odd.

"A new friend, Wade?"

He only seemed to notice that he had Lucy with him when she started to play with one of his sideburns. "Oh," he chuckled. "Well, I needed the ladies to focus this morning and all of their attention seems to be on this one." Mr Wade could pretend all he liked, but Cassian could see fondness in his eyes. He had a soft spot for Lucy.

"Give her to me," instructed Cassian, rising from his chair and extending his arms. "All I have to do today is correspondence. I can look after her."

"Very good, sir."

Cassian accepted Lucy from Mr Wade and he held her close to his side to support her. She had a very curious look in her brown eyes. They so mirrored her mother's. Cassian had not really seen much of Lucy since she had arrived with Faith. Perhaps concealing her was Faith's way of ensuring that she would not be a bother to Cassian. But he did not mind.

If Lucy had managed to get Mr Wade onside then she was an angel.

"Do you remember my name?" Cassian asked her, sitting back down in his chair and sitting Lucy on his lap.

Lucy cocked her head, her sweet curls bouncing. "No."

Cassian smiled. He had only ever introduced himself once. "My name is Cassian," he told her again. "Your Mama is my friend."

"Cassian," she repeated. Lucy's attention quickly shifted to the papers that were strewn across his desk. Her little hand travelled over to a stock report and she lifted it up, pretending to read. "A story?" she asked, looking up at Cassian.

"A very dull one," he chuckled.

Lucy frowned, confused. "Read?" she persisted.

Cassian supposed he could have a go at turning his dull stock report into a story. He took the page from Lucy, who promptly grinned excitedly. He cleared his throat and began. "Once upon a time, there was a man named Gerald Hockley, who lived in a faraway land called Yorkshire. Mr Hockley had a very important job in Yorkshire. He looked after all the workers in the village. One day, Mr Hockley wrote a letter, a very important letter to his master. His name was Cassian."

Lucy gasped excitedly.

Cassian was bewildered. How was she finding this interesting? Nevertheless, he continued. "He wrote to Cassian telling him how many shipments of ..." cotton was not very interesting, "... fancy dresses were ready to be sent to ..." not manufacturers, "... Princess Lucy."

Lucy beamed. "Me?" she squealed.

Cassian relaxed a little. "Yes, you, Princess Lucy." He smiled. "There were ten fancy dresses ready to be sent. Blue ones, and pink ones, and all sorts. Princess Lucy needed the dresses for all the parties she was going to attend, after all, she now lives in London."

Lucy shifted herself on Cassian's lap so that she was standing up on his thighs. She was holding on to the collar of his shirt and her face was level with his. She looked so excited to be hearing his waffle of a story.

There was a look of youthful wonder in her brown eyes. Cassian had never seen anything like it.

"And one day, Princess Lucy met a handsome prince," Cassian continued. "The prince was very charming, and kind, and clever. Only the best for Princess Lucy."

Cassian was near hypnotised by Lucy. He had never before witnessed real childhood innocence. He had never been privy to it himself, and so this was completely foreign to him. Cassian felt compelled to protect this quality in her. Innocence was fleeting, and too often taken. Faith had done such a wonderful job to protect Lucy's. Cassian would help her.

"But Princess Lucy would not accept any old prince, no matter how charming. She decided she would stay with her mama and her new friend Cassian for a little while longer. The end."

Cassian discarded the stock report on his desk and leaned back in his chair, Lucy still standing up on him. The dead weight on his legs was slightly painful but he did not mind.

"Was that a nice story?" he asked, hopeful that he had turned a banal report into something interesting.

Lucy nodded. "Oh, yes," she said dreamily. "Again."

Cassian exhaled. Would he be able to recall what he had just said? Probably not. Instead, he picked up his cheque book and began to read about Princess Lucy and her horse, Sunshine.

Two hours later, Cassian had read Lucy half a dozen fantasy stories, and was now immersed in a game of dolls. He was sitting on the floor in his study, completely neglecting his work, mesmerised as Lucy played around him, making up a story in her broken toddler speech.

At midday, there was knock on the door.

"Yes?" Cassian called.

His study door opened and Faith entered carrying his lunch tray. Her brown eyes immediately softened at the sight before her. "Mr Wade told me she was in here. I hope she is not bothering you."

"On the contrary," Cassian countered, "Princess Lucy, here, has given me my next business idea. I am going to write children's stories. Apparently I have a gift for them," he teased.

"Princess?" Faith arched an eyebrow. "My, aren't you being spoiled, Lucy?"

Lucy trotted over to her mother and hugged her legs, just as Faith set the lunch tray down on the table.

"Lucy likes her stories. I wish I could buy more of them," Faith confessed.

"I could –" Cassian started but Faith interrupted him.

"That was not a request for charity," she said firmly. "Her birthday is in a few months. Then and only then," she instructed.

Cassian sighed, wishing it were not so difficult to help. "You know, Faith, there is grace in accepting charity. You are an angel. You deserve it."

Cassian could tell Faith did not agree with him as she changed the subject. "Thank you so much for entertaining her this morning, Mr Kensington. I do sincerely appreciate it. Everyone has been so kind to her," Faith said sincerely as she lifted Lucy up into her arms.

Cassian climbed to his feet and straitened his waist coat. "She really is an awful child. It was such a chore," he teased.

Faith laughed lightly. Cassian noticed a sudden change in Faith's facial expression as she chewed on her bottom lip nervously. "I ought to tell you something," she started nervously.

Cassian furrowed his eyebrows. "What?" he asked curiously.

Colour drained from Faith's cheeks. "You have been so kind to us, and you are such a good man, that I feel that I ought to tell you the truth," Faith stammered.

Cassian was starting to feel ill. What on earth was she worried about?

Faith's lips parted but no words escaped. After a few moments, she found her voice. "I ... I ought to tell you that ... I am not sure I like that painting." Panicked, she pointed to the painting he had purchased the day before of Mrs Forster's sister-in-law.

Cassian frowned. "Oh ... that is alright," he murmured. Why was she so nervous to tell him that? He did not mind. His taste in artwork was not to everyone's liking.

"Yes, well, I will leave you to your luncheon," she mumbled, scurrying from the study.

"Oh, you coward," Faith cursed herself. "You big, lying coward!"

Faith had been about to tell him, but the words tasted like ash on her tongue. Cassian thought of her as an angel. Angels were perfect. Faith was the farthest thing from perfect.

Faith was selfish and deceitful and there could be no redemption for her. She had gone too far.

She certainly did not deserve charity. Lucy, on the other hand, deserved everything. Faith felt guilty for denying her daughter the storybooks, but Faith felt as though she needed to be the one to provide, seeing as she was the one who had taken the away the life Lucy could have had.

Faith often thought of her niece, Olivia. She would be eleven now. She was the most gorgeous child, brought up with riches and fine things, yet she cared only for her books, and had a very clever head on her shoulders.

Lucy could have been just like her. By birth, she was Lady Lucy Pendleton. The daughter of an earl. Entitled to anything and everything.

But Faith only had to think of her son, her poor, lost son, to know that she could not have lived with the fear of the same thing happening to Lucy. She would not have survived that pain twice.

Just as she was about to open the door to descend to the kitchen, she heard her name being called.

"Faith!" cried Cassian.

Faith turned around to see Cassian standing in the doorway of his study.

His brow was furrowed and his dark eyes were fixed on her. My, he was handsome when he was concerned. "Are you alright?"

Faith nodded, but she was certain her facial expression resembled more of a grimace as she disappeared down the stairs.

Lucy, not surprisingly anymore, was taken by Mr Wade just as soon as she arrived downstairs for luncheon. She was grateful that the butler did not seem to mind Lucy anymore, and selfishly, she was hopeful that the attachment meant that there would be job security for her.

Faith smiled. Lucy seemed to like Mr Wade. She had a fistful of his collar as he sat down at the head of the table to eat.

Walking in on Cassian and Lucy had warmed her heart. Cassian was sitting on the floor, playing make-believe with Lucy. She could see it in his eyes; he was mesmerised. Cassian genuinely enjoyed playing whatever toddler babble Lucy was spouting and it brought tears of joy to her eyes just thinking about it.

Faith needed to quickly brush those away before anyone noticed.

Cassian was so good. He was the angel. There was a part of her, a very large part, which felt so drawn to him. Perhaps it was what had drawn her to him three years earlier. He was good, and kind, and warm, and safe.

She and Lucy were safe with Cassian.

Her husband could never have been the kind of father she Faith would have wanted for Lucy, but nevertheless, Faith had denied Lucy the right of a father. Whatever connection Lucy was developing with the gentlemen in this household, she hoped it could compensate.

"You alrigh' there, milady?"

Anne jumped, and quickly wiped her eyes with her lace handkerchief. She had not expected to be found by anyone here. She was hiding down by the lake. Their estate had such a pretty lake, surrounded by tall grass and wildflowers.

It was here, under a cluster of tall, red flowers, that she had buried her son a year ago. It was her secret. Nobody knew. Not even George. What would he do if he knew she had lost a son and heir? He would never accept that it was his fault that their boy had been lost. He had been so tiny; smaller than her palm.

And yet here she sat, with child again, and what was she to do? If she even looked at George the wrong way she was sentenced to a shove. That was all it had taken with her son. A shove, a trip, and a fall down the stairs.

Anne looked up at Mr Carne, their driver. He was an older, portly man, who loved his horses, and did not mind sitting atop fine carriages if it meant driving them.

"Oh, yes, I am fine," Anne lied. She climbed to her feet and brushed the dirt and pollen off of her skirt.

Mr Carne pursed his lips and crossed his arms over his chest. "You've been cryin', milady," he stated.

Since when did men notice tears?

"The pollen," she murmured. "It itches my eyes."

"Did you know I got a daughter abou' your age, milady?" Mr Carne said casually. "Sian, she is. Do you know wha' I would do to any creature who laid an ill hand on her?"

Of course the servants knew. They were not blind.

"What would you do?" Anne asked powerlessly.

"I would string 'im up," Mr Carne growled. "Enough is enough, milady. You need to leave."

Anne's eyes narrowed. "What are you talking about?"

"I am talkin' about leavin' that lout you are wed to and makin' a life for yourself elsewhere!"

"No!" exclaimed Anne. "You cannot understand." Instinctively, she placed a hand on her stomach. Mr Carne was obviously insane. Wives did not leave their husbands. Ever. And what of her child? What would she do? "George would never let me leave."

"Milady, I was not suggestin' that you ask the master's permission."

CHAPTER 11

It became somewhat routine that Cassian would entertain Lucy during the day while the servants went about their business.

Much to Faith's reluctance, Cassian had purchased several story books for Lucy, and read them to her frequently. She never seemed to tire of the repetition. Lucy could also please herself playing make-believe when Cassian did have to pull himself away to complete the work that was piling up.

It was amazing how quickly he could fall behind in his correspondence when he was playing tea parties.

That was something else that he had purchased for Lucy – a tea set. Faith had protested, of course, but Cassian had simply quipped, "Faith, how can we possibly have a tea party without a proper tea set?"

Cassian had eventually persuaded Faith to join one of their tea parties. He loved to see her relax, and simply enjoy a few moments in time, without worrying about money, or Lucy being a bother, or whatever other worries lived inside her pretty head. Faith always seemed to have something on her mind.

Faith was so beautiful when she smiled. She was beautiful all the time, but even more so when she smiled. Cassian realised it did not happen often. He wanted to change that. She did not need to worry, if only she would let him help her.

Cassian's fleeting moments with Faith, and his time with Lucy, had quickly become the favourite parts of his day. Cassian forced himself to get through his work, and complete his correspondence so that he could spend more time with them.

He had been putting off visiting Angel Faith and his other nearby factories but he knew it was not fair to neglect his workers. He dreaded when he would need to travel north and be away for weeks at a time. It was nearly alarming how attached he was becoming.

When Tuesday came, Cassian skipped his weekly card game for a story about a princess and a frog. Cassian had no desire to drink whiskey and win money from those men when he had a better offer.

Cassian did not have any memory of his father. His memories of his mother were sad and brief. But he liked to think that Lucy was benefitting from his time with her. He knew he was not her father, but perhaps it was good practice for him in the future. Cassian had no desire to be the kind of father that Townsend, Hounslow, and Weatherby were, the kind that had staff to care for their children.

That thought made him laugh. A mere few weeks ago, he was scoffing at the suggestion that he would ever marry. Now he was thinking about the sort of father he would be.

Cassian found himself opening his bedside table drawer the following Sunday morning. He had not told Faith that he had kept her ring all these years. He was not sure why. Was he waiting for a special moment?

He held the little diamond ring between his thumb and forefinger. It was such an exquisite piece of jewellery. It had to be special to Faith, which only made it more important that he return the ring to her.

"Today is the day," he decided, as he slipped the ring into his pocket.

Just as he had slipped his arms into his coat, there was a knock on his door. Cassian wondered who that could be. His breakfast had been brought up an hour ago. About this time he usually locked himself in his study for a few hour's peace while the servants walked on down to the church for the morning service.

Cassian opened the door to see Faith standing before him, wearing her travelling cloak, with Lucy in her arms. Her cheeks were flushed and pink, making her especially lovely.

"Good morning," he said cheerfully.

"I am sorry, I know this is inappropriate," she apologised immediately, "but I wanted to ask if you wanted to attend church with us this morning?"

Cassian smiled at her thoughtfulness, even if her idea sounded dreadful. Cassian was not a churchgoing man. He had a very complicated relationship with God. Going hungry for twenty years did that. "That is really kind of you to ask but ..." Cassian stopped himself. Was he really about to turn down a few hours with Faith where she did not feel the need to dust around him? "I would love to. Shall we?" Cassian collected his thick winter coat from the wardrobe and donned it, before joining Faith and Lucy in the hallway.

Cassian patted his pocket. Smiling as he felt the outline of Faith's little ring, he walked out into the cool winter morning.

He did not pay much attention to the sermon. His attention was solely on Faith. Her singing voice was sweet as she followed along with the hymns, and she swayed ever so slightly as she did so, almost as though she were dancing.

Cassian wanted to take her dancing.

When Faith finally noticed that Cassian was staring at her and not the hymn book, she smiled at him mid-verse and urged him to pay attention playfully.

When the sermon ended and the congregation dispersed, Faith stayed behind. Cassian was curious. Faith was greeted by the old reverend warmly.

"The children will be happy to see you again, Mrs Rowe," he said cheerfully.

"We will be happy to see them again, too," she replied. Faith then looked back at Cassian. "May I introduce Mr Kensington? Mr Kensington, Reverend Atwood."

Cassian bowed his head respectfully. "How do you do, Reverend?"

"Very well," he replied. "I have not seen you here before now."

Cassian cleared his throat awkwardly. "Mrs Rowe persuaded me. It was wonderful sermon." He prayed that the reverend did not ask him questions about the sermon because Cassian had no idea about the subject.

"Oh, thank you," replied Reverend Atwood. "Are you here to help with the children as well?"

Cassian was missing something. "What children?"

"The children that are looked after by the church," replied the reverend. He motioned for both Faith and Cassian to follow him.

"You know I only asked you to attend church with us. You did not have to agree!" Faith hissed in an amused tone so that the reverend could not hear them.

Cassian smirked. "I did not need much persuading to say yes to you, Faith." He would not pretend to be displeased at the blush filling her cheeks.

They were led into the back room of the church. It was a relatively large room, with a crackling fire, and several pieces of mismatched furniture filling the space. Also filling the space were a dozen young children.

Cassian knew immediately who they were. Orphans. Orphans who had not lost all hope yet.

Cassian's heart jumped to his throat as he stared at each and every one of them. Their ages varied. Some were very young, toddlers Lucy's age. Others were grown, getting to the age where they would need to leave.

A boy looked to be the oldest. He was tall, skinny, and had a solemn expression on his face. He was huddled in the corner, watching the others.

But the others ... they seemed happy. What did they have to be happy about? They were orphans. They were alone. If nobody claimed them they would be sent out into the world to starve, just as he almost did.

Cassian had always been told to avoid orphanages. His mother had been convinced that he would be beaten or starved, or taken in by someone who only wanted a servant. He had best rely on himself.

But really, where had that gotten him?

Cassian received a shock when Faith's small hand held his for the briefest of moments. He had not realised his fists had been clenched until then.

"I did not think," she whispered. "You do not have to stay."

Cassian shook his head stiffly. He would stay.

Lucy trotted over to the children her age, who accepted her into their toddler babble conversation. The other children flocked to Faith. They seemed to adore her. How long had she been spending time with these children?

Faith and Cassian were left with the children. Faith sat down on one of the small sofas and she children gathered around her, one handing her a book.

Cassian relaxed a little, smiling. She read to them. She truly was an angel.

"Before we begin, can you all say hello to my friend, Mr Kensington?" Faith asked the children.

A dozen heads suddenly turned around and shouted hello at him excitedly.

Cassian chuckled as he returned the greeting, though that word bothered him. Friend. It did not seem like the accurate word to describe their relationship.

It took Cassian a few moment to realise that the boy he had noticed before had not joined the others. He was still huddled in the corner, watching the others.

The boy noticed Cassian looking at him, and he met his stare with a pair of wary green eyes. Those eyes were nearly covered by the untidy mop of curly blond hair that fell across his forehead. He was pale, skinny, and tall, so tall that his trousers and sleeves were too short for him. He needed new clothing, but Cassian wondered how often tailors frequented parish orphanages.

Cassian took a deep breath and walked over to the boy. A defiant look started to appear on his face. By the time Cassian was standing before him, the boy was scowling.

"What do you want?" he asked rudely.

"That is not the tone to use when speaking to an adult," Cassian scolded. The boy seemed a little taken aback at the firmness. "Now, what is your name, boy?"

The boy climbed to his feet. Cassian was again astounded at his height. He could not be that old, but he still stood just shy of Cassian's chin. "Kit, sir," the boy replied.

"Kit?" repeated Cassian. "Is that short for something?"

Kit nodded stiffly. "Christopher," he replied.

"And your surname?" prompted Cassian curiously.

Kit pursed his lips. "Don't have one, sir. Got no father."

Cassian sucked in a breath. The boy was nameless. "Who gave you your name, Christopher?" asked Cassian.

"Kit," he snapped. "I don't like Christopher."

Cassian held his hands up. "Who gave you the name?"

Kit chewed on his lip nervously. "The matron," he stated. "She found me on St Christopher's Day when I was a baby."

Cassian's heart sank. Kit had been abandoned. Cassian had only been alone since the age of ten. This poor child had been alone all his life.

"Is the matron here?" wondered Cassian. He had only seen the reverend.

Kit shook his head. "No, she sent me away. Got too old," he said bluntly. "The reverend, he ... he is letting me stay." Kit sounded unsure.

Too old. Cassian shook his head. He was not old enough to look after himself. Cassian would never employ a child his age, no matter how tall he was. He looked young and skinny. Not strong enough for a trade, not yet anyway.

"How old are you, Kit?"

"Fourteen," he replied.

Fourteen and cast out. How was that fair?

"Why aren't you listening to the story with the other children?"

Kit scowled. "I hate books," he said bluntly.

"You might like this one," Cassian urged.

Kit ignored Cassian's suggestion. Instead he changed the subject. "Is she your wife?" he gestured subtly to Faith, who was still reading to the others.

Cassian practically coughed up his tongue. The sound caused Faith's brown eyes to flick up at him in concern. Cassian waved away her worry. "No, no," Cassian replied. "She is my ... housemaid," he said awkwardly. Housemaid, like friend, did not seem like the right word to describe Faith.

She was so much more. But wife?

"Well, if she ain't your wife, she must be somebody else's, so you should quit looking at her the way you do."

If Cassian were not already offended at the tone and attitude that Kit used when speaking to him, he was now. He also could not comprehend the astuteness of this child. He was sharp to catch Cassian's stare, but then Cassian supposed he had not been looking much elsewhere today.

"Ain't is not a word," was all he could say in retort.

"What does it matter to you what I say?" Kit demanded to know.

"Because making something of yourself starts with improving yourself," replied Cassian simply. That was a subject in which he was an expert.

Kit just stared at him as though he were speaking a foreign language.

Cassian sighed. "Mrs Rowe will not be here all day. You really ought to go and enjoy the story."

Kit stubbornly crossed his arms. "I told you I hate books."

Kit had been abandoned as an infant, taken in by a matron and cast out at fourteen, most likely because his orphanage was overrun. It was highly likely Kit did not receive any attention, let alone education. Cassian deduced that Kit did not hate books because he did not enjoy them, he hated books because he could not read them.

"Have you ever learned to read, Kit?" asked Cassian.

Kit's green eyes flashed to Cassian's. Cassian saw shame in them. But Kit did not reply. He only stormed away, marching through the door that led back into the church.

Cassian sighed. He had made something of himself, but what was he? A rich man? Was that it? He only had to look over at Faith to know that it would be far better to be rich with generosity and kindness, then to be rich with money. Faith was the richest woman in the world in that sense.

When Faith had finished reading and cuddling each individual child, she joined Cassian.

"Are you alright?" she asked, concerned. "I did not even think when inviting you here. It was very callous of me."

"You do not have an unfeeling bone in your body, Faith," Cassian said sincerely. "But it was very good to come here. It really opens one's eyes."

"It is hard for the reverend and his wife to give them all attention and love. The least I can do is spare a half hour to read a story. Who was that boy you were talking to? I do not recognise him."

"His name is Kit," said Cassian. "He is fourteen years old and has just been cast out of his last home for being too old. And I embarrassed him about his not being able to read." Cassian was the callous one.

Faith frowned. "Oh, the poor boy. I know you did not mean to embarrass him, Mr Kensington."

"I have had enough of that, Faith," groaned Cassian.

Faith's brown eyes widened. "What?"

"It is obvious to anyone that you are more to me than just a housemaid." He took a step away from her and ran a hand back through his hair as he exhaled. "Faith ... you and Lucy have quickly become the best part of my day."

Cassian could not make sense of his life before. How could he have been content? He supposed he was not content. He spent his nights drinking and gambling with gentlemen who were not really his friends. He filled his house with faces to help with the loneliness, as Faith had said. He worked from dawn until dusk.

When did he live?

Cassian had waited three years to find Faith, to thank her, and to show her he had made something of himself. But had he? He was rich, but was it in the right way?

Cassian had waited three years to find Faith, and she had awakened him to a life he had never known he wanted. Faith was good, kind, generous, and impossibly beautiful.

"I imagine my life, even a month ago, without you, and I cannot stand the thought of it."

Cassian looked down at Faith. She was standing before him, her fingers knitted together, her bottom lip trembling. Lord, she was beautiful. Faith was an angel. His angel.

"I have been searching for a term to describe our relationship." Cassian was suddenly aware that he was in a room full of children, some who were old enough to understand their conversation. Cassian took hold of one of Faith's trembling hands and pulled her through the doorway and back into the empty church. Kit was nowhere to be seen. He stopped, and turned back to her. "And I think I know the one I want to use. In fact, that boy, Kit, he put me on to it." He chuckled, reaching into his pocket and wrapping his hand around the Faith's ring. He could not believe what he was about to do. But the words were coming naturally. That had to mean that it was right. "Faith, you have changed my life in countless ways. I only hope I can do the same for yours." Cassian pulled the ring from his pocket and held it up to her.

Faith gasped and clapped her hands over her mouth.

Cassian smiled. She had not been expecting that he would hold onto her ring. "I will buy you another ring, but for now, the one you entrusted me with will have to do. Will you marry me, Faith?"

CHapTer 12

The idea of Anne keeping her head down and going unnoticed was quite impossible when she was travelling in her husband's ostentatious, atrociously expensive carriage.

It had been Mr Carne's idea to travel in that carriage. Her whole escape had been because of Mr Carne's careful instruction. He wanted the Countess of Runthorpe to be seen by everyone. The more talking about having seen her travelling in the carriage, the better.

George was under the impression that Anne was travelling to London to see a dressmaker to order a new seasonal wardrobe and peruse the new collections. George was not aware that ladies usually sent away their measurements. He did not bother himself with such frivolous things. Anne simply had to play the sweet, loving, obedient wife for a few days before she asked permission.

And when that did not work, George requested another sort of favour from her.

A few moments of displeasure for a lifetime of freedom was not too high a price for Anne. She had a child in her belly to think about. This child she would protect. She would not fail this child as she did her first.

Anne packed a trunk, the normal sort that a lady would take to London. She packed gowns and gloves, bonnets and boots. She then packed a secondary bag, one filled with every kind of valuable she could get her hands on that would not be noticed.

She had been saving her pennies for years. Even though she was married to a very rich man, she was not rich at all. Her dowry had been paid to her husband upon her marriage. She had never controlled a shilling.

Every so often, George gave her a small stack of coins to spend in the village. Anne had never spent anything, and had instead saved them for a rainy day.

Today, although sunshiny, was pouring.

Anne sat across from Mr Carne in a little pub in a village she did not know the name of somewhere in Hertfordshire, drinking milky, lukewarm tea. She would never be able to thank this man for his kindness towards her. She had thought about naming her child after him if he was a boy. But then she did not quite like the name "Magnus". Second name, she decided.

"Have you changed your mind, milady?" asked Mr Carne. "I can help you in London."

Anne had already refused this offer twice. "No, I cannot accept. If we are seen together in London, then no one will believe our story. You need to return to Leicestershire and sell the tale. You must convince every that I am dead." Anne still could not believe she was saying those words aloud. It did not seem possible. Would people believe that she had died? Well, she was going to try.

Mr Carne sighed. "Alrigh'," he said, defeated. "Have you decided what you will call yourself? Have you decided what you will do or where you will go?"

Anne brought her tea cup to her lips and decided against taking a sip. It was too cold. "I have not decided on what I will call myself.

I suppose I could use my maiden name. Rowe. It is common enough, though I could never say that to my parents."

Anne's parents were Gloucestershire nobility, or at least they thought of themselves in that way. They were rich, but untitled, which made the Earl of Runthorpe the perfect candidate for a husband for their daughter. They ignored Anne's early pleas for help. Eventually, Anne abandoned them. She had not written to them in over a year.

"And your Christian name?" prompted Mr Carne.

Anne was not so much concerned with her alias as she was in knowing where to go to birth her child. Her golden wedding band would tell any employer that she was not an unwed mother, but she worried about finding work whilst with child.

"I will think of something," replied Anne.

"We really ough' to get goin', ma'am, if you want to reach London by nightfall. We should reach the cliffs in two or so days."

That was their final destination. The White Cliffs of Dover. Where they would stage Anne's tragic and dramatic death. The story would be that Anne instructed Mr Carne to take her to Kent so that she could see the seaside. Something would spook the horses, and Mr Carne would release them and jump for his life, while Anne would plummet to her death.

"Let us go." Anne paid for their tea, and then was followed by Mr Carne out to the carriage. She really hated the thing. George had covered it in gold filigree detailing. He had spent thousands on it.

Mr Carne opened the carriage door for her and Anne climbed inside. Despite the hideously over the top façade, it was a very comfortable carriage to travel in.

Anne slipped on her white gloves and smoother the silk of her cornflower blue skirt as Mr Carne moved the horses on.

Anne was unsure of how long they had been travelling. She had moved several times in the carriage, lying down and sitting up, reading to try and pass the time. Eventually she just stared out the window at the sparse, yet green surroundings.

There was really nothing to look at. She was looking forward to passing through a village. All she could see was trees and grass and trees and ... what was that?

Anne squinted her eyes and the black figure she could see in the distance. She pressed her face against the glass of the window in order to see the figure. Was it a dead animal?

No! It moved!

Was it a person? What would a person be doing on the side of the road?

Anne knew if she waited any longer, they were going to pass this person. Mr Carne certainly was not halting the horses. Anne found her voice as she cried, "Stop the carriage!"

Mr Carne obeyed her immediately. He pulled hard on the reins and the horses skidded to a stop. The carriage had stopped right beside the black figure.

Anne released the latch on the window and it dropped down into the door. As soon as she did this, the figure, the man, lifted his head ever so slightly. He was a man, and he was alive, but barely.

Oh, good God. What had happened to him? Was he injured?

Anne opened the carriage door and she climbed out. As quickly as her skirts would let her, she rushed towards the man and knelt down beside him.

Anne had never seen a more tragic sight. This man was barely alive. His skin was sunken, pale, and grey. His skin looked thin, and it clung to his bones as there was not muscle. He was emaciated. He looked like he was starving.

He was lying face down in the dirt, and though he had fallen from weakness. He could barely move, but he made every effort to look up at her, to keep her gaze.

This man's body was failing him, but she could see him in his dark, almost black eyes. There was such desperation in his eyes. But there was no malice in his eyes, nor anger. Just desperation. He wanted to live. He had something to live for.

Anne knew the exact feeling.

Mr Carne interrupted her appraisal when he grunted, "Don' touch 'im, ma'am. You don' know what crawlers he's carryin'."

Anne glared at him angrily. How could he be so dismissive? "Oh hush," she said in a warning tone. "Can you not see that this poor man needs my help?" Carefully, she placed her hand on the man's cheek. Even though she wore gloves, she could still feel how cold his skin was. She could see that he was willing himself to keep his eyes open. He refused to leave her gaze. He was strong. Determined. "Oh, you poor thing," Anne said sadly. "What must have happened to you?" How could he have ended up on the side of the road? She needed to help him. He deserved to live. She could feel it. "Mr Carne," she said, turning back towards him, "fetch me the water from inside." And food. He needed food, too. "I have some biscuits, too. Bring them."

Mr Carne did as he was told, and Anne did her best to prop the man. Even though he was emaciated, he was still tall and relatively heavy. She was only a small person, herself.

"Here, drink," she instructed, just as soon as Mr Carne had handed her the silver flask.

The man drank gratefully, and ran his now moistened tongue over his bloodied and chapped lips. How long had it been since he had had a drink of water?

Mr Carne removed the lid from her tin of biscuits and she began to feed him. She prayed this would help him. He ate gratefully, but weakly. He struggled to chew, as if it pained him.

"We need to go, ma'am," urged Mr Carne.

"One minute," Anne insisted. "He needs to eat."

"Ma'am, he's just an urchin. Ain't nothin' you can do for 'im. He's half dead already. Just look at 'im!"

Anne pursed her lips together angrily. How could Mr Carne have such concern for her and none for this poor stranger? Could he not see the decency masked by desperation in his eyes? This man needed her. "He is not just an urchin, Mr Carne," Anne insisted. "He is important to somebody." She pushed some of his dark, matted, curly hair away from his forehead, his eyes never leaving her. She smiled down at his reassuringly. "And I am familiar with the feeling of desperation." The child inside of her was the evidence. She was faking her death to save him or her. Desperation could not begin to describe how she felt. "What is your name? I can write to your family if you wish." He wanted to live, she could see it in his eyes, which meant that he probably had people somewhere who cared about him.

The water had helped the man find his voice. "No family, ma'am, and my name is Cassian. Cassian Kensington."

That made her even sadder for him. He had no one but he was desperate to live. He could be something, she just knew it. He had the determination and the heart, but had been dealt the wrong lot in life.

Perhaps they were meant to meet.

"I am glad we met, Mr Kensington," Anne said sincerely. "My name is —"

"Ma'am, we need to go!" Mr Carne urged, interrupting her. Mr Carne was watching the sun, concerned about reaching London on time.

Anne regretfully nodded. "I am afraid Mr Carne is right, Mr Kensington. It is essential for me to reach my destination by sundown." Anne could not leave him here with nothing. How could she do that? She needed to help him. Anne looked down at the flask in her hands and she knew exactly what to do. "This," she said, holding up the flask, "is made of silver. You will fetch a fine price for it." Anne reached into her pocket and pulled out her coin purse. In it was nearly everything she had saved during her marriage. She could not stop herself from giving him the money. Everything inside of her was telling her it was the right thing to do.

She still had possessions to sell, but she could not hold on to this money. It was meant for better things. She just knew it.

"Take this as well," Anne insisted.

She could see that Cassian was struggling with the weight of the purse. He had little strength.

"Ma'am, no," he said weakly.

"Yes," she insisted. "You will take this." Cassian would do good with the money. Anne knew exactly what else Cassian could make good with. She removed her glove on her right hand and stared down at the ring that George had presented her with upon their engagement. At the time she had been happy, excited to be receiving such a beautiful ring, unaware of just how miserable she would be. That is what the ring now was. A symbol of misery. "And this," she decided, removing the ring and placing it inside the coin purse for safe keeping. "You will take this, too." She hoped something good would happen when Cassian used the money from the ring.

"Why?" Cassian struggled to ask.

Anne could tell that he was asking her why she was helping him. The disbelieving tone in his raspy voice told her that not many people had offered him the helping hand that she had. No one had seen the decent person that he was underneath his poor appearance.

Anne slipped her glove back on and smiled down at him. "I have good intuition about people, Mr Kensington." She wished she had developed this intuition before she had married George. "You are a good man who just needs a little help. You will take this money and you will make something of yourself. I have faith in you."

"How can I ever thank you?" he rasped. He looked so grateful.

How could he thank her? "Thank me by living a better life," she said sincerely. Anne placed her hand on his cheek once again. She knew in her heart this was the right decision. She had faith. "I know what it is to be desperate, but yours is a far greater need than mine." Anne would survive. She and her baby would be just fine. Anne climbed to her feet and brushed the dirt off of her skirt. About a half mile back, she remembered seeing a road that led into a village. "There is a village that way, not a half mile. Rest a little, and when you have your strength, you will find a bed and a meal there." Anne did not want to leave him, but she had done everything she could in that moment. She needed to be in London by tonight so that they could reach the cliffs on time.

Anne Pendleton was on a tight schedule to die.

"May I have your name, ma'am?" he asked.

Her name? She turned back to look at him once more. She had been spreading her real name about, just as Mr Carne had instructed, to ensure that it was known that Anne Pendleton, the Countess of Runthorpe, was passing through in her fine carriage.

But it did not seem right to use Cassian as another tool in her ruse. And then suddenly, she knew the right Christian name to use going forth. "I suppose you may call me Faith." She smiled. "Good luck, Mr Kensington. May we meet again."

Faith stared at the ring in Cassian's hand. She never thought she would see that symbol of misery again. George had given her that ring years ago, and it came to represent every toxic second of her wretched marriage.

But Cassian had asked her something, and just as soon as he had brought out the ring, she had not heard anything. "Forgive me, what did you say?" she asked Cassian.

Faith could see just how vulnerable Cassian looked. His eyes read like books. His shoulders were tense and his gaze was fixed on her.

"I ... I asked you to marry me, Faith."

Faith sucked in a tight breath. Where on earth had he got an idea like that? Why on earth would he want to marry her?

Faith was not the sort of wife that Cassian deserved. She was difficult. Nothing about her was clear or honest. She had a child. Did Cassian understand what that entailed?

Not to mention she was already the wife of another man in Leicestershire.

But Faith had never meant to give Cassian any ideas of affection. That would not be fair. Faith was not blind; she thought Cassian was incredibly dashing and handsome. But she had never led Cassian to believe that she felt more for him than friendship.

Or had she?

Faith began to question everything. It was not normal to have tea parties in one's master's study, was it? Was that an indication of his affection for her? Had she really not noticed?

Oh, no. What had she done? Faith had ruined everything. She had ruined everything! She had managed to stay hidden, go unnoticed, for three years! Nobody knew who she really was. Anne Pendleton was dead, and long forgotten about. But with that came a price. It meant that she could never remarry. Love was out of the question.

Love was out of the question. She had been treading on dangerous ground with Cassian and she had not even realised. Faith cared deeply for Cassian. She had since the moment she had laid eyes on him. But did she love him?

"Faith?" prompted Cassian.

"What?" she replied quickly.

Cassian laughed nervously. "I have asked you to marry me twice now and you have said nothing."

Cassian had proposed marriage. He wanted to marry her. He wanted Faith to be his wife. Cassian wanted Faith. Lord knows why, but he did. But he could not have Faith, because she did not exist.

"Cassian ... I," Faith began, but she did not know where to begin. She had been meaning to tell him the truth for nearly a fortnight, but every time she came to it, she could not find the words. Still, her tongue betrayed her.

Even without words, Cassian knew that Faith was refusing him. She watched as his eyes, his shoulders, his heart, sank. Faith was breaking his heart, and it felt like a knife right through hers.

Cassian truly cared about her. How could she have let this happen?

"Cassian ..." Faith tried again, but Cassian held his hand up to stop her.

"You do not need to say a word, Faith. I understand." He put the ring away in his pocket and nodded his head stiffly. Cassian was trying to compose himself but Faith could tell she had truly wounded him.

No, no, she had never meant for this to happen.

"Will you be alright to walk home? Perhaps ask the reverend to escort you," Cassian said emotionlessly. "I need ... I need to go." Cassian marched from the church cursing himself, and Faith fell to the floor in a sobbing heap.

Faith was not entirely certain how she returned to Cassian's house. She had somehow managed to take Lucy back whilst drenching her sleeves with her tears. Lucy constantly wondered aloud why her mother was crying, and Faith did not really have an answer for her.

She managed to compose herself for the rest of the day, whilst still feeling like a terrible person on the inside. Faith went about her responsibilities, whilst Mr Wade dutifully watched his new favourite person in Lucy.

It did not escape Faith's attention though that Cassian had not returned home. He had missed luncheon. Several hours passed, tea time came and went, and Cassian had still not returned.

Faith had started to worry hours ago. Now she was feeling physically ill. Where was he? Had something happened to him? He was on foot. He did not even have a carriage. What if he was set upon by thugs in the night?

The servants began to retire at about nine o'clock. Faith had long since put Lucy to bed. She could not bring herself to go to bed when Cassian was not home. The others did not know what had transpired. They would not understand.

Faith pretended to retire, but had snuck downstairs to the foyer carrying a lamp. She sat down on the bottom step and turned down the light so as not to alert anyone she was not in bed.

The foyer clock chimed ten o'clock, and then eleven, and then twelve. Faith leaned against the banister of the stairs and stared at the front door, willing it to open.

She needed to apologise. She needed to do something to make things right.

Shortly after the clock chimed one, there was a loud bang on the door. Faith nearly jumped out of her skin. She immediately turned up the flame in her lamp which illuminated the foyer.

There were a few more successive bangs before the door opened and a large figure fell through. He laughed at himself and clumsily climbed to his feet.

It was Cassian, and Faith could smell the stench of whiskey from where she was sitting. He was drunk. She had driven him to drink.

"Cassian," she said quietly, alerting him to her presence.

Cassian looked up and smiled dopily. "Faith," he slurred. "My housemaid and not my fiancée." He laughed at himself, but Faith winced at his words. He was hurting.

Faith stood up from her step and stretched her legs. She had been sitting for three hours. She walked over to him slowly, bringing the light from her lamp with her. As she approached him, Cassian's face and clothing became clearer.

His clothing was dishevelled, and his face was covered in red smudges. Faith frowned as she peered at him more closely, until she saw a clear mark on the collar of his shirt. It was red lip paint. Only two types of people wore red lip paint. Actors and prostitutes. Something told Faith that Cassian was not just in a theatre establishment.

The red smudges all over his face made sense. She knew exactly where he had been, and just whom he had been with. Cassian must not have been hurting that much after all.

Faith had rejected him, and Cassian had run right into the arms of another women, a prostitute. Faith felt her heart sink and bile rise in her throat. She felt the urge to punch something, and Cassian's idiotic grin seemed like the perfect target. She felt like she was already the recipient of a punch, a punch right in the gut which had knocked the wind out of her.

It was a betrayal. It felt like a betrayal. She wanted to scream at him. He had proposed marriage to her and had jumped right into the arms of another woman. What kind of husband would that make him?

Faith could not find any calm words. All she could think of to say was, "You really ought to launder your shirt, Mr Kensington. You seem to have gotten a little tart on it."

Faith turned on her heel and tried to control her breathing as she marched up the stairs. The new tears that fell from her eyes were different. She was not feeling sadness for hurting Cassian. She was feeling sorry for herself. She felt betrayed because Cassian's affections were not one-sided. The enormity of that realisation made her heart ache.

And it had taken Cassian betraying Faith for her to realise just how she felt.

CHAPTER 13

Faith did not have to say the words, but Cassian knew her answer just by looking into her regretful eyes. She did not want to marry him. The proposal had come as a complete shock to her. She had no romantic feelings towards Cassian at all.

Cassian felt utterly humiliated.

Worst of all, he felt completely heartbroken.

It had taken Faith walking back into his life for Cassian to realise that he never wanted her to walk out of it again. How many times does one encounter an angel?

It had not taken Cassian long to hold Faith far above anyone else in his acquaintance. Perhaps he had been slightly infatuated, hypnotised by her beauty, but it had never occurred to him to think that Faith might not share his regard.

Cassian knew that was arrogant, but surely there had to be some romantic feelings inside of her? All those afternoons spent with Lucy, he and Faith had shared such blissful exchanges. It was almost like they were a little family.

But clearly he had imagined it. Cassian had just offered Faith the opportunity to step back into the world she had previously known, with a husband that would vow to look after her and her daughter for ever, not just until his death as her previous husband had. Cassian would love her, and he would love Lucy as though she was his own. Anything her heart desired would be hers in an instant.

But Faith had refused. Her good heart would not allow her to say the words, but Faith had no desire to become Cassian's wife.

But then why would she want to? Cassian knew that Faith did not value money or things. She had shown him this from the very beginning of their renewed acquaintance. Faith valued humility, kindness, and selflessness. Cassian knew that he was not good enough for Faith. He liked to think himself a kind man, but he could be as selfish, materialistic, and vain as the next man with money to burn.

Cassian felt such a surreal pain, concentrated right in the middle of his chest. It was as though a giant hole had formed where his heart had once been. This hole was filled with agonising emotions such as despondency, hopelessness, and misery.

With just the look of rejection in her eyes, Faith had all but ripped his heart out with her own tiny hand.

This pain was more real than any other pain Cassian had ever experienced. He had experienced starvation, the utter feeling of his stomach caving in on itself, but it did not hold a candle to the burning agony he felt in his chest.

If this pain told him anything, it was just how deeply his angel had infiltrated his heart and soul. This was love, it had to be, and if he was honest, he would rather feel this pain and be reminded of Faith, then to not feel anything at all.

Love.

Cassian had never known it. Not in the real romantic sense. He had been loved by his mother, and he had loved her in return, but he had never known true, passionate, fervent, longing, defence-less love.

The isolation in which Cassian had grown up had all but sealed his fate. He had been destined to die as a young man who had barely lived. He would never know friendship, or family, or love. Perhaps the way he had grown up, despite his wealth now, would always hold him back from securing those things for himself.

What a joke. He now had all the money in the world to buy things, but what he truly needed was just beyond his reach.

She would be gone. Cassian knew that to be true. Now that he had made an utter fool of himself, Faith would pack her things and take Lucy, never to be seen again. He hated himself for speaking so zealously. He had driven away the only person who had ever shown him genuine friendship.

Cassian was unsure of how he wound up at the club. His feet had carried him there from the church. He wondered if it was some mortal sin to be gambling and drinking on a Sunday, but in truth, after his third whiskey, he did not care.

Cassian had entered into a game with a table of gentlemen he did not know. It was not Tuesday, and so his usual party were elsewhere. He was playing with the other sad London folk who had nothing better to do on a Sunday then throw away their money and drink to their sorrows.

At the bottom of his sixth, or perhaps seventh, whiskey glass, Cassian was starting to see double. He could not coherently speak, nor was he sure of what cards he was holding. Before he could make any grave mistakes, he was pulled away from the game by a mysterious hand.

There was a sweet scent that was suddenly permeating the air around him, which was masking the stink of alcohol on his breath. "Fanny?" he slurred.

Fanny giggled. "Can you not see me, Mr Kensington?"

Cassian endeavoured to focus his blurry eyesight on the blonde woman in front of him. "I ... I think I need spectacles."

Fanny giggled again. "I think you need to leave the whiskey alone, Mr Kensington. I have never seen you indulge so." Cassian felt Fanny wrap a comforting arm around his waist as she led him away from the smoking room. Cassian managed to stay upright despite his stumbling feet. Before he knew it, Fanny was sitting him down on a soft surface.

A bed. His eyes fluttered shut at the thought of it. He was so tired. He wanted to sleep and forget this day ever happened.

"Oh, no you don't, Mr Kensington. What will Madame say if you suffocate on your own sick in this room? You stay awake now, you hear?" Fanny ordered, before thrusting water at him.

Cassian drank, although the water did not have the comforting burn that whiskey did. "Did I not give you the money to get out of this place, Fanny?" Cassian mumbled grumpily.

Cassian's vision was still distorted, but he could see a distinct sad frown on Fanny's face. "Your kind gift went directly to my father's creditors," she replied. "He is imprisoned in the Marshalsea, Mr Kensington. He owes three hundred pounds. So no, I cannot get out of this place anytime soon."

The Marshalsea. Drunk as he was, Cassian knew the debtor's prison. Filled to the brim with starving inmates who suffered if they could not afford to pay their prison fees. If Cassian could coherently remember this conversation in the morning, he would send three hundred pounds to the Marshalsea for Fanny's father.

"Why are you here, Mr Kensington? I noticed you were not here with your particular circle last Tuesday."

"She doesn't want me. Doesn't love me," he muttered.

"Who?" Fanny pressed.

"Faith."

"Who is Faith?"

"An angel."

"An angel?"

Cassian nodded, a spluttered through a pathetic, tearless sob as his head fell on to Fanny's chest as though he were a child seeking comfort. Fanny immediately enveloped him in a hug. "Proposed," he slurred. "Said no."

"Oh, dear," said Fanny. Before Cassian knew it, he could feel Fanny's lips on his person. In his hair, on his forehead, his cheeks, his neck, and finally his lips. Between kisses she was telling him how she would make him feel better.

Cassian closed his eyes, but he did not feel as relaxed as he was a moment ago. Every fibre of his being was telling his alcohol distorted mind to leave. This was not right. The gaping hole in his chest was screaming at him, telling him he was being unfaithful.

"She said no," Cassian told his conscience. "I can do what I please."

"Who are you talking to?" Fanny ask breathlessly.

"No one," Cassian murmured as he seized Fanny's face in his hands and crushed his lips to hers. It did not take Fanny long to climb on top of him to start unbuttoning his shirt.

The feeling on her cold fingertips on his skin brought him back to earth, or at least back to the room he was in. He was laying down on a bed with a woman who was nor Faith. Rejection or not, how could he ever look her in the eye again if he did this?

"No!" he cried.

The volume of his voice startled Fanny so much that she quickly climbed off the bed. "Are you alright?"

"No." Cassian shook his head. "No, this will not help. I don't want this. I want her. I want only her."

"But she doesn't want you?" Fanny's words were not said with malice. If anything, she sounded as though she was concerned.

The gaping hole filled with agony was going to constantly remind Cassian of this face. "She would never have me like this."

"Who the bloody hell is ringing that bell?" Cassian groaned.

Cassian's eyes fluttered open. It took him a moment for his eyes to focus, but he realised he was at home in his bedroom. How had he gotten home? The last thing he remembered was vaguely talking to Fanny.

There had been a lot of whiskey consumed. He remembered playing cards. He remembered Fanny pulling him away. Why was Fanny there? Had he not given her money to leave? That thought sparked a memory of the Marshalsea. Debtor's prison. He needed to rectify that. Cassian thought hard, though it hurt his pounding hear, to recall vivid memories of him kissing Fanny. But it had not gone any further.

His conscience demanded his fidelity to a woman who had rejected him.

But the rest was gone. He truly wondered how he had gotten home. Had Mr Green fetched him?

Cassian climbed out of bed, and promptly tripped over his own breeches, which were still gathered around his ankles. Clearly he had failed dismally at undressing himself the night before.

He needed water. Cassian kicked off his breeches and walked over to his basin. Thankfully, the pitcher was filled with water. He poured the water into his basin and began to wash his face. Cassian nearly had a heart palpitation when the water began to turn red. Was he bleeding? He looked at his reflection in his small mirror above the basin and saw that there were red marks covering his face, neck, and collar. Fanny's lip paint.

Cassian smirked as he washed away the evidence of his drunken stupidity.

Once Cassian finished cleaning his face, he dressed. He collected a clean pair of breeches from the wardrobe, and selected a fresh shirt. Once dressed, Cassian collected his discarded clothing from the night before off of the floor. As he lifted his waist coat into his arms, something small fell from the pocket.

Cassian's eyes settled on the small diamond ring, which stood out against the plain rug on his floor. The pain he had forgotten about for the briefest of moments had all but sucked the air out of his lungs.

Cassian picked up the ring and threw it in his drawer, slamming it shut all too aggressively.

Cassian left his bedroom before his breakfast had been brought up. He would have it in his study, where he would remain for the day.

He wondered if Faith would still bring Lucy to him. The thought of Faith keeping Lucy away from him frightened him more that he thought it would.

Just as he turned the corner towards his study, he saw Faith leaving it. Faith cleaned his study in the afternoon, so that she could spent time with Lucy and Cassian, or so Cassian believed.

Dusting before eight o'clock in the morning meant that she was endeavouring to avoid him.

Faith noticed him immediately, and as soon as her brown eyes met his, that aching agony that he was becoming accustomed to reared its ugly head.

But this time, Faith did not look at him with sympathy or regret. She looked at him with contempt. She was angry at him. Cassian stopped in his tracks as Faith stormed away from him, not even bothering to talk to him, or to make nice with him.

Why was she angry? Had his proposal offended her so? "Right," he mumbled. "Enough of this." He would not sit around in his house, feeling like he did, while Faith had the audacity to be angry at him.

No. Cassian had been putting off a trip to his northern factories. Perhaps it was best he left for a while.

CHAPTER 14

Cassian spent the next three weeks travelling through northern England, visiting and inspecting all of his factories, and ensuring that his workers were all in good health and spirits after the installation of the wheels.

He discussed business with each of his factory controllers right into December, ensuring that production was going to be efficient, of good quality, and financially prosperous come the New Year. Cassian's factories were some of the biggest employers across the north, so it was vitally important to hundreds of families that he maintained a successful operation.

The business talks were a welcome distraction. Cassian did not have a moment to think about anything or anyone back in London while he was away.

That was a lie.

Cassian thought about Faith all the time. Every time he turned around and saw a woman with a thick, brown braid of hair, he thought it was her. He kept hearing her voice across rooms and he had himself convinced on several occasions that Faith had followed him up to Yorkshire to reconcile.

But, of course, she had not.

Cassian and Faith were not meant to be. Faith had made that very clear.

Cassian only wished he did not miss her as much as he did. Every day, while discussing distribution plans, or machinery improvements, he found himself thinking about what he would be doing were he at home.

Cassian would have been with Lucy for starters. They would have been reading, or playing make believe, or Lucy would have been happy entertaining herself while Cassian worked. Having Lucy in his study made for a happy work space. Spending time with Lucy was like a reward. If he finished his correspondence then he got to sip pretend tea. He never could have imagined that he would enjoy sipping air but he did.

And then sometime in the afternoon, Faith would bring Cassian and Lucy luncheon, and she would join in on their games. Cassian never liked her to clean around him. He preferred to help her dust and wipe down the surfaces afterward. That precious, fleeting time felt almost like what a family would.

Cassian liked to think that at some point while his father had been alive that he, Cassian's mother, and Cassian all played together similarly.

By mid-December, the snow had begun to stick on the ground, and the weather was extremely cold. Cassian knew that if he delayed returning to London any more then he and Mr Green would be stuck in the middle of nowhere for Christmas. While Cassian did not have any desire to celebrate the season, he would not have Mr Green away from his family purely because Cassian was in a foul mood.

Their journey took them south, and the trek was more arduous thanks to the slippery road. It was late on December twentieth when Cassian's carriage pulled into the little village of Norwood, a picturesque town not a mile from Derbyshire's famous peaks. The sun was setting as Mr Green halted their carriage outside of a blacksmith.

"We ought to rest the horses, sir," called Mr Green to Cassian. "I shall talk to the smithy, see about some new shoes and a stable."

Cassian climbed out of the carriage and came to stand at the front. He placed a hand on the back of one of his horses. The poor beast was awfully sweaty, even though the air was icy. "Yes," he agreed. He handed Mr Green some money and turned to look about the long main street of Norwood.

It was quite quaint. All the shops and businesses were shut, of course, but he could see from the signage and advertising that there seemed to be just about everything. There was a blacksmith across the road, a post office, a tailor, a general shop, a bank, a library and even a magistrate's office. He could see the bell tower of a church at the end of the road.

Finally, Cassian saw an inn and pub. "I shall be over there," he informed Mr Green, pointing at the long white building. The windows were all illuminated and he could hear the faint sound of jolly conversation. "I shall get us rooms."

"Very good, sir," replied Green as he began freeing the horses from the carriage.

Cassian made his way over to the inn and was welcomed by the warmth of a roaring fire just as soon as he crossed the threshold. The interior of the pub was very simple. There were several tables that were occupied by the local villagers, each with a pint of ale in their hands. A long bar serviced the far wall, and a portly, older gentleman with a rather chipper smile was serving the patrons on the stools. The narrow staircase beside the entrance led up the inn, Cassian assumed.

"Can I help you, dear?" asked a female voice.

Cassian jumped, not seeing the tiny woman. He looked down to see an older, bespectacled woman, with greying blonde hair and small, clear blue eyes. Before Cassian could answer her, she was pulling his cloak from his shoulders and was hanging it with the others. "Yes, Mrs ...?"

"Mrs Porter," she replied. "What is your name?"

"Kensington, Mrs Porter."

"Welcome to Norwood, Mr Kensington," Mrs Porter said kindly.

"Thank you," he replied. "Mrs Porter, I don't suppose you have two rooms available?" he asked hopefully. "I understand you will be busy, what with the festive season upon us, but my driver and I only require lodgings for one night."

"Oh, yes, Mr Porter and I will be happy to have you, Mr Kensington. Will Mrs Kensington be joining you?" Mrs Porter looks around their immediate area for a companion.

"Oh ... oh, of course." Mrs Porter tried to sound sympathetic, but Cassian saw the glee in her eyes. Cassian wondered if the woman had an unmarried daughter.

Mrs Porter arranged rooms for Cassian and Mr Green, and ensured that her husband provided Cassian with a pint of ale at the bar.

Cassian, who was used to the searing taste of whiskey, enjoyed the ease at which the ale went down his throat. It was refreshing and comforting, and he demanded another within minutes. Mr Porter was only too happy to oblige his paying customer.

Cassian knew the behaviour was irresponsible, but the haze of alcohol clouded his ever racing mind. He could not miss Faith when he was concentrating on staying upright.

"Perhaps you ought to retire for the night, sir," encouraged Mr Green as Cassian finished his fourth pint.

Cassian nodded, the motion clouding his vision. Oh, he felt ill. Cassian climbed down off of the stool, and immediately lost his footing. His balance was non-existent as he stumbled across the floor and into one of the Porters' tables. Cassian's weight crushed the table and the glasses of ale went flying, shattering on the floor and splashing their contents over several customers.

In Cassian's drunken haze, he heard the shouts and cries of angry men before his world went black.

"A woman, money, or both?"

Cassian groaned. The inside of his mouth tasted like vomit. He had been sick at some point. His head was pounding, with much of it centred on his cheekbone. He brought his hand to the area and winced. It was sensitive. Had he been struck? With great difficulty, he sat up and opened his eyes.

Cassian was lying on a cot in a small, square, concrete room, with only a pot in the corner. The bed was hard and uncomfortable, with only a scratchy woollen blanket for warmth. The voice had come from the other side of the bars.

Cassian's eyes flared. Bars? Oh, good Lord. He was in jail. "What?" he croaked, his voice thick with sleep.

"A woman, money, or both?"

Cassian saw the man sitting next to the door of the jail. He was leaning against a wall, sitting on the floor, with his legs outstretched and his ankles crossed. He was finely dressed. He wore cream breeches with polished, expensive black boots. His green waist jacket was embellished with gold embroidery, and Cassian could see a golden watch poking out of his pocket. He wore no coat, but Cassian assumed that was just as fine. The man was rich.

He climbed to his feet and approached the door of the cell. He looked down at Cassian with calm green eyes. He had a fine face, not weathered at all like Cassian's. His skin was clear and pale, his jaw was strong and masculine, and his hair was copper in colour, and curled slightly at the ends, not at all like Cassian's own ratty black curls. He looked to be around Cassian's age, perhaps a year or two older.

"I have found that men only drink themselves stupid over a woman, money, or both," he said calmly. "So which is it?"

This man's theory had merit. "A woman," replied Cassian truthfully.

The man smirked. "Spurned you?"

How many drunks had this man imprisoned? "I asked her to marry me and she refused." Why he was divulging any of this, Cassian did not know. His situation was already embarrassing enough.

"Why?"

Cassian frowned. "Why do you want to know?" he retorted.

He shrugged. "Curiosity. My usual drunkards are in here after irking their wives or refusing to pay Mr Porter for their drink."

"I am not a drunkard," spat Cassian.

"And look where you are," he shot back. Cassian was silenced. "So, why did she refuse you? You are not ugly looking, and your pocket watch alone would feed a family here for a year so you have some money. Do you have an odious nature?"

Cassian did not know whether to be grateful for or offended by the man's candour. "Not that I know of," Cassian muttered.

"Then why did she refuse you?" he pressed.

Lord, he was nosy. "I have no idea," snapped Cassian. "I do not pretend to know the minds of women. Do you annoy your own wife in this way?"

He laughed lightly. "Oh, no, I am not married. I have not met a woman who could put up with me."

"I wonder why," mumbled Cassian.

He ignored Cassian's comment. "You are not my usual sort of drunkard, Mr Kensington. Your servant assures me that you are a good master and the word of a subordinate is good enough of a testimony for me."

Cassian needed to increase Mr Green's wages. "Testimony?" replied Cassian. "Are you with the law?"

"Of a sort," he replied. "My name is Finnegan Kelly. I am the county magistrate. I never really have any interesting cases so you can imagine my curiosity. A foreigner, like yourself, wanders into Norwood and winds up in our little prison. You are the talk of the town."

Cassian shuddered. He had gone twenty years without being noticed. This was not how he wanted to build a reputation. "I am from London. Hardly foreign."

"Foreign enough to us," replied Mr Kelly. "Not that I can talk." He chuckled. "Irish by birth. But I have acclimated. I am a Norwood native."

Cassian could detect the faintest of Irish accents on Mr Kelly's tongue. The way he flicked certain words gave off hints of an Irish twang. Cassian sighed and climbed to his feet slowly. "You should know that this is not a normal behaviour."

"According to your servant, this is not the first time you have overindulged," countered Mr Kelly.

Cassian scowled. He had changed his mind. He needed to sack Mr Green. "I have never before been in prison."

"Then let this be the last time," Mr Kelly replied calmly.

Cassian did not like how he felt after a night of drinking. He did not like the fact that this feeling was becoming somewhat familiar to him. He always enjoyed whiskey with his card games. But this was ridiculous. Cassian knew it needed to stop. "How may I repent, Mr Kelly?"

"Compensate the Porters for any damage. They are good people. All will be forgotten afterwards."

It was the least Cassian could do after such an embarrassing display of behaviour. "Oh, course, Mr Kelly," agreed Cassian.

Mr Kelly produced a set of keys and selected the right one to unlock Cassian's cell door. "We are very friendly folk here in Norwood, Mr Kensington. No one person higher than the other, no matter their station or fortune. To my friends here I am Finn. Mr Kelly is back in Ireland."

Cassian exited his cell stiffly. He thought it odd for a magistrate to be so informal. From what he knew of magistrates, they sent poor, desperate thieves to Botany Bay.

"I am Cassian," he replied, returning the gesture.

Finn's office was very simple and functional. All that occupied the room was a large desk. On it was Cassian's coat, cloak, purse and watch.

"What are you doing in Norwood?" asked Finn as Cassian gathered his possessions.

"Just passing through," he replied. "I had business in the north. I am travelling home to London."

"What is your business?" Finn asked, learning against his desk and crossing his arms.

Cassian wondered if Finn was deprived of social company. Surely he was not so interesting. "I own several factories," he said. "Cotton mills in the north. Textiles in the south."

"Ah, you must earn a tidy profit a year then," Finn surmised.

Cassian was not about to disclose his income to a stranger.

"My family's fortune was made in farming. I learned to operate land before I was in the schoolroom. We left Ireland when I was a boy and purchased several thousand acres of land off of a bankrupt aristocrat. Made it profitable again. My parents are back in Ireland now, and I run the business here."

Clearly Finn did not have any trouble in disclosing his business to a stranger. "Then how are you a magistrate?" Curiosity was now getting the better of Cassian.

"The people trust my judgement," Finn said simply. "I was only too happy to oblige. Does your father help with your business at all?"

"My father is dead." Cassian's tone let Finn know that he would not elaborate on the subject.

Finn winced, looking regretful. "Well, you know, I still cannot understand it," he said, changing his tone to a more light-hearted one.

"What?"

"You seem a decent enough man. You have a clever head on your shoulders. You run a successful business on your lonesome. What would provoke your woman to refuse you?" he pondered. "Did you strike her?"

"Of course not," snapped Cassian.

"Did you insult her? Is she ugly?"

Finn would not ask such a stupid question if he had ever seen Faith. "Faith is an angel," Cassian said firmly.

"Faith is her name? How odd," Finn murmured.

Cassian liked it. It suited her.

Finn pinched the bridge of his nose and appeared to be thinking deeply. "You did not strike her. You did not insult her. Apparently she looks like an angel. That I would like to see." Cassian growled under his breath. "Well, you must have scorned her then. Did she catch you with another woman?"

"No!" Cassian immediately retorted, but he then paused. His mind went back to that night with Fanny. He had never betrayed

Faith, not that there had been any formal understanding between them, but he had remained faithful. Cassian had come close to disaster with Fanny, and she had covered him with her red lip paint.

He did not remember anything else from that night, but he had woken up covered in evidence of a supposed indiscretion. His first encounter with Faith after he had proposed to her was the following morning. She had looked at him with utter contempt. Disgust. She would not do that without a reason. Could she have seen him in such a state?

That still did not explain why Faith had refused him, but if it upset her to think he had been with another woman, it had to mean she cared. Cassian knew the theory was unlikely but it felt nice to hope.

"Ah, so you are a cad. That explains it," realised Finn. "Well, you know how to solve this. Flowers, decadent sweets, expensive gifts. They all work."

"Clearly you have never met Faith," murmured Cassian. "Faith values simple kindness and selflessness. And I am not a cad."

"Kindness and selflessness?" mused Finn. "I might just have an idea then. Come along, Cassian. You can pay the Porters, and then I will help win back your Faith." Finn slipped his arms into his own green coat. "What?" he asked, noticing that Cassian was staring at him. "I am a romantic, what can I say?"

Whatever his idea was, it needed to be bloody romantic.

Norwood was awake when Cassian stepped out onto the street. Despite the cold, the townspeople were busy and bustling about their daily business. The noise was nice in a way that the London noise was not. The people knew each other. They cared about each other. Each person wondered about how the other was doing.

"It is a lovely village," commented Cassian.

"I always thought so," replied Finn. "I complain about the idleness of the magistrate's work but then I would not like it if it were any worse. It is a good place to raise a family, I think. If I ever have the pleasure."

Cassian quite agreed. "Yes. It seems to have a sense of familiarity in the way that London does not."

Cassian apologised profusely to the ever accommodating Porters, and paid them handsomely for the damage that Cassian's irresponsible behaviour had caused. They were only too happy to forgive him.

Finn seemed to be well liked by the residents of Norwood. It was refreshing to see a kind and fair magistrate, despite his nosy questioning.

When Cassian and Finn left the inn, Cassian spied Mr Green readying the horses. Finn marched over to Mr Green and shook the man's hand, as though they were old friends. He then whispered something quietly to Mr Green, who nodded.

Finn opened the door for Cassian while Mr Green climbed up onto the driver's perch.

"Where are we going?" asked Cassian.

"To the place that would win any woman over," replied Finn confidently.

Cassian was not at all confident.

They travelled for about a mile. The scenery outside the carriage windows was beautiful. Cassian found himself getting lost in the hills, majestic and unending with the white layer of snow that sat atop them.

Finn opposite Cassian. "What makes Faith value such things?" he asked curiously.

Cassian opened his mouth to reply, but he found that he did not really have an honest answer for him. Faith liked the things she liked, and never really offered any explanation for them. Cassian had snippets that he had managed to extract, but Faith had never really confided in him. "Faith has had fine things," Cassian believed, "and she has had nothing. Faith values people, and what people can do for others. She reciprocates than tenfold. She saved my life."

"Really?" Finn raised his eyebrows. "How?"

Cassian was not in the mood to rehash his poverty stricken youth. "Another time."

"I may just hold you to that. Well, Faith sounds like a very extraordinary sort of woman. I can understand why you want to marry her."

Cassian managed a small smile.

"Ah, we are here." Finn unlatched the window and let it drop down. A gust of icy air filled the carriage.

Cassian stuck his head out of the window to see just where "here" was. They were driving toward a house, passing through the iron gates on its border. House was really an understatement. This house was enormously grand, with three storeys of white washed stone, covered in a majestic layer of ivy. Several of the windows, there had to be a hundred of them, were illuminated, beckoning them in to the inviting home.

The grounds were flat and extensive. Trees, bare from the winter, littered the estate.

But the house. Cassian had never seen such a house. Not even his house in Kensington could compare.

"Welcome to Norwood Cottage," said Finn.

"Cottage?" repeated Cassian. One could fit twenty cottages inside this house.

Finn laughed lightly. "I own this house," he informed Cassian. "I do not live here. I have tenants who will no longer be requiring it. I live a mile or so from here at Forsyth House, so I really have no need of this house anymore. I would be willing to sell it for the right price."

Cassian nearly choked on the freezing air. Buy a house? He already had a house.

"You said that Faith valued kindness and selflessness. You will find that in the people here. But they do need help. There is poverty. There will always be poverty. Norwood has no school. The village children are educated by the vicar at the church but a school is needed." Finn looked out the window. "I do not know Faith, but I think if you buy her this house, you will be giving her a life in which she will have value and purpose."

Just thinking about Faith with the orphans at the church in London made Cassian certain that Faith and Lucy would thrive here. Anyone would fall in love with such a house.

But he could not force her to fall in love with the man that came with it. There were still so many questions surrounding Faith. There was so much that he did not know, and he really needed those answers.

"Well?" prompted Finn.

Chapter 15

"Hark! The herald angels sing. Glory to the newborn King!" sang Cassian's household as they stood around the long kitchen table that was so decadently laid out with such exquisite looking food.

The cook, Mrs Simpkins, had prepared a feast for the servants at Cassian's request. Glazed ham, pork, roasted vegetables, gravy and pies, both savoury and sweet, were all set out for them to enjoy.

Faith had not seen such a meal in a very long time. The food was an incredible sight, and her stomach screamed with excitement just to see it, but what made her heart melt was seeing Lucy.

Lucy had never really celebrated Christmas. Faith had always taken her to a church service, but she had never been able to afford to buy a decent meal, or to give her a special gift.

Lucy had never minded. Of course, she was too young to know different, or have expectations, but it made Faith's heart happy to see her daughter in receipt of something that Faith could not have given her without help.

Lucy was gleefully clapping, sitting on the forearm of Mr Wade as he held her during the song. She was so happy and excited, her brown eyes darting around the room with wonder as they took in the wonder.

Faith was very grateful to Cassian's butler, Mr Wade. Lucy had become so used to spending her days with Cassian. She had been so unsure and distressed at the sudden change to her routine when Cassian had abruptly left London without so much as a goodbye.

Perhaps Lucy was not the one who missed receiving the goodbye, but she certainly did miss spending time with Cassian. She and Faith shared that feeling.

Mr Wade had only been too happy to step in to help with Lucy in the interim. To Faith's understanding, Mr Wade was unmarried, and had no children. He had formed a special attachment to Lucy, and Lucy seemed to like him in return. She often played with Mr Wade's ears and nose, and he did not seem to mind at all. In fact, he laughed.

Faith sat down at the table as the meats were carved and served. She had been certain that Cassian would have returned for Christmas. He had been gone a month. That time had given Faith enough of a chance to gain some perspective.

She had been angry that he had gone to another on the day he had proposed marriage to her. She still was. But she now could understand why he had behaved this way.

Cassian had lived a life filled with rejection. Cassian had survived on his own, never having experienced acceptance, and being cast aside and dismissed as a filthy urchin. Faith had shown him kindness in a way that Cassian had never before experienced.

Cassian had therefore carried this image of Faith ever since, an image that she could not possibly live up to. He thought her an angel. He had named his factory after her! Cassian held Faith in such high esteem that when she disappointed him, he responded in a way that was entirely out of character.

Faith needed to tell Cassian the truth. She needed to tell everyone the truth. She had known that she owed it to Cassian to confess, but she had always resisted, failed at the crucial moment.

She would not fail if she were given another chance. Faith trusted Cassian with her child. To anyone else, it might simply be a kind act of child minding, but to Faith, trusting another with her child was no simple feat.

Faith had experienced the immeasurable agony of losing a child. She would not survive the loss of another. In fact, she felt as though she was tempting fate by even entertaining the thought.

Faith had been very careful with whom she chose to trust with Lucy's care since the day she was born. But none had ever had such involvement in Lucy's life than the people in this house. Faith trusted them. She trusted Cassian. She knew in her heart that these people would protect her child from the monster that was Lucy's father.

That realisation had hit Faith the minute she had learned Cassian had departed London.

"Merry Christmas, everyone."

For a moment Faith thought she might have been hallucinating, but when the household all stood up to greet the new arrivals, Faith knew that Cassian had really returned. Mr Green followed behind him, greeting the others and hungrily filling a plate with the delicious food.

"Merry Christmas, sir," greeted Mr Wade warmly. Mr Wade bowed his face respectfully to Cassian, as Lucy eagerly reached out her arms. Mr Wade obliged the toddler, and handed her over to Cassian.

Cassian smiled warmly at Lucy and cuddled her to his chest. Lucy immediately began to play with a few of Cassian's black curls. "Hello," he cooed, "I missed you, Lucy."

Faith froze, her heart melting in her chest. Cassian had not looked at her yet. Was it in purpose? She did not know. Of course it had occurred to her to seek new employment while Cassian was away, but selfishly, the feeling of safety and security was too tempting.

"You will all find an additional fifteen shillings in your week's wages," announced Cassian. "Merry Christmas."

Cassian's gift was met with elation from everyone. Faith, too, was touched at the gesture. While everyone was celebrating, Faith remained silent. This was when Cassian met her eyes for the first time.

Faith's heart stopped as she felt the intensity of his gaze. The sounds in the room disappeared as they stared at each other. There was so much to say. Faith could tell that Cassian felt the same way.

Cassian motioned subtly towards the stairs. He wanted her to follow him. "Well, excuse me. I am sure my correspondence is a mile high by now. Enjoy your meal."

"Oh, won't you stay, sir?" asked Mr Wade.

Cassian shook his head. "No. I have a gift for Lucy upstairs. I will return her shortly." Cassian retreated with Lucy still in his arms.

Twenty seconds later, Faith said, "I had better ensure that the gift is not too generous," before quickly flitting from the kitchen and following Cassian up the stairs.

Once on the main landing, Faith began searching. She opened the door of the drawing room and the dining room, before finding Cassian and Lucy in the library. Cassian's library was a small, cosy room. The shelves, much like the ones in his study, were half-filled here and there. He had yet to amass a collection.

Lucy was sitting on the settee absolutely enamoured with her new china doll. The doll was beautiful, from the corn silk coloured curls on her head and the painted pink flush of her cheeks, to the exquisite lace of her dress.

Cassian was standing beside the fireplace, watching the flames and listening to the crackle of the wood. "I did not think that you would accept an additional wage. I thought you might accept the money to use as a donation to the children at the church. Perhaps you might purchase books or toys. Something lovely for Christmas."

Faith had not even comprehended the fact that he had gifted everyone an additional fifteen shillings, but Cassian had guessed her exact thoughts before she had even had them.

But before she could even thank him for his kind thought, the truth rushed out of her. She could not control it. "My name is not really Faith," she stammered quickly.

Cassian's eyes flashed to hers within a second. He wore a look of complete and utter shock. Of all the things he had expected her to say, Faith could wager this was not it. Her story was truly fantastic.

"I beg your pardon," he said slowly.

Faith chewed on her bottom lip nervously as she crossed the room towards him. She passed Lucy, who was still incredibly engrossed in her new doll. She would not heard, nor comprehend, a word.

"My name is not really Faith," she said again, this time attempting to control the speed of her voice.

Cassian exhaled shakily. "And what, pray tell, is your name?"

Faith had not said this name aloud in three years. She had not felt like that person since the moment she had made the decision to leave that life. "My name is Anne Pendleton," she confessed.

Faith's heart was pounding in her chest as she watched the information pour over Cassian. She wondered if he could hear her pulse.

Cassian's eyes were fixed firmly on the ground, as if there were something incredibly fascinating about the patterns in the rug. He did not speak for several minutes.

Faith kept her eyes on him. She needed to continue or else she would lose her nerve. "I was born Anne Elizabeth Rowe on the nineteenth of June in seventeen hundred and eighty-two. My parents are Harold and Frances Rowe. They live in Gloucestershire. My father is very wealthy. He made his fortune in banking. I have no brothers or sisters. When I was seventeen I was presented into society in London where my father arranged a betrothal to George Pendleton, seventh Earl Runthorpe."

Faith took a breath. The information she had just divulged seemed so simple really. It was the same identity that hundreds of girls in the aristocracy possessed. Rich girls were betrothed to even richer men who could boost their position in society. It was an age old practice.

Faith, however, had been wed to a barbarian.

Cassian stood motionless.

"I was happy at first, I think," Faith continued quietly. "George was not at all unattractive, and he bought me fine things." That miserable ring, for example. "But George liked to indulge. In alcohol, and in women." Faith's lip began to tremble as she thought back to the first time her husband had struck her in anger. "I had not at all been expecting it. I was not prepared for it. I told George that I did not appreciate his infidelity. He ... he laughed at me ...

and he slapped me to the ground ... and then he forced himself upon me."

Faith had grown up with a false sense of entitlement. She had always assumed that her wealth, her station, protected her. She was safe from everything. But in that moment, Faith realised that she was powerless. Her entire identity had shattered into oblivion and everything she knew was a lie.

From that day, until the day she ran away, Faith lived in a state of constant fear.

Faith was shocked to feel Cassian's hands on her cheeks, his thumbs brushing away the tears she did not know had fallen from her eyes. She met his angry eyes. Cassian's irises were nearly black normally, but she had never seen them like this. But she was not afraid. She could never be afraid of him, and her heart told her that his anger was not for her.

"You need not say anything else," he whispered.

"Oh, but I do," Faith insisted. "I owe you an explanation."

"You owe me nothing," Cassian said firmly.

"Please, listen," Faith begged.

Cassian nodded, and motioned for Faith to sit down on the floor beside him. They both sat in front of the fire, and Faith welcomed the warmth. It felt as though the blood had drained from her body.

"From that day onwards, my life at the Runthorpe Estate became a vicious cycle. I would tread so carefully. I would not say a word. But he would find fault with me always. He always found some reason to discipline me as he called it." Faith looked down at her hands. They knotted themselves together. She concentrated on the lines in the palms of her hands as she spoke. "I tried writing home to my parents. They did not want to be bothered with it. As far as they were concerned, their son-in-law could do no wrong. He was a wealthy earl." Faith did not often think of her parents. She wondered if they had grieved for her. "George had a younger brother. His name is John, and he is married to a woman called Ruth. They often visited with their daughter Olivia. I think she would be about eleven now," Faith recalled. "But they knew exactly what was going on. They condoned it, I think, or they ignored it. I hate to think how many in our circle knew and pretended to be none the wiser.

"Eventually George began to pressure me for a son. An heir. I did not fall pregnant straight away, and that was another reason for me to be disciplined. My sister-in-law, Ruth, had lost a child shortly after Olivia and had lost her ability to bear children. I was so terrified that it would happen to me that I did not tell a soul when I learned I was with child."

Faith had been so happy during those first few months of pregnancy. Knowing that she would have a child made George's behaviour tolerable.

"It seems very foolish now to have kept the news to myself. I was afraid that if George knew, and then I lost our child, that he ... he would kill me." That had been Faith's genuine fear. It had been selfish. Her fear should have been for her unborn child. Youthful ignorance.

"Your son," murmured Cassian quietly in recollection.

Faith nodded helplessly. "Yes, I told you about him. I do not precisely remember the reason, but I remember George becoming angry with me and he shoved me. I tripped and I fell down the stairs. He left me and went on with his day, but I remember feeling such surreal pain. I was certain that I would die." Faith did not want to describe what happened, but if Cassian was going to understand her motivation for everything that happened afterward, she would tell him. "I started to bleed. I knew something terrible was about to happen. I went to my bedroom and screamed into my pillow to muffle the noise. I do not understand how or why. I never spoke to a doctor. I do not know how I survived, but I did. But I gave birth to my first born child on the third of March, in eighteen hundred and one, and he was dead before he entered this world."

Her son would have been five upon his next birthday.

"The physical pain was nothing compared to what I felt whilst holding him. He was no bigger than the palm of my hand. He was tiny and perfect, and denied a chance at life because I was not brave enough to tell his father that he existed." Faith knew that it was George's fault that their child had been lost, but she could not help but put blame on herself for being a coward. "The feeling of heartbreak is a very real experience. I was in pieces knowing that nothing could ever fix me."

Faith was shocked that she was able to get the words out. She had never spoken of this before. She had never described the pain before. She had healed, or attempted to heal, on her own, and had never spoken to another soul about what had happen on that day nearly five years ago.

"You will think the name I gave him is silly," Faith continued, though she felt a fond smile filling her face. "Nothing else seemed appropriate really. I named him Sky, for that is where he was born to."

"I think it is perfect." Cassian spoke for the first time in a while, and his voice was cracking, filled with emotion.

Faith dared to look up at him, and she could see his eyes were filled with tears, just as hers were. He was a man of great feeling. Faith longed to reach out to him, to seek comfort in his arms. She longed to belong to him, so that Cassian could tell her that everything would be alright, and she would never have to live a day in fear again.

"I wrapped him in lace, and I placed him in a beautiful Cherry-wood box. I feigned illness so that I would be left alone. When I was well enough to stand, I burned the bedding, and took him down to the lake on the estate. It is beautiful there. Especially in spring. I said my prayers, and I buried him beneath the wildflowers."

One day, when George was long dead, Faith would go back to the Runthorpe estate to visit her son. It had been three long years, and three birthdays, since she had sat with him, and prayed for him.

"I grieved for a very long time. My melancholy disposition only angered George further." Faith brought her hand up to the scar on her hairline. "You asked me about this once. I was trembling at the dinner table, rattling my cutlery, and irritating George," she explained quietly. "But everything changed when I became pregnant with Lucy." Both Faith and Cassian looked over to Lucy, who was still merrily playing with her doll. Her beautiful daughter, who had not a care in the world, seemed to be making up voices for her doll, and was thoroughly enjoying playing make believe with her. "I had to protect her. I would not let her suffer her brother's fate." Faith gritted her teeth at the recollection of her determination. "It was our driver who helped me, who gave me the idea to escape. I will forever be indebted to Mr Carne.

"His plan was simple. Gather everything of value, anything that would fetch a price, and all money that I could get my hands on. I did just that, and I convinced George to let me travel to London to purchase gowns for the next season. I travelled in his finest carriage. It was Mr Carne's idea to have my travelling be noticed. It would have been difficult not to notice George's carriage. He had spent five thousand pounds on it.

"The plan was to travel to Kent, under the guise that I wanted to see the seaside. The story would be that the horses spooked, and Mr Carne cut them free and jumped for his life, but was unable to save me. My husband spent five thousand pounds on that carriage and I pushed it off a cliff." Faith chuckled at the ridiculousness. "Mr Carne and I rode the horses back to London where we separated. I left to start a new life, and he sold the story that the Countess of Runthorpe had died in a tragic carriage accident. I monitored the newspapers for a while and the story was believed. I gave birth to Lucy, sourced employment, and eventually found myself working at Angel Faith Textiles, where we were reunited.

"You have to know, Cassian, I was so proud of you. To know that you had built yourself such an empire with only a mere purse of coins was just so incredible. No matter my objections to things, you have to know that I speak the truth."

Faith took a breath and studied Cassian's face. She felt like she had been talking for hours, and Cassian had been taking in revelation after revelation. He still appeared incredibly shocked and in awe. His tears were gone, but his lips were parted, as though he were about to speak.

"Those coins," he whispered, "they were meant to ensure a life for you and Lucy?"

Faith helplessly nodded. She still had enough in the way of valuables to support herself, but she could not leave with the money knowing another needed it more.

"Why would you do that? Another hour, had you passed me then, I would have been a corpse on the side of the road."

Faith winced at his words, though they made her all the more grateful that she had passed him when she did. "I do not regret my decision, Cassian. I became Faith the moment I met you. Your will to live inspired the person I became."

"I ..." Cassian exhaled, "what do you want me to call you?"

"Faith," Faith said firmly. "As I said, I became Faith the moment I met you. Anne is in the past."

"But she isn't," Cassian countered.

Faith's little dream of Cassian telling her everything was going to be alright shattered. In her heart, she knew it was not going to be alright. People could not make themselves disappear without consequences.

"You are Anne Pendleton. You are a countess! A great lady. I honestly do not know what to say. I cannot comprehend what you have endured. I cannot fathom your pain. I could never have predicted that this was your story. And selfishly, all I can think is that I am coveting another man's wife." Cassian climbed to his feet and marched over to one of the bookshelves. He selected a book and looked at it for a moment before showing it to Faith. "Have you ever read this book?"

Faith looked at the title. Utopia by Thomas More. "No, I have not."

"It was one of the first books I ever read. It is about a society on the island of Utopia. They have their own set of rules, laws, customs and the like. No one man better than the other. Wealth does not mean status. Everyone works. The people are given what they require. Wives are answerable to their husbands, just as husbands are answerable to their wives." Cassian flipped through the pages absently. "I remember reading this as a starving child thinking that there is so much I could do if I was just given the chance. If a man, much higher in society and station than me, could give me a helping hand, then I could show the world my worth. And it happened. I was found by an angel, the most beautiful woman my weary eyes had ever laid eyes on, and I was given the opportunity to show my worth. But the world cannot be like the one in this book. We are not equal. Wealth matters. There is, and always will be, poverty. Husbands will never be answerable to their wives. Incredible, generous, caring women are bound to beasts. I cannot understand it!"

Faith wrapped her arms around her legs and rested her chin on her knees. She watched as Cassian wrestled with this knowledge. "It is the only reason why, you know."

Cassian looked down at her. "What?"

"Why I could not say yes to your proposal," she confessed. "In the eyes of the law I have a living husband."

Cassian's dark eyes softened. He immediately crossed the room and came back down to the floor beside her. He took hold of her hands and kissed her knuckles softly. Faith's hands were trembling, and Cassian warmed them between his. Such a simple action invited that addictive feeling of safety.

"Can you ever forgive me?" Faith asked fearfully.

Cassian frowned. "Forgive you for what? It is I who should be asking forgiveness."

"I do not blame you for that," Faith promised him. "I understand why you did it. I do not have any right to feel hurt by it anyway."

"What are you talking about?" Cassian asked quizzically.

Faith felt her cheeks flushed. "That night you came home ... covered in another woman's lip paint. I know what you did, and I understand why you did it."

Cassian recoiled. "I never did anything. I left before I did any-thing I would regret," he promised her.

Faith felt relief spread through her as Cassian spoke those words. As much as she had convinced herself that she did not mind, it was nice to know that Cassian had not spent time with another.

Faith felt herself edging closer to Cassian, her face not ten inches from his. "I am sorry for hiding the truth."

Cassian copied her movements, his eyes not leaving hers as he moved closer to her. Neither one dared to blink. "You do not have to apologise," he said softly.

"I need to tell everyone downstairs. I owe them the truth, too."

Her words provoked a gasp from Cassian, and he pulled away immediately. "You will do no such thing," he said firmly, all subtle intensity to their words gone. "This will stay between you and me. I will protect you Faith. I promise you. You and Lucy will be safe with me. I will never let that man harm you again."

Faith could see the sense of duty in Cassian's eyes, and she knew he was speaking the truth. He would endeavour to protect them. Faith felt that addictive sense of safety once more, but she could not deny that she felt a sense of apprehension as well. Now that the truth had been spoken, a small part of Faith was telling her that something terrible was imminent.

Chapter 16

It had been an odd week since Cassian had learned the truth of Faith's identity. Never in his wildest dreams could Cassian had ever have predicted Faith's tale.

Cassian had always known that there had been some underlying facts about herself that Faith had been concealing. Perhaps an unfortunate relationship with her parents, or her late husband's gambling debts, but never this.

Faith was really Anne Pendleton.

Anne was the wife of George Pendleton, the Earl of Runthorpe.

Lucy was truly a lady. She was Lady Lucy Pendleton. She was entitled to such riches and society. She would be a prize when it came time for her to marry.

The Earl, despite his wealth, was a barbarian. He had caused the death of Anne's first child, and his cruelty had led to Anne creating the ruse that had led her to Cassian.

But most of all, the Earl was alive.

Cassian could recall the story. What a story it had been at the time. It had been all over the newspapers: Countess Killed in Carriage Catastrophe. Of course, at the time, he had not made any connection with the story. The newspapers had been floating around the public houses Cassian frequented as he regained his strength after near starvation. But everybody had been talking about the dead Countess.

But she was not dead. The Countess was dusting Cassian's study.

Cassian sat back in his chair on the second of January, eighteen hundred and six, as he watched Faith flit about his study as she normally did. Lucy played on his study floor as she normally did.

Everything was normal. Except everything had changed.

Cassian felt such overwhelming anger and sympathy for Faith. She had endured an animal. Being wed to such a man must have been like eternal fire for her. It enraged Cassian that in the eyes of the law, Faith was powerless against such a tyrant. It enraged Cassian that nobody had protected Faith. Not her parents, not her brother and sister-in-law. Not anybody except for Mr Carne, and even he had been too late to save her son. Her Sky.

But here she was, pottering about her usual chores, seemingly peaceful. Faith had resumed the life she was accustomed to in Cassian's household. She had been such a wealthy, great lady, and here she was, in a black maid's uniform, wiping every surface in his study.

Cassian now fully understood why Faith did not appreciate material things. She had once been in possession of everything, and yet she had nothing. Faith now possessed everything she could have ever needed right here in this study.

And yes, Cassian did include himself in that equation. In his heart, he was Faith's, and she was his. It seemed so simple. Cassian could love Faith for the rest of his days. Cassian would happily step into the role of Lucy's father. He would ensure that she received the very best education, and the protective love of a father.

But it could never be. Faith could not be his. Anne was George Pendleton's. No matter how barbaric the possessive term seemed, it was true in the eyes of the law. Faith was another man's wife, and the truly selfish part of Cassian's heart loathed that fact.

Cassian felt such jealousy, disappointment and self-pity. And he hated every inch of himself for feeling that way.

Cassian had wanted to speak to Faith when he had returned home on Christmas Day. He wanted to seek the truth, and to properly discuss everything, as per his new friend Finn's advice.

Once everything was settled, Cassian was going to drop down on one knee and propose properly. He had not purchased a ring. Faith had not responded positively to the last ring that Cassian had presented her with. Instead Cassian had spent fifteen thousand pounds on a glorious new life for them.

Cassian had been planning on presenting Faith with the key to their new home in Norwood, Derbyshire.

And now that key was settled in his desk drawer, never to be utilised.

Cassian was most unsettled. He had promised Faith that he would protect her and Lucy, and he would keep that promise, but he had a funny feeling. Life could not go on as it once had. Too much had changed.

This secret was of huge proportions. If it was ever discovered that Anne Pendleton was still alive, the repercussions would be enormous. George Pendleton's embarrassment was what concerned Cassian the most. The shame and humiliation that a man experienced after the abandonment of his wife was great. What would George would do to Faith if he ever got his hands on her again?

Cassian would give his own life before that happened.

"What are you staring at?"

Cassian was snapped out of his daydream when Faith had spoken to him.

Faith had finished her chores and was now sitting on the floor with Lucy. She was smiling at him, looking as beautiful as ever, and she was as married as she always would be. Cassian willed himself to stop thinking so impurely. What sins he was amassing.

"What do you say we wander down to the church and gift those books to the children," Cassian suggested, though he was not entirely sure how sensible it would be for him to walk into a church coveting as he was.

Faith had ordered enough books for each child to have two with her fifteen shilling Christmas present.

"I suppose the weather is better today," Faith agreed, peering out his window. It had been pouring with rain all week and Faith had not wanted to take a risk in bringing Lucy outdoors.

Faith smiled at him again, the same smile she had been giving him at least half a dozen times a day since she had revealed to him her true identity. They seemed to say "I am sorry, but thank you." Cassian knew that Faith was grateful to him.

The selfish part of him again was telling him that George Pendleton had to die someday. Perhaps Cassian could marry Faith when they were in their fifties.

Thirty years. What a horrible thought.

"Go and fetch your cloaks. I will meet you downstairs."

Faith left the study carrying Lucy and Cassian made his way down to the foyer. He ducked into the library and went to collect his copy of Utopia. His mother, the good woman that she was, had ensured that her son had been taught to read. Utopia had inspired him as a young man. It helped him to believe that those of simple means and low birth could amount to something when given the chance.

Cassian's thoughts went to the boy he had met upon his last visit to the church. Kit reminded Cassian so much of himself. Cassian was certain that this book could help him. As Faith would put it, it could inspire Kit to make something of himself.

"Oh, forgive me, sir." Mr Wade had begun to retreat out of the library when he had seen it was occupied.

"No, no, Wade. Please," beckoned Cassian. "I am just leaving. In fact, Mrs Rowe and I will be out this afternoon if you could excuse her."

Cassian knew exactly what Mr Wade was thinking. He knew what all the servants thought. Cassian was not well practiced in concealing his particular favouritism for Faith. He knew it was not conventional for a master to spend such time with a housemaid. Cassian trusted his household not to talk, but to outsiders, he knew what it would look like.

"Of course, sir," he murmured.

Cassian tucked the book in his coat pocket and left the library. When he returned to the foyer, Faith and Lucy were waiting for them, protected in their warm travelling cloaks.

Cassian took the package of books from Faith. "Shall we?" he proposed, offering Faith his arm.

Faith held onto Lucy's hand and then took Cassian's arm. It felt so natural to leave the house like they were, as though they were a family on an outing.

Together they walked the short distance to the church. As it was freezing, Cassian felt a fool to not have ordered his carriage. Not ten feet had they walked before he lifted Lucy up into his arms so that he could keep her warm.

As it was a Friday, the church was relatively empty, except for the Reverend who was practicing his Sunday sermon. "Mrs Rowe," he remarked. "Mr Kensington."

"Good afternoon, Reverend," greeted Faith. "Mr Kensington has seen to it that I can gift these books to the children." Faith gestured to the package of books that Cassian was still holding.

Reverend Atwood smiled warmly. "How kind," he remarked. "I am sure the children would be very grateful to receive such a generous gift."

Cassian placed Lucy on the ground as Reverend Atwood led their party towards the back of the church where the children were housed.

The children were elated to see Faith and Lucy. Faith was quickly taken by the hand and led away towards the settee. Cassian placed the package of books beside her and Faith set about in pulling them out and showing them to the children.

Cassian smiled. Faith was so good. She had such a big heart for people. If Norwood was the type of community that Finn had described, Cassian was certain that Faith would have thrived there. He was so disappointed now that she would never know it and the people would never know her.

Cassian quickly noticed that Kit was not among the children that Faith was entertaining. He momentarily panicked, thinking that even Reverend Atwood might have expelled the boy because of his age. Cassian knew that was a wicked thought when he noticed Kit outside in a little courtyard that adjoined the church.

Kit was outside in the freezing weather in nothing but a thin, worn shirt for warmth. He was playing with a well-loved football, kicking it from end to end of the courtyard. If it were possible, Kit had grown in the weeks since Cassian had last seen him. He was taller, but still just as skinny. His untidy blond curls were longer, too, nearly reaching his shoulders.

Cassian entered the courtyard and closed the door behind him, so as not to let the warmth escape. It was so cold outside. Cassian knew that Kit was going to catch the death if he was not careful.

It was then that Kit noticed that he was not alone in the courtyard. He stopped the football by placing his foot on top of it. He stared at Cassian with his distrustful green eyes.

"What are you doing here?" he demanded to know.

"Mrs Rowe has brought books for the children," replied Cassian.

"Why?" Kit muttered. "They are all too stupid to know how to read."

Cassian pursed his lips. He knew that Kit did not really think that the children were stupid. Kit thought that he was stupid after Cassian had embarrassed him upon their first meeting. "Perhaps those books will inspire them to learn," he suggested. "Come now, do not stop on my account." Cassian pointed to the football at Kit's feet.

Kit's hard exterior softened, only just, as he kicked the football towards Cassian.

Cassian stopped the football with his right foot, before kicking it back to Kit. "Are you not cold?"

Kit returned the football. "A little," he admitted.

Cassian stopped the ball. "Do you have a coat?" he asked before kicking it again.

Kit shook his head before kicking the ball against the wall of the courtyard, allowing the ball to ricochet directly towards Cassian's feet. Cassian was impressed.

"I am afraid I embarrassed you at our first meeting, Kit," Cassian said regretfully, stopping the ball.

Kit squared his shoulders and stared directly at Cassian. "Not as much as the lady embarrassed you," he countered, motioning indoors. "I heard her refuse you." The boy was trying to be cruel, to wound Cassian just as Cassian had wounded him.

Cassian's eyes narrowed. "You need to understand something, child," he said firmly. The change in Cassian's tone caused Kit to stiffen. "You are of no significance to anyone." Cassian took a step towards Kit. "Nobody knows that you are here." Another step. "I understand that this attitude you possess protects you from truly feeling." Another step. "But it will not serve you well in future. If you are not careful you will end up on the side of the road. Dead." Cassian was now standing three feet from Kit. Even though he was fourteen, he was still a child. The boy had tears in his green eyes. Cassian's words were hurting him.

"Why are you saying these things?" Kit asked, his voice breaking.

"Because I was just like you when I was your age." Cassian had never been as rude as Kit, but then he supposed he had not experienced abandonment as Kit had. But Cassian had been just as poor, just as alone, and just as angry at the world for his situation.

Kit scoffed in disbelief. "Please. A rich man like you?"

"I was not always rich," Cassian countered. "I was an orphan. I had no money and no home. No prospects at all. I was starving, and I was dying. Were it not for a helping hand, I would not be standing before you today."

Cassian could tell that Kit was still very unsure about him. Cassian supposed the tale was quite fantastic. Not many people could boast from having been hours from death to being one of the wealthiest men in London.

"The trick, young man, is to accept help when it is offered," Cassian continued. Cassian reached inside his coat and pulled Utopia out from his pocket. "Merry Christmas," he said, holding out the book to Kit.

Kit tentatively accepted the book, and looked down at the cover. He then looked back up at Cassian with angry eyes. "Are you teasing me, sir?" he demanded to know.

"Not at all. I thought you would enjoy that book as I did when I was younger."

Kit's grip on the book tightened. "But you know I cannot read," he seethed through gritted teeth.

Cassian smiled. "When you read this book, you will learn that every man, no matter his station, has the ability to contribute to society if he is given a chance to prove himself. I am giving you that chance, Kit."

Cassian could see the turmoil and embarrassment on Kit's face. "But I cannot read this book, sir!" he exclaimed.

"Then I shall teach you," replied Cassian calmly.

Kit clamped his mouth shut and stared at Cassian. "What?"

"Do you want be able to read, Kit?"

Kit's lip trembled as he nodded his head. "Yes, I do, sir," he whispered.

Was this how Faith felt when she was helping Cassian? Cassian felt as though he was truly about to change this boy's life with such a simple act. "Then you will come to my house three times a week from now on," he decided. "I will give you a lesson and then I will insist upon you staying for dinner."

For the first time, Cassian saw such a genuine smile spread across Kit's face. He looked back down at the book and flipped through the pages with such excitement in his eyes.

Men of all stations could do wonders if only they were given the opportunity. Cassian wondered what this boy would do.

Cassian gave Kit directions to his house, and instructions to come on Monday afternoon. Lastly, Cassian shrugged out of his coat. "You will grow into this within the month, I am sure. But you need a coat."

Cassian saw genuine gratefulness on Kit's face as he accepted the expensive coat. He slipped his arms inside and fixed the buttons. Cassian was right, it was a little big, but the boy needed something warmer than a calico shirt.

Cassian kicked the ball one last time. "I shall see you on Monday, Kit."

"Yes, sir. Thank you, sir," replied Kit cheerfully.

CHAPTER 17

"The b ... big d ... do ... dog is ... b ... br ... brow ... brown."

Faith listened as Kit sounded out the sentences in his reading book. As soon as Faith had learned that Cassian was to give Kit reading lessons, Faith had immediately sourced some teaching material for children learning to read. She had tried to find the least childish renditions for Kit, so as not to make him feel behind.

Cassian had been planning on teaching him to read from Utopia.

"Excellent," commended Cassian. "See, now that you have memorised what sounds the letters make, it is easier to put them together to make words."

"If you say so," murmured Kit as he leant on Cassian's desk and turned over the page.

Faith had experience with impatient children. Granted, her daughter was just shy of three, but she still knew that when children wanted things, they wanted them immediately.

When Faith had learned that Cassian was to give Kit reading lessons, she was elated. He was determined to give Kit an opportunity to better himself. It seemed so perfect. Faith had found

Cassian. Cassian had found Kit. If this was to be the pattern, she wondered who Kit would find.

There was a selfish part of Faith that was glad that Cassian had a distraction. It had not escaped her attention how unsettled it had been between herself and Cassian since she had revealed herself to him. Faith knew that Cassian would ensure that no harm would come to her or Lucy, but that still did not make things any easier.

Cassian had proposed marriage after all, but their relationship could never go beyond where it was now. And exactly where that was, Faith was not sure.

So she was happy that Cassian had somewhere else to direct his attention.

Faith had kept Lucy away for the first few reading lessons because she had not wanted to intrude. After each lesson, Cassian always insisted that Kit stay for dinner. It was during this time that Lucy had attached herself to yet another.

Lucy had been curious about Kit at first. And as soon as Kit had given her the time of day, Lucy was besotted. She seemed to adore Kit's curly blond hair, and loved it when Kit lifted her up onto his shoulders. It was one of the sweetest sights Faith had ever seen.

Faith had not given much thought to Kit when she had first seen him at the church, and she chastised herself for it now. He had seemed like a sour boy. But Cassian had persisted, and he had extracted a decent and deserving young man.

This had been the first lesson in which Cassian had invited her and Lucy inside. Lucy played like she usually did, though Faith knew she was itching to climb atop Kit's shoulders. Faith cleaned as she usually did, repeated where she had already been so she did not have to leave.

The sight before her was special. Cassian had such patience and compassion. There was not a single man in her acquaintance who could boast such qualities.

Faith had grown up in a society where men were rich, proud, belittling, self-righteous, rude and haughty. These gentlemen would never have looked an inferior in the eye, let alone take one into their homes for literacy lessons.

"Th ... th," hesitated Kit.

"You had the word before. The, remember?"

"Oh, yes," Kit mumbled. "That sound is hard. I keep thinking it is the 't' sound."

Faith suddenly remembered something from her own time with her governess. She abandoned her dusting cloth and went over to the desk. Kit looked up at her with wary green eyes as Faith looked down at the words in the reading books.

The 'th' sound was repeated often. "Do you know, Kit, when I was a child, my governess taught me that the 'th' sound was the only time I was ever allowed to stick my tongue out." Faith grinned sheepishly. She had loved learning that sound as a child, and often used 'th' words in everyday conversation just so she could poke out her tongue. Her parents were none too pleased.

Kit chuckled, some of the stress leaving his face.

Faith caught Cassian's eye in that moment. He was staring at her with such a sense of pride.

"So whenever you see these letters coupled together, you re-member that they make the 'th' sound, and that you have per-mission to poke out your tongue." Faith winked and a wide smile spread across Kit's face as his attention returned to his reading book. Faith smiled with satisfaction as she heard Kit read the next 'th' word without difficulty. Faith bent down to collect Lucy in her arms to take her down to the kitchen for afternoon tea.

Faith set Lucy down with a cup of milk and a biscuit while she sat down next to Hattie who was folding the linen. Faith took a pillow slip and began to fold it.

"Is that boy still upstairs with the master?" asked Hattie.

Faith nodded. "Yes. It is really very good of him to teach Kit to read," she said fondly.

Hattie smiled knowingly. "Oh, is it?" she teased.

Faith rolled her eyes. She often responded flippantly to the teasing comments of the other servants. She successfully concealed her true feelings on the matter. They never saw her true devastation at her situation.

"I often wonder about the master, you know," Hattie mused once the folding was complete. "He used to frequent those clubs in London. You know the sort. Drinking, smoking, gambling, with fallen woman flitting about the tables."

Faith clamped her lips shut as she listened.

"But ever since you have arrived, I think he has only been once. He is home more. He used to practically live in his factories. I have always wondered as to why he never married. But then I suppose, he is in the fortunate situation of being able to select whomever he pleases as a bride."

"Really, I do not think it appropriate to be discussing Mr Kensington's private business," muttered Faith.

Hattie giggled. "Oh, come now. You can tell me. Everyone knows the master is in love with you. He has been besotted from the moment he brought you here. He singles you out. He takes you on outings. You are his favourite, and you spend an awful amount of time cleaning his study." Hattie raised her eyebrows in disbelief. "Do you return his affections?"

Faith stared into Hattie's kind but curious eyes. She trusted this woman. She was her friend. But Cassian had instructed her not to share her secret. "No," Faith lied. "I think him kind and generous, but that is all."

Faith could tell that Hattie did not believe her. She only prayed that Hattie thought that Faith was being bashful.

The entire household celebrated Lucy's third birthday on St. Valentine's Day.

Mrs Simpkins prepared a glorious cake and handmade gifts were presented to Lucy. Among the gifts were beautifully stitched clothes for her doll, and a brand new pink dress for church, lovingly made by the housemaids. Hattie had embroidered the bodice with daisies. Poor Mr Wade could not sew, and so funded the material for his favourite little girl.

Cassian had purchased a gorgeous dolls house for Lucy, which he had positioned next to her bed, so that when she woke up on her birthday, it was the first thing she saw.

Faith had not objected to the expense. Not on Lucy's birthday.

Cassian had invited Kit to Lucy's birthday dinner, which was being held in the infrequently used grand dining room. All of the servants were invited, and all were terribly excited to dine like a rich Londoner for the first time.

Lucy proudly wore her new dress as she gleefully enjoyed the attention she received. She enjoyed twirling, fanning out the skirt of her dress, and lapped up the praise and admiration of those watching her.

Faith helped Mrs Simpkins to lay the table, positioning the dishes just so. Mrs Simpkins had prepared a delicious roast dinner, with every trimming imaginable. The aroma was mouth-watering.

"Kit!" Lucy screamed excitedly.

Faith's head turned to see Cassian entering the dining room with Kit at his side. Cassian had been teaching Kit three time a week for six weeks now. Every time Faith saw Kit, he seemed to be a little taller. However, an explanation for that could be that he stood a little taller with each ounce of confidence he gained from his reading lessons.

"Have you missed me, Goose? I only saw you yesterday," Kit chuckled as he lifted Lucy up onto his shoulders.

Kit had taken to calling Lucy "Goose" every so often. Lucy adored it. It would take Faith a little longer to be comfortable having her daughter referred to as poultry.

Lucy wrapped her little arms around Kit's forehead and she rested her chin on top of his head. Her smile was as bright as the sun.

For so long, Faith had had a funny feeling that something would go wrong now that her secret had been revealed. But it would not. It could not. They were too happy here.

Faith stole a glance at Cassian, who was laughing along with the others up at Lucy on Kit's shoulders. Happy enough, she corrected.

"For she's a jolly good fellow," boomed Mr Wade in a powerful singing voice nobody knew he possessed. But everyone quickly joined in. "For she's a jolly good fellow. For she's a jolly good fellow, and so say all of us! And so say all of us, and so say all of us! For she's a jolly good fellow, for she's a jolly good fellow. For she's a jolly good fellow, and so say all of us!"

The dining room was filled with cheers and applause, and joyful wishes of birthday felicitations. It filled Faith's heart so fully knowing how treasured her child was by the people in this room.

"For you," whispered Cassian.

Faith jumped, not realising that Cassian had come to stand beside her. Cassian was discreetly holding up a snowdrop flower. He was staring down at her, his gaze so tender.

"What for?" she asked softly as she accepted the delicate little flower.

"It is St. Valentine's Day," he replied simply. "I love you, no matter sinful, and no matter our situation."

Faith trembled as she heard the words. Not one person had ever said those words to her before. And yet here she stood, hearing them for the first time from a man she could never have. Cassian's words washed over her, filling her with such feelings of warmth, comfort, and disappointment.

Faith pushed the snowdrop through one of her buttonholes, and as she did so, she caught sight of her wedding band on her left ring finger. It might as well have been a noose around her neck for it had stolen her life from her.

"Let us eat!" she exclaimed, motioning for everyone to take their seats. Jolly conversation filled the dining room as plates were filled with the divine meal. Faith cut up Lucy's food for her into little pieces.

Cassian had taken the seat next to Faith, choosing not to sit at the head of the table. Underneath the table, Cassian took Faith's hand. It was not a gesture of longing, or a gesture of romance necessarily, but one of comfort. His touch was understanding, and Faith felt herself relax as she enjoyed the evening.

"What does that say?" Lucy asked as she pointed to one of the signs that hung above a shop door.

Cassian, Faith, Kit and Lucy, who sat atop Kit's shoulders, were walking back to the church the following morning.

"A ... poth ... e ... cary," read Kit carefully.

Faith smiled as Kit remembered to stick out his tongue at the 'th' sound.

Faith then noticed Cassian's proud expression. He really cared about this boy. Faith then thought that she should not refer to Kit as a boy. He was a young man, and a foot taller than her.

"What does that say?" Lucy persisted, choosing another sign.

"Mill ... i ... ner," read Kit. "What is a milliner?" he asked, puzzled.

"They make fancy hats," replied Faith.

They passed the milliner's and saw all the fine hats on display in the window.

"Surely women would tip over wearing some of them," chuckled Kit.

Faith smiled. She had attended many an afternoon tea with ladies wearing such extravagant hats. The tulle and feathers and ribbons were all quite ridiculous.

The party arrived back at the church and Kit lifted Lucy off of his shoulders and placed her down on the ground. Lucy appeared quite put out that she was now standing back at her original height.

Kit smiled. His smile was happy, Faith thought, as it reached his eyes. He looked so much healthier, too, for having spent time in Cassian's company. Kit was still a skinny young man, but he did not seem to be so thin anymore. Three hearty meals a week certainly helped in that respect. His clothing was no longer ill-fitting. Cassian had seen to that. Poor Reverend Atwood had not the resources for a boy with such long limbs. Cassian had commissioned clothing for Kit, and he was now dressed appropriately for his height, and the cool weather.

"Thank you for inviting me, sir," Kit said gratefully to Cassian. "Thank you as well, Mrs Rowe."

Cassian frowned. "How many times have I told you to call me Cassian?"

"Just don't seem fitting, sir," replied Kit.

"You are welcome, Kit," interjected Faith. "Lucy quite adores you."

Kit feigned a playful gasp and knelt down to Lucy's height. "Do you, Goose?" He then tapped the side of his cheek. Lucy giggled as she kissed Kit's cheek. "Happy birthday, Miss." He tapped Lucy's nose and stood back up again. "Will I see you on Monday, sir?"

Cassian nodded. "Absolutely."

Kit beamed and waved goodbye as he walked back into the church.

Faith stood there with Cassian for a moment, who was watching after Kit.

"I will do right by him, you know," Cassian murmured quietly. "He is getting to the age where even the good Reverend will not keep him. There are not many employers that will take on a child in his situation. Believe me, I know."

Faith pursed her lips. Cassian had not divulged much of his childhood struggles to her. She supposed that was a story for another day. "I know you will do right by him. There is not another man in this city that would do for that boy what you are doing."

"I keep thinking that I should give him a job in one of my factories. Create a new role at Angel Faith Textiles for him. But it does not seem enough," continued Cassian. "I have all this wealth for a reason."

"You will know the right thing to do when the opportunity presents itself," replied Faith.

Cassian nodded. "I suppose you are right," he agreed. "Come now. Let us get home and out of the cold." Cassian scooped Lucy up into his arms and held her on his hip as he led them back in the opposite direction.

Cassian and Faith chatted animatedly. That was something that Faith truly enjoyed about Cassian. She could tell him the darkest, most intimate moments of her life, and then she could chat about something so inconsequential, and he would listen intently to both.

Faith was laughing as they walked back past the milliner's, and so she did not see the young girl who had just exited the shop. Faith bumped right into her, knocking the young girl to the ground.

"Oh!" cried Faith. "Oh, I am so terribly sorry! Let me help you!"

Instead of carrying hat boxes, she had been carrying a book, which had flown out of her hand and landed open a few feet from where they were gathered.

Faith knelt down on the ground to help the girl up. She was dressed ever so finely. Her gown was a lovely pale green, adorned with white lace and embellished with such intricate embroidery. Her over coat looked just as expensive. It was white, or it was had Faith not knocked her to the ground.

The girl wore her hair down which was odd. Her hair was truly lovely, though. It was the most brilliant shade of red, and had a gorgeous natural wave to it.

"That is alright, ma'am. Mama always says that I need to keep my nose out of books and to watch where I am going," she said casually. At that moment, she looked up at Faith with the most brilliant pair of blue eyes that Faith had ever seen.

Except Faith had seen them before.

The young girl was beautiful. Her blue eyes were framed by light coloured eyelashes. Her nose was small and straight, and her skin was smooth and pale. Her face was heart shaped, and she would only grow more beautiful with age.

Faith had always thought so.

The last time Faith had seen her niece, she had been eight of so years old. She had to be nearing twelve now.

Faith was not the only one to recognise. Olivia Pendleton's eyes widened as well. Olivia recognised her aunt. She looked as if she were seeing a ghost.

"Aunt ... Aunt Anne?" she asked in disbelief.

CHAPTER 18

"Is it really you, Aunt Anne?" asked Olivia again.

Faith wanted to say something, anything, to convince Olivia that she was not the aunt that she remembered, that she was a stranger, someone who merely looked like her aunt.

But all Faith could manage was to stare at the twelve year old girl with her mouth open.

Faith could feel herself going into shock. Her mouth was completely dry. She could feel the blood draining from her face. Her heartbeat was erratic.

Faith could see what was going to happen. Olivia was going to tattle to her mother. Ruth would ensure that George found out the truth. The biggest scandal of the century would erupt across Britain and George would be humiliated.

Worst of all, Lucy would be discovered by the father that Faith had never wanted her to know.

What would happen to Lucy when George killed Faith?

Before Faith could find her voice and beg Olivia to keep her mouth shut, she heard and all too familiar voice.

"Oh, Olivia, for goodness' sake. If you took your nose out of that hideous political nonsense for one moment and actually looked where you were going —" Ruth Pendleton stopped just as soon as she noticed who Olivia had knocked into.

Ruth Pendleton had not changed one bit since Faith had last seen her. She was just as severe and as proper as ever. Her face had always been very thin and angular, which made her disapproving expressions all the more unsettling. Unlike Olivia's loose waves, Ruth's red hair was fixed just so. Intricate curls were visible below her lacy, expensive bonnet. She, too, wore a fine white overcoat, protecting her royal blue gown from the weather.

Ruth's blue eyes widened as she gasped. "Anne?"

"Ruth," said Faith, finally finding her voice.

Ruth shook her head. "I do not understand. How is this possible?"

A figure past Ruth and Olivia caught Faith's attention. It was Cassian. He was standing with Lucy, nonchalantly outside the apothecary. She said a silent prayer in thanks for his quick thinking. Cassian had removed Lucy from any danger of being associated with Faith. It was exactly what Faith would have done.

"You are supposed to be dead," Ruth said slowly, though her eyes were still wide with shock.

Knowing that Lucy was away from danger made Faith relax a little. "I am dead," replied Faith.

Ruth scoffed. "Do not insult my intelligence. You are standing here before me. Flesh and blood. I can see it!"

"Ruth, you must stay quiet," pleaded Faith. "As far as anyone is concerned, I am dead. I died in that carriage accident and that is how it must stay." Faith looked down at Olivia, who had since righted herself and collected her book. Faith squinted as she read the title: Declaration of the Rights of Woman and of the Female Citizen. It was written in French. "And you, too, Olivia."

Ruth's eyes flared. "You will not involve my daughter in this sickening affair. Where is he then?" she demanded to know. Her head immediately turned around, surveying the immediate area.

Faith's heart stopped as Ruth looked directly at Cassian, but she did not seem to take any notice of him. Faith was thankful that Cassian was entertaining Lucy, and so Lucy was not looking after her mother. "Where is who?" Faith lied coolly.

"Your lover!" she said accusingly. "You must have run off with a lover."

"I did not such thing," snapped Faith. "You know exactly why I made myself disappear. You only pretended not to notice."

"Oh, hush," spat Ruth. Ruth seized Faith's wrist and pulled her inside the milliner's shop. Olivia quickly followed. "I will not air dirty family laundry on the streets of London. You never know who is listening." Ruth glared at the milliner's who sat behind their craft tables stitching lace and all sorts onto the bonnets of rich women. "Be off with you!" she ordered.

The two workers quickly abandoned the stations and run up the stairs at the back of the shop.

Ruth paced the small length of the shop, moving between the two craft tables. "Yes, I knew. Of course I knew," she admitted gruffly. "Everyone did. You were such a sour girl. Everyone knew of your unhappiness." Ruth sucked in a deep breath. "How did this not occur to me?" She sighed.

"So you understand my decision?"

Fire returned to Ruth's ice cold eyes. "Understand?" she repeated. "Of course I do not understand, you selfish, selfish girl!" she seethed.

Faith was taken aback. Even Olivia flinched away from her mother. Faith would never tell Ruth as to why her decision was completely unselfish. That reason was safe in the arms of the man she loved.

"Did you ever imagine the sort of effect that your decision would have on the Earl?" Ruth asked accusingly.

Faith tensed. "I am sure he had his half a dozen whores to comfort him," she retorted. Immediately she regretted her choice of words in present company. "Excuse me, Olivia," she apologised.

"He was heartbroken," emphasised Ruth.

Faith had a hard time believing that.

"It took him nearly two months to find another bride," Ruth continued. "That is how forlorn he was."

Faith resisted laughing. Two months? He must have been terribly upset in between bedfellows.

"You are lucky that the engagement fell through or else you would have made a bigamist out of the Earl!" she cried.

Faith had never really given any thought to George remarrying. He was allowed to. Faith was legally dead.

"You are returning to Leicestershire with Olivia and myself today. This charade will not continue."

Faith took a step back, only to bump into the craft table. She shook her head determinedly. "Ruth, I am living an honest life in London." Relatively. "I cannot go back to Leicestershire," Faith insisted. "More than my body was beaten and bruised in that house."

Ruth held up her hand to stop Faith. "You are the one who married the man, Anne," she replied. "You are married. That is not something than can be undone."

Olivia cleared her throat awkwardly. "Actually, you could apply to parliament for a divorce," she informed them. Both Faith and Ruth turned to look at Olivia, clearly dumbfounded. "It is difficult and costly, but Uncle George has the money, and it would not be hard to find witnesses of adultery, combined with your accusations of cruelty, Aunt Anne."

"I will pretend that that filthy word did not just come out of your mouth, young lady," growled Ruth. Ruth glared at the book in Olivia's hands. "That is going in the first flame we come across."

Olivia's grip tightened on her novel as her blue eyes narrowed. Faith could quickly tell that Olivia Pendleton knew her own mind.

Despite her good intentions, Faith knew that divorce would never be an option for her. Divorce was scandalous business and was never entered into by the aristocracy.

"Anne, the way I see it, you have two options. The first," Ruth began, "is to leave this shop and carry on with whatever life you have created for yourself here, while I inform our circle of your whereabouts and you are shrouded in scandal and humiliation."

Faith wanted nothing more than to run out of the milliner's and directly over to Cassian and Lucy. But she knew if Ruth returned home with this story then there would be a witch hunt for her. They would find her. People with money always got what they wanted. Connections would be made. Mr Carne would be interrogated. Her alias would be discovered, and Lucy could be discovered.

Ruth pursed her lips and her eyes narrowed. "Can you imagine, Anne? Can you imagine the utter humiliation that the Earl will endure? Scandals outlive and outlast us all. Perhaps it will outlive you a little faster," she hinted.

If she was dead, then Lucy would be at the mercy of George. No, that was not an option for her.

"Or," Ruth continued, "you can return with us now and I will tell everyone that I happened upon you in a London hospital suffering from memory loss. All will be as it was, and none will be the wiser."

Faith felt herself trembling at the thought of returning to what was once her home in Leicestershire. She felt sheer and utter panic at the thought of being once more at the mercy of her husband.

But her decision was an easy one. Which would keep Lucy safe?

Faith knew that Cassian would protect Lucy. Lucy might not even miss her mother what with her friends in Cassian's home. That thought broke her heart. The whole notion of leaving Lucy behind broke Faith's heart.

But Lucy's life, and her happiness, were more important than Faith's. It was a selfless nature one acquired when one became a mother.

"Just look at you, Anne," remarked Ruth distastefully, as she gestured to Faith's attire. "What are you wearing? Come to your senses. Just think of what you could be wearing as the Countess of Runthorpe."

Faith's eyes narrowed. "I care not for such things," she said flatly.

"Well, you always were of a haughtier disposition," muttered Ruth. "Anne Rowe, the darling of society."

Faith knew that Ruth's bitterness resided in the fact that she had married the second son, the clergyman, and Faith had wed the Earl. Ruth could not understand how lucky she truly was.

"I will go back with you," Faith informed Ruth emotionlessly.

Ruth smiled, triumphant. "I am glad you have made the right decision, Anne. All will be as it was."

That was what Faith was afraid of.

"Do not fret. I shall tell everyone that you were only injured in the carriage accident, and that you lost your memories. Perhaps you might act slightly simple when we return," Ruth suggested.

"I need to write a letter," Faith insisted. "I need to inform the matron that I will no longer be requiring living arrangements," she lied. She needed to beg of Cassian the biggest of favours. She needed him to raise her daughter.

It took all of Faith's strength not to break down sobbing at the thought of her child being brought up by someone that was not her. When would Faith see Lucy again? Would she see Lucy again?

"Do it quickly," snapped Ruth. "I hate London in winter. But thanks to Olivia, a trip to London was necessary." Ruth glared at her daughter.

Faith frowned as Olivia looked away guiltily. "I gave away all my bonnets," she confessed. "I have no need of such silly bonnets anyway, Mama," Olivia insisted. "What need to I have for a bonnet? It is not as though I am out in a field and needing protection from the sun."

Ruth huffed angrily, and snatched the book from Olivia's hand and tossed it over her shoulder. Olivia cried as it landed on the floor some ten feet away. "Out," she ordered, smacking Olivia in the centre of her back. "Write your letter. We will be waiting."

Faith began to cry and she hurried to collect Olivia's book and tucked it inside her cloak. The enormity of what was happening was overwhelming her. How had she gone from celebrating Lucy's third birthday with such wonderful people to making the decision to return to hell on earth?

Faith wiped her eyes with her sleeves and noticed several scraps of parchment on the craft tables. The milliners were using them to sketch designs. Faith immediately seized a fresh piece and a quill and began to scrawl.

Faith was effectively signing away her child. She felt as though she was losing Lucy, even though she was saving her. It brought on memories of such immeasurable grief. How could she survive feeling this way once again?

"Hello?" she called once she had finished writing. "Hello there?"

Faith heard movement as the milliners returned to their shop. They appeared very uneasy.

"I am so sorry for interrupting your day," Faith said sincerely, sniffing through her tears.

"Are you alright, ma'am?" asked one.

"Was that woman horrible to you?" asked the other. "She is horrible to her poor daughter."

"Aye, she is," agreed the first.

"No, no," Faith lied. "But please, I beg of you one small favour," she pleaded. "I need this letter delivered to a man outside the apothecary. He has dark, curly hair, and is holding a small girl. Could one of you please take this to him?"

"Yes, I will take it," volunteered the milliner.

Faith breathed a sigh of relief. "Thank you. For Mr Kensington," she instructed.

"We will see that he gets it, miss."

"When will Mama be back?" asked Lucy for the tenth time.

Cassian watched as the older, redheaded woman summoned a carriage. She pulled on the arm of her young daughter, and pushed her inside. Faith had not emerged from the milliner's, but Cassian dared not approach.

Those people knew Faith, or rather, they knew Anne. Cassian had realised it the moment the young girl's eyes had found Faith, even before she had called Faith by her former name.

Cassian had immediately wanted to pull Faith away. To hide her. To keep her safe and away from these people she had run away from. But he knew that Faith's concern would only be for Lucy, which is why he had immediately removed her from Faith's side.

Cassian prayed that Faith would be able to talk her way out of this. He prayed that these people were sympathetic, and would understand Faith's reasons for fleeing from her husband.

From the sour look on the woman's face, Cassian was not optimistic. But they had left the milliner's without Faith. In a few moments, the carriage would away, and Cassian would storm that shop and take her into his arms.

"I want Mama!" Lucy said impatiently.

Cassian looked down at the little girl in his arms for the briefest of moments before his eyes went back to the shop door. Lucy was frowning, her chocolate brown eyes staring at him accusingly, as if he were the reason she could not be with her mother.

"Lucy, what colour are my eyes?" Cassian asked.

It was a little game that Cassian had thought up a few weeks ago when he had been teaching Kit to read numbers and colours. Lucy felt included, and she also learned something.

"Black!" she cried excitedly, her mood suddenly improved.

Cassian kept watch. "And how many ears do I have?"

Cassian felt Lucy's hands on his ears. "One," she counted. "Two."

"What colour is your hair?"

Lucy clapped her hands on her head. "Brown!"

"What colour is Kit's hair?"

"Yellow!" They had not quite achieved 'blond' yet.

"How many noses to I have?"

Lucy's hand flew to Cassian's nose. "One!"

"What colour —"

At that moment, Faith emerged from the milliner's. She looked awful. Her eyes were red, her mouth was downturned, and her head was low. She did not look up at him or Lucy, but he watched as her hand nearest to them outstretched and waved for a split second.

Cassian's heart stopped as Faith climbed into the carriage after the redheaded mother and daughter. "No," he gasped. "What are you doing? Where are you going?"

The carriage moved away and Cassian and Lucy were left standing in the street. Cassian stared after her, his mouth open, utterly shocked.

"Are you Mr Kensington?"

It took Cassian a moment to realise that someone was standing before him. He looked down at the woman. She was about fifty or so, wearing dark, practical clothing.

He could only nod.

"This is for you." She held out a letter to him. It was not sealed.

"Thank you," he murmured, readjusting Lucy on his hip so that he could flip open the letter.

Cassian, wrote Faith.

The woman is my sister-in-law, Ruth Pendleton, and her daughter, Olivia.

I have to go back. It is my only choice. If I do not, then George will find me, and then he will discover Lucy. I have to go back to protect her.

I need you to look after her for me. I need you to raise her. I need you to love her. I need you to tell her every day that Mama loves her and longs for her.

I know this is such a terribly selfish request, and that I am giving you no choice. It is utterly unfair of me, but I pray you will not resent me for this.

I do not know when I will be able to write again. I do not know if I will ever see you again.

Know that meeting you changed my life, Cassian Kensington. You are extraordinary.

I love you.

Faith.

The letter was tear stained. Faith and Cassian's tears were indistinguishable. Cassian could not hold them back. Whatever was said, whatever had gone on in that shop had convinced Faith that she had no other choice but to return to a monster.

Her request was a given. Lucy would always be safe with him. Of course he would love her. He loved the little girl already. She had every member of his household wrapped around her tiny, little finger.

At that moment, Faith was on her way back to a man who had beaten her, whose cruelty had caused the death of her unborn son. What would he do to her when he had his hands on her again? He would kill Faith. Cassian was absolutely certain of it.

Cassian had been a poor, poverty stricken man all his life, and yet he had never felt more powerless than he did in this moment.

He looked down at Lucy, who stared up at him with her mother's trusting brown eyes. But what could he do? Faith was married to the man. She could not fake her death twice.

Cassian had a sudden thought. An idea that just might work.

CHAPTER 19

Naturally, Cassian's arriving home and announcing to everybody that they were moving to Derbyshire had been a big surprise to everyone.

Cassian's plan was simple. He was now the owner of Finn Kelly's estate in Norwood. Of course, he had only been a "resident" of Norwood for a night, and that night had been spent in their jail, but he had found the place to be very lovely, quiet and secluded. It was out of the way, and gave off the impression that the people looked after one another.

"Faith Rowe" had been an alias. "Faith Kensington" could be one too.

Faith could not fake her death again, but by God Cassian would help her get away. Cassian would take her to Derbyshire where she would be safe. She and Lucy would live with the protection of Cassian's name. If he introduced them as his family then there would be no reason to doubt him.

It would not be legal, and it would be terribly sinful to live in such a way, but what was the alternative?

At this very moment Faith was travelling back to her barbaric husband. Cassian could not stand the thought of Faith being in that man's clutches for even a minute.

Cassian had explained to his household that he had purchased an estate in Derbyshire and had immediate plans to relocate. The house needed to be packed up and moved immediately. Those who could relocate with him would be welcomed. Those who could not leave London would be compensated while they looked for work elsewhere.

Cassian took his butler into his study after this conversation, under the guise of discussing the move. Cassian closed the door behind Mr Wade, who immediately lifted Lucy into his arms.

"Where is Mama?" Lucy asked him.

"I was going to ask the same question. Did not you and Mrs Rowe leave together, sir?" he asked.

"What I am about to tell you must stay between us. Do you understand?" Cassian asked seriously.

Mr Wade frowned and nodded his head. "Of course, sir. I always operate under the strictest confidentiality. Is this concerning Mrs Rowe?"

"Yes," confirmed Cassian. "Please, sit." Cassian gestured to one of the chairs before his desk.

Mr Wade tentatively sat down and sat Lucy on his lap. Cassian walked around to the other side of his desk and sat down. He took a deep breath and began.

"You know how I feel about Faith?" he asked.

The butler pursed his lips guiltily. "We had an inkling, sir," he admitted.

Cassian was not surprised. He had never made any deliberate effort to hide his feelings. "Do you remember the story that was in the newspapers a few years ago?" he asked. "The carriage accident that killed the Countess of Runthorpe?"

Cassian saw the recollection in the butler's eyes. He nodded slowly. "Of course. It was a tragic accident. She was very young."

"Yes, she was twenty years old," confirmed Cassian, "and she is three and twenty now."

Realisation dawned on Mr Wade as his jaw dropped. "I ... I do not understand," he stammered. "Mrs Rowe is –"

"Mrs Pendleton ... or Lady Pendleton. I do not know. I am not familiar with how to properly address peers." Cassian shook off the thought. "Faith is really Anne Pendleton, the Countess of Runthorpe. She faked her death three years ago to escape her husband's cruelty."

Mr Wade looked down at Lucy who sat absently on his lap, disinterested in the conversation. "Faith is the Countess of Runthorpe?" he asked is disbelief.

"Yes," confirmed Cassian.

"Does ... does that mean that Lucy is the daughter of an earl? She is Lady Lucy?"

"As far as I am concerned, Lucy is my child," Cassian said firmly. "Faith left her in my care and I will abide by her wishes. Faith never wanted that man to have anything to do with her daughter and I shall keep it that way. She is mine. That is final."

At the mention of her name, Lucy looked her. Her brown eyes found Cassian's and she smiled. Cassian could not help but smile back at her. Lucy was so innocent. Her mother had protected her from so much.

"I purchased the Derbyshire estate for Faith while I was away in the north," explained Cassian. "It is a sanctuary, or it will be a sanctuary for her. I want my household moved to Derbyshire so that I can bring her there for safety."

"Of course, I understand, sir. But what about the earl?" asked Mr Wade quietly. "I am sure he would not take too well to his wife leaving again."

"That is why I am telling you this, Wade," continued Cassian. He would not have dreamed of breaking Faith's confidence were it not important. "When I bring Faith home to my estate, it will be as my wife."

It took a moment for the information to sink in. Mr Wade's eyes widened. "Your wife? But —"

"Yes, I know." Cassian nodded. "It will not be legal, but this is how it has to be. I am telling you so that you can sell the story to the servants. Tell them that Faith and I are eloping and moving to Derbyshire and we shall all reunite in a short while."

"But you would be living in sin, sir," cautioned Mr Wade.

Cassian's eyes darkened. "Better to be living in sin than not to be living at all," he snapped defensively. "I am trusting you to organise this move, Wade. I want everything in Derbyshire within a week. Arrange transport. Arrange everything. Pay whatever. I care not for the cost." Cassian stood up from his desk. "Lucy and I are leaving immediately," he decided.

If Cassian could not intercept Faith on the road, he would find a way to steal her from her husband's home.

Ruth had commanded that the carriage take them directly back to the Runthorpe Estate. They stopped only to change horses and the drivers rested intermittently.

Faith, Ruth, and Olivia all slept in the carriage, sporadically and poorly. The jolt of the roads did not promote restful sleep.

Faith could hardly sleep anyway. She was too anxious. She watched out the window as more and more of the countryside passed her by. London was long gone, and she felt the ominous feeling of hell pulling her back in.

Her only comfort was that Lucy was safe. Cassian would protect her. That assurance was almost enough to mask the feeling of her broken heart. Almost.

"Aunt Anne?" whispered Olivia when Ruth was sleeping.

Faith turned her attention back to her young niece. "Yes?"

"You could really do it, you know, obtain a divorce," she encouraged.

Faith appreciated Olivia's optimism but she knew it was impossible. George would never consent to a divorce. The shame and expense would be far too much.

Faith produced Olivia's book from inside her cloak, at which point Olivia's eyes lit up. She accepted the book gratefully and held it to her chest.

"Why do you like it so much?" asked Faith curiously.

Olivia pursed her lips. "I suppose it started with my parents not being able to have a son," she said quietly. "My father's estate is going to a cousin and not to me because I am a girl. And so I started reading about other things I was not allowed to do. I cannot vote. I cannot own property. Whatever money I have will belong to my husband upon my marriage. I cannot attend university. My last lesson with my governess was how to curtsey in the presence of a royal." Olivia rolled her eyes, frustrated. "Have you ever heard of a locomotive?"

Faith frowned and shook her head.

"It is a new steam engine. Faster travel," Olivia replied. "Papa took us to see it last year. He and Uncle George are investing in them. But when I asked to ride in it I was told that "women's bodies are not fit for travel at great speed". Bah!"

Olivia spoke with such passionate disdain, all in a hushed whisper so as not to wake her mother. She was much changed since

Faith had last seen her, a mere eight year old child who liked to read into the night.

Olivia had fire.

"I am going to change the world one day, Aunt. You shall see," Olivia said confidently.

Faith smiled slightly. "I hope you do." She truly meant that. Olivia's vision for the future surely was better than the one that awaited Faith.

Faith sat in exhausted terror for the duration of the journey. It was early Monday morning when Faith began to recognise Runthorpe land, and midday by the time the carriage was travelling through the gates and down the driveway towards the great house.

"Now, Anne. I am fully committed to the tale of memory loss. It will be your prerogative to tell your husband the truth, of course," Ruth said as the carriage came to a stop. "But none in our circle will know what really happened. Everything will be as it was."

That was what Faith was afraid of.

Faith peered out the window and she felt her stomach drop. The house seemed so familiar, as though she had only left it the day before. Had it really been over three years? And yet she still felt as though she was seventeen, and entering this harrowing house for the first time.

Faith was no longer seventeen. She had survived. She had survived here, and she had survived on her own in London with a little daughter to provide for. She was stronger now. She could survive anything knowing that Lucy was safe.

Footmen began to surround the carriage. They were servants Faith recognised from before. As soon as the carriage door was opened and the steps were lowered, they began to realise just who had returned.

One footmen fainted. The others looked as though they were seeing a ghost.

Faith took a deep breath and moved past them, climbing the steps up into the house. The house had not changed a bit since she had last been there. The same paintings of the people she had once used for company still hung on the walls. She could still see her reflection in the black and white marble floor. She looked tired.

"Your Ladyship?" gasped a familiar voice.

Appearing from nowhere was the Runthorpe butler, Mr Kirkham. He was old, traditional, and had served the last three earls.

"Oh, good, Kirkham," said Ruth, looping her arm through Faith's as though they were dear friends. "Tea, I think. And tell His Lordship that Lady Runthorpe has been found safe and well in a London hospital. We shall be in the drawing room."

Tea and one's undead wife. What an agenda for the day.

"Yes, Mrs Pendleton." Mr Kirkham, still clearly bewildered, nodded his head slowly and disappeared.

"Come along, dear," urged Ruth forcefully, as she pulled Faith towards the drawing room. Olivia followed along behind.

The Runthorpe drawing room was the type of setting one was afraid to be relaxed in. The furnishings were ornate and uncomfortable. The pianoforte was decorative, and the people who frequented it were insufferable.

"Mama, surely this is wrong," appealed Olivia. "Aunt Anne does not want to be here. We ought to leave."

Faith jumped when she heard the sound of skin forcefully meeting skin. Ruth had slapped Olivia's cheek. Olivia was now clutching her cheek and crying. Faith's heart broke for the poor girl.

"Quiet, you stupid girl," she snapped.

No sooner had Olivia sat down, the door of the drawing room opened again and the devil walked in.

He had not changed at all. He was still just as handsome as he had been the day Faith hair married him. His sand coloured hair was still perfectly coiffed and his clothing was just as spotless and expensive as ever, draped over his ever lean physique. And his eyes, his grey eyes were still just as cold.

George's eyes found Faith immediately. Faith saw the shock and confusion there. He was just as surprised as everybody else that Faith was alive. And then came the ire. The all too familiar ire. Faith had seen it many a time she had been offensive to him. That look had preceded many, many cruel acts.

But Faith was not as afraid as she had once been. Of course, she was terrified of what could happen, but she no longer saw it as definite. Faith took a deep breath and rose to her feet. This man was her husband, but that did not mean that he could have her like he once had.

"Get out, Ruth," ordered George. "I need to talk to my wife."

Kit could not contain his smile as he half skipped, half jogged, towards Cassian's house in Kensington. Kit's reading lessons were the favourite part of his week.

Kit had never really had anything to look forward to. As an orphan, he had had a cruel introduction to life. There had never been a surplus of food to go around. There was never adequate clothing, though nothing really ever fit Kit's long arms and legs.

And there was never any love. Kit would never admit it, but sometimes it was a nice idea to imagine someone putting an arm around his shoulders and uttering "I am proud of you" or "You can rely on me, son".

The "son" part was a particular fantasy.

Kit's name was just that. Christopher. Kit. No surname. No father to give him one. Kit was not really even his true name. Perhaps it was John. Perhaps it was Michael. He did not know the name his mother had given him upon his birth.

All he knew about his mother was that she had left him on the doorstep of an orphanage on the twenty-fifth of July fourteen years ago. St Christopher's Day.

Kit had never experienced the feeling of being wanted. Not until he had encountered Mr Kensington. Of course he had not liked the man at first. Kit had a horrible habit of being suspicious of adults.

The only adults that had ever been interested in taking him were those after a strong, young man who could provide free labour.

But not Mr Kensington. Mr Kensington cared. Mr Kensington was a rich man who cared about poor people. Mr Kensington wanted Kit to learn how to read. Mr Kensington wanted the best for Kit. Mr Kensington wanted Kit to make something of himself.

Kit knew it was silly to think so, but he could not help but look up to Mr Kensington as a father. Fathers cared about their sons in the way that Mr Kensington cared for Kit, did they not?

Too many people knew the embarrassment of illiteracy. Of course, Kit was not expected to know how to read. He was insignificant. He did not matter. School was not important for the likes of him.

Kit lived in a church and could not even read the bible. It was humiliating.

Kit could not understand that logic. School was for the rich, and not for the poor. And yet, how could the poor change their circumstances without a proper education?

Kit could not wipe the smile off of his face. He had such a surprise for Mr Kensington. In his pocket was Mr Kensington's copy of Utopia. Kit had been working so hard of a night time to learn the words on his own. He had managed to read the first page almost fluidly. He hardly stumbled. He could not wait to show Mr Kensington.

In his other pocket was a small gift. Insignificant really, but Kit had little to thank him with. Kit had always had the knack for whittling, and so he had whittled away making an ornate letter "F". The gift was twofold. To show Mr Kensington that he recognised the letter, and to represent Mr Kensington's affection for Faith.

Kit liked Faith very much. She was so kind and caring, and she always seemed to have time for him. In a church full of children less independent than him, time was scarce.

And then there was Lucy. Little Goose. Kit had always been around younger children, but he had never thought of them as siblings. Kit had an affection for Lucy, and he cared about her as an older brother.

Today was Monday. Monday had quickly become one of his favourite days.

When Kit saw Mr Kensington's house come in to view, he felt as though he was coming home. These people were good people. These people were the kind of family that he had always wished for.

Kit knew it was wishful thinking, but he could not help but hope. Hope that reading lessons would become frequent dinners. Hope that he would be included on significant occasions like Christmastime.

Hope that one day they might come to love him, too.

As Kit climbed the stairs, he furrowed his eyebrows. The front door was wide open and he could see the servants scurrying about inside, arms filled with different objects.

Kit pushed the door open and was nearly flattened by a maid carrying a painting that was quite nearly taller than her.

"Oh, mind out!" she exclaimed, huffing and puffing. "Are the paintings being wrapped in the drawing room, Hattie?" she called up the stairs.

"Yes, yes," confirmed Hattie, who descended the stairs carrying another painting.

Kit looked around the foyer with wide, confused eyes. Where was everything? The walls were bare, and the furniture pieces were gone. What was left was covered in large, white sheets.

"Oh, hello, Kit," greeted Hattie, who blew a piece of hair out of her face.

"What ... what is happening? Where is Mr Kensington?" asked Kit nervously.

Hattie rolled her eyes. "Oh, he is eloping," she muttered in an annoyed tone. "He has run off with Faith and left us to pack up the house in a matter of days."

Kit nearly choked on his tongue. "Eloping?" he gasped. "Packing up the house? I don't understand. Where are you going?"

"Derbyshire of all places!" Hattie exclaimed. "We are all leaving this week for Mr Kensington's new estate."

Derbyshire? Where on earth was Derbyshire? Why were they all leaving? Why had Mr Kensington not told him?

"Listen, Kit, either pick up some furniture or make yourself scarce. We have to be in Derbyshire within the week." Hattie moved past him with the painting and went into one of the rooms off the foyer.

Mr Kensington was gone. That was obvious. He was eloping with Faith and moving away to start his own family. Kit was not part of that life. Mr Kensington owed him nothing. He owed Kit nothing.

That was realisation sent a tremor down Kit's spine as a sob threatened to escape from his throat.

"Alright, then." Kit pursed his lips and turned on his heel. He marched out of Mr Kensington's house and left behind whatever hope he had once had for a family.

Chapter 20

George had been startlingly pleasant to Faith upon her return. He had sent Ruth and Olivia away to welcome her home. That was all he had said.

But Faith could sense his displeasure, his anger. Her actions were humiliating to him. Of course, the hospital story would be believed by the public, George would see to that. But in private?

Faith was certain that the shock had prevented his true ire.

George was not the sort of man to allow a woman's disobedience.

It was odd moving back into the routine she had once kept. Three and a half years and things were suddenly just the same as they always were. George kept to himself as Ruth chaperoned Faith, not so subtly ensuring that she did not run away again.

Faith's bedroom was unchanged. Clearly there had been no other woman staying. Everything she had left behind was still neatly folded in her wardrobe. Her scent bottles were all still perfectly aligned on her dressing table. The jewellery pieces she had left on purpose so as not to attract suspicion were all still where she had left them, strewn casually atop her table.

But everything was not the same. Faith would not allow it. She would not allow her daughter to grow up in a world where her mother sat down and simply let atrocious things happen to her.

That night, Faith's eyes shot open at the all too familiar squeak of her bedroom door.

It was not a loud squeak at all. It was not a squeak that warranted attention due to the annoyance. It was a slight, barely audible creak.

But to Faith, it had always been as loud as a church bell, alerting her to the opening of her door. And there was only ever one person who frequented her bedroom at all hours of the night.

Her heart started to hammer in her chest as her grip tightened on the bedclothes.

Creak. Creak. Creak.

The wooden floorboards shifted beneath the intruder's feet, screaming a warning.

The hairs on the back of Faith's neck stood up as the squeaking stopped, indicating that the intruder was now standing on the rug.

He was standing right behind her.

"I am sleeping," Faith murmured into her pillow. It took all the strength she had not to stammer.

"Well, I am awake," retorted George firmly.

His voice sent a shiver down her spine as Faith bit down on her bottom lip. This night would not end how George was planning. Absolutely not.

Faith screamed as her hair was pulled from behind. George had grabbed a fistful of her hair and had yanked her so that she was on her back and facing him. The safe cocoon of her bedclothes were then pulled away from her, leaving her feeling very exposed in her old nightdress.

It was dark, and Faith could only faintly see the outline of George's body.

"Quiet, dear. We do not want to wake the servants," George sneered as he seized Faith's wrists and wrapped his large hand around them both. He held her hands above her head. "Speaking of," he continued as he climbed onto the bed. His weight dipped the mattress and Faith involuntarily turned towards him. "I had an interesting discussion with a friend of yours today. Mr Carne."

Faith gasped as the blood drained from her face.

"Oh, yes. He told me everything."

Everything? Mr Carne had never known of Faith's pregnancy. Faith had never spoken of it directly, but had he known? Did George know that there was a child somewhere?

"He told me all about your plan to fake your death, how he took you to Kent, and how you planned on going to London," George mocked.

Faith resisted sighing with relief. No mention of Lucy. She thanked God. Her focus returned to her struggle to free her wrists. She writhed but George would not relent.

"He is lucky that his actions only cost him his job."

Oh, poor Mr Carne!

"Did you really expect that you could leave forever?"

"Clearly I was unsuccessful," Faith snapped.

"Listen to you. You have become common." He laughed. "Now, for your punishment," he began. Using his free hand, Faith heard the sound of his belt buckle unfastening. It was quickly discarded.

"No, I do not think so," Faith said firmly as she tried to pull her hands free again.

George laughed again. Even though she could not see him, she felt his close proximity. The bile rose in her throat. The mattress moved as his weight shifted to hover over her. "Oh, dear Anne. You forget yourself. You have denied me three years of my conjugal rights. Just lay still."

But Faith was not afraid. How many times had she been in this position? Subjected to her husband's brutality because she had naively promised to obey him on her wedding day. She was strong. She survived. She would not allow him to take advantage of her anymore.

"No," Faith said again, giving him one last chance.

She did not see it, but she felt it. The cruel sting that his hand left upon her cheek only made her angrier.

"I am no longer the type of woman to just lie here, George," Faith snapped as she brought her knee up to her chest and aimed. She drove her foot into the general direction of his groin and prayed that her aim was true.

George immediately released Faith's wrists as he leapt off the bed, crying and cursing, shouting profanities.

Faith immediately turned up the flame in her lamp and her bedroom illuminated. Her husband, the man she had always feared, was curled up on the floor, cupping his manhood like a child. "You dare to touch me again and I will cut it off," she threatened darkly.

His grey eyes flew to Faith's, testing her. "You would not have the gall," he spluttered.

Faith did not break. She smiled. "Shall we see?" she said calmly, extending her hand to him.

George stared at her hand as though it were poisoned. He made no move to test her. "You ... you devil woman!" he exclaimed, his voice still riddled with pain. George ungracefully climbed to his feet and stumbled out of Faith's bedroom.

Faith climbed back into bed and smiled in her misery. She stared at the canopy above her and prayed that her daughter was sleeping soundly in her bed in London. "Mama is going to make you proud, Lucy. I promise."

George avoided Faith like the plague the next day. The man was used to snapping his fingers and having whatever he wanted. He had never before been challenged like he had been the night before.

Faith knew her victory would be short lived. George was cautious of her, but his fear would soon be replaced with rage and resentment. Faith knew that the previous night's visit would not be the last, no matter her threats.

Ruth had launched into planning a ball to celebrate Faith's return, and Olivia had made herself scarce while they all awaited the arrival of George's brother, John, from his parish.

Faith used this time alone to wander down to the lake. It was a miracle that she was not followed, though she would never allow herself to be seen there. As she came closer and closer to the lake, she felt the overwhelming sadness that was always there, buried deep in her heart.

She felt the pain, as fresh as it had been five years ago, as she approached the place where her tiny boy was buried.

The spring flowers were not out yet. The weather was still far too wintery. But it was peaceful. The water was still and the long grass had frozen dew drops clinging to the blades.

When she came to the spot, a loud sob escaped her throat. The earth was bare, but that was only because the bulbs had not flowered yet. In springtime, daffodils would bloom all around him.

Faith knelt down and placed her palms in the earth, right above him. She pressed her fingers into the soft ground and closed her eyes. For what purpose, she did not know. But it felt right to be here, to sit with him, to be close to him, and to just breathe. Breathe for him. Breathe for both her children.

Sky would have been five in March. What would that have been like? To have a five year old little boy? An older brother for Lucy?

"Mama!"

Faith laughed. For a moment she could have sworn she heard Lucy's voice.

Faith suddenly sat bolt upright when she realised that she had not imagined Lucy's voice. She wiped her eyes free from tears so that her vision was not clouded.

Was she hallucinating?

Lucy had emerged from the wilderness that accompanied the Runthorpe estate, followed closely by Cassian. Lucy trotted happily, wearing her thick travelling clothes. Her curly hair was fixed poorly in ribbons.

Cassian wore a stern expression as he looked around, but they were alone. It was only the four of them.

Faith's heart leapt with a brief moment of pure happiness as she saw the two people she loved most in the world. Lucy tore through the long grass, stumbling as he went, crying out Faith's name.

"Mama!" she cried as she came closer. Moments later, Lucy threw herself into Faith's arms.

Faith nearly crushed her daughter as she held Lucy so tightly to her chest. Had it only been a few days? She pressed her face into her hair, committing Lucy's scent to memory. She brushed her hands over Lucy's face, memorising every little freckle.

"I thought you would be here."

Faith looked up at Cassian knowingly. His dark eyes were sad. He knew the reason she was here. He knew what this place was to her.

Cassian dropped to his feet as his stern façade melted away. He enveloped Faith and Lucy in his long arms. Had her bedclothes been a cocoon the night before? They could not beat the safety of

Cassian's embrace. Faith rested her head on Cassian's chest and listened to his heart as it beat rapidly in his chest. She felt him press his lips into her hair.

A moment's serenity was quickly clouded by the danger in their presence. "What are you doing here?" Faith suddenly asked.

"What else do you think? We are here to rescue you," Cassian said simply, caressing her cheek, which was still sensitive from George's strike the night before.

Rescue. How brilliant. How fanciful. How impossible.

Faith stared down at Lucy in her arms. Lucy was standing on the grounds of her father's estate. Lucy was standing on the ground in which her brother was buried. Lucy was standing where she, too, would have been buried had Faith lost her the same way.

That thought made Faith want to vomit violently.

"How could you bring her here?" Faith asked accusingly. "She was safe in London!"

"But you were not safe here," Cassian retorted. "Come. Now. I have a carriage waiting just a mile through those trees on the road," he urged. "I have a sanctuary for you. For all of us."

A sanctuary? How could she possibly be safe anymore? Knowing Ruth and her powers of gossip, the news that Anne Pendleton was alive had probably crossed the Atlantic. Anyone and everyone would know her and be talking about her. Her portrait would be printed again, just like it was the first time.

"Do you trust me?"

Cassian's question caught a troubled Faith off guard.

"Of course," she breathed.

"You had faith in me once. Have faith in me again," he said sincerely, helping Faith to her feet. "I will keep you and Lucy safe for the rest of your lives."

Faith believed him. She could feel his truth. And he was right. She had faith in him. She would always have faith in him. He would keep them safe.

Their conversation was interrupted by the sound of a cocking pistol. Both Faith and Cassian spun around to see George, who had appeared suddenly, holding a loaded pistol.

The pistol was not pointed at Faith or Cassian. It was pointed at Lucy.

"A bastard child?" George was turning red, his body was shaking as his finger rested on the trigger of the weapon aimed at Faith's child.

Faith screamed an unholy noise as she threw her body on top of Lucy. Lucy was tackled to the ground, and had started to cry, but Faith did not care, so long as she was the one in the way of the bullet.

George believed that Lucy was Cassian's child.

"You!" exclaimed George irately, his pistol moving to Cassian. Cassian raised his arms as he casually stepped in front of Faith and Lucy who were lying on the ground.

"Do not make any hasty decisions, sir," Cassian said calmly. "The law still applies to gentlemen."

"Gentlemen?" The word seemed to strike a chord with George. "You are right. There is only one way to kill you as a gentleman. I challenge you to a duel," he spat, throwing his handkerchief down on the ground at Cassian's feet.

Faith's eyes widened in terror. A duel? Oh, good God! No, Cassian, she willed. Do not pick up that handkerchief! Do not accept the challenge! Go now with Lucy and do not come back!

"When I win, Faith comes with me," Cassian said darkly as he bent down to pick up the handkerchief, accepting the challenge.

"When I win, your whore will never leave my bed, and you and your bastard will share a coffin," sneered George. "Dawn, tomorrow."

Cassian twitched at George's evil words. "Dawn then," agreed Cassian.

CHAPTER 21

F aith felt sick.

A duel? How could Cassian agree to a duel? How could he be so foolish? George was a proud gentleman! Did Cassian think that he had never engaged in a duel before?

George had engaged in three duels while Faith had lived at Runthorpe, all over money. Two opponents had been fatally wounded, and one had managed to survive. Duels were ended when the challenger was satisfied that there was no longer an offense. George had never been satisfied with only a single shot.

"She has been living as a whore, John," exclaimed George irately as he paced the drawing room before Faith, Joh, Ruth, and Olivia.

Faith was hardly listening.

As Cassian was the challenged party, he had the right to choose the weapon. George and John had grown up fencing. Faith prayed that Cassian did not choose the sword. There was no possibility of George being satisfied at first blood. He would run Cassian through.

"I always knew she was a loose woman," mused John. "Never the holy type of wife."

It had to be pistols. That was his only chance for survival, and even then it would be through sheer, dumb luck.

What if he died?

"I bet you Anne was with that man and their bastard when I discovered them in London!" added Ruth. "He probably hid like the coward he is."

In the grand scheme of things, Faith had only known Cassian a few months, but in that time he had changed her life. Faith had only ever known one sort of life, and one type of man. Cassian had opened her eyes to the kind of life that she had never known existed, the kind of life that she wanted for Lucy.

"All will be settled tomorrow," said George. "I am an excellent shot."

And most importantly, he had quickly become the exact sort of man for her. Faith had never been in love before. And she thought she loved Cassian.

Only now, at the possibility of losing him, was she aware of just how incredibly she loved that man. The thought of being without him was unbearable. This was not how it was supposed to be.

"Have you any defence, woman?" exclaimed George.

Cassian was supposed to be in London looking after Lucy. They were both supposed to be safe.

If Cassian was killed in the duel, Faith had no doubt that George would put Lucy in the ground with him. And over Faith's dead body was that happening.

Faith looked up, only to realise that everyone was staring at her. "What?"

"Have you any idea of the shame you have brought upon this house?" seethed George. He shook his head. "I had no idea of the depth of your selfishness. How dare you birth his bastard?"

Faith watched as George clenched his feet, his anger making him shake. He was going to strike her. Faith's eyes narrowed. "I am still here tonight, George. You touch me and I cut it off. That was a promise, mind."

George hesitated. "What do I want with you anyway?" he snapped. "You are spoiled goods now."

"We must thank God that the law is relaxed around duels," preached John. "The good Lord understands that we are men of honour, and our honour must be maintained."

"If you kill him, it will be murder," stated Faith.

George grinned darkly. "Not for the likes of gentlemen," he retorted. "You should be thanking me, Anne. With him and your bastard gone, there is no chance of your shame being spread about."

Faith flinched. "Hear me now, George," she threatened. "If you lay a hand on my daughter, I will do far more than cut off your prick," she cursed. Faith got to her feet and squared her shoulders, standing as tall as her small frame would allow. "I will cut out your pathetic excuse for a heart and cook it for breakfast. Do not think that I won't do it. You take away my daughter and I have nothing to lose. I will end your life and dance on your grave." Faith's voice did not shake, nor did she blink.

The room was silent, and Faith momentarily felt guilt that Olivia was present to hear her threat. But Faith meant every word. George would draw his last breath on this earth if he laid even one finger on Lucy.

George smirked. "I broke you once, Anne. I will do it again. A bastard is not the same as a real child. Women do not love bastards. You will soon bear my heir whether you like it or not."

"And that is why you will never be a father," countered Faith. Little did George understand her true meaning. "I would rather die than give you a child."

Again, George twitched with anger. "That can be arranged, my dear."

Faith barely slept. Every time she closed her eyes, her mind thought of all sorts of horrid, frightening scenes. She could see Cassian's death so vividly, and so she had emptied her stomach into her chamber pot twice.

She rose before dawn, dressed warmly, and stuffed whatever jewellery she could get her hands on into her pockets. She prayed Cassian did not bring Lucy to the duel, but if he did, then Faith would grab her and run.

The rest of the house was awake as well. Much to Faith's disgust, the servants were tasked with preparing refreshments for the witnesses. Fruit and pastries were to be served while two men possibly killed each other. It was utterly barbaric.

Faith, alongside George, walked down to the green beside the house. John, as George's second, Ruth and Olivia followed.

The air was cold, the clouds were low, and the rain was drizzling. It was a miserable morning.

The servants were assembling sheltered chairs and tables. A footmen had always carried down George's prized set of duelling pistols, as well as his fencing swords, depending on Cassian's choice of weapon.

Usually, Cassian's second would arrive with a note before the duel, with his master's choice of weapon on it. Both seconds would attempt to solve the issue of the offense without violence, but if no amends could be made, then the duel would go ahead. The duel was ended when the challenger was satisfied that the offense was no longer, and honour had been restored.

Cassian had never duelled before, and so he was unaware of this. Had he ever even fired a pistol?

Cassian was already standing on the green with a man Faith did not recognise. Lucy was nowhere to be seen. Faith said a silent prayer of thanks.

Cassian's eyes immediately went to Faith. He appraised her diligently. He was searching her for injury.

"Lucy?" was all Faith mouthed.

"Mr Carne," Cassian replied silently.

Faith relaxed as much as the situation allowed. Somehow Cassian had found her initial saviour. Lucy was safe and away from danger. Now she could focus all her worry on Cassian.

"I think I ought to have the name of the man I am about to kill," announced George in front of everyone.

Cassian looked relaxed. "My name is Cassian Kensington," he replied. "This is my second, Mr Finnegan Kelly." Cassian gestured to his stern, copper-haired companion.

"Kensington," pondered George. "I have heard of you."

"Funny," replied Cassian. "I have never heard of you."

Again, George twitched. Cassian was provoking him. George stepped towards Cassian and glared at him with such hatred. George snapped his fingers and John stepped forward. "My second," he snapped. "Reverend John Pendleton."

"Gentlemen," said Mr Kelly, holding up his hands and stepping in between Cassian and George. Faith detected a slight Irish accent. "It is my duty as a magistrate to inform you that any deaths here today are classed as murder under the law."

"You brought a magistrate?" barked George.

"I sensed you were not one to follow the rules," retorted Cassian.

Out of the corner of her eye, Faith spied another joining the party. Doctor Sampson, the local surgeon, had been summoned. She uttered another thankful prayer.

Even though it was technically murder to kill another in a duel, the courts seemed to respect the honour in a duelling death. Nobody was ever brought to justice.

"Your weapon?" asked George stiffly.

"Pistols," replied Cassian.

Faith watched in horror as John went to collect the pistols from their ornate box. He brought them over carefully, giving one to George, and one to Mr Kelly, to inspect for Cassian.

As Mr Kelly conducted the inspection, Cassian stared at Faith. Faith could tell that he was trying to appear reassuring. He was confident.

George would not fire more than three shots. Any more than three was childish and not gentlemanlike. Faith only feared it would not take him three shots to kill Cassian.

Mr Kelly was satisfied with the pistol, and had handed the weapon over to Cassian. He then joined John in the centre of the green to pace out the distance.

Faith was shaking. She watched Cassian as he moved into position, standing opposite George. Both men glared at each other. This was going to end in blood, only Faith was unsure of whose it would be.

Faith felt a small hand take hers. She looked to her left to see Olivia standing beside her. Olivia looked just as frightened as Faith was.

"Any last words?" challenged George.

Cassian looked directly at Faith. "I love you," he said sincerely. Cassian was not afraid.

Faith was frozen. She could not even respond to him. She could not comprehend what was about to happen. In a matter of minutes he could be dead. She would never forgive him for that.

"Take your aim!" cried John, as he raised his handkerchief in the air.

Both George and Cassian cocked their pistols and aimed at each other.

Faith stopped breathing.

"FIRE!" John dropped his handkerchief and an almighty bang echoed around the green.

The pistols fired and a cloud of gunpowder concealed their masters.

Faith screamed soundlessly as she searched the cloud desperately for Cassian. The gunpowder quickly cleared to show that both men were still standing.

They had both missed.

Cassian was still alive. Oh, thank God! She would kill him for putting her through this!

"Are you satisfied, George?" called John.

Oh, no.

"Absolutely not." George waved John over, indicating that he wanted his pistol to be reloaded.

"You have both fired!" cried Mr Kelly. "You have both risked your lives to restore honour. Is this not enough?"

"Get out of the way, Mr Kelly. A duel is not over until the challenger is satisfied. I am not satisfied." George aimed his pistol at Cassian once more.

Cassian reloaded his pistol and raised it again. He took a deep breath, staring directly at George.

"FIRE!" shouted John again.

Once again, the green was filled with the noise of gunshots. The air was permeated with the smell of gunpowder. Faith anxiously searched the cloud for Cassian. As the gunpowder haze cleared, Faith saw that Cassian was on the ground.

She screamed this time. She screamed an ear piercing scream, the sound only one who was truly suffering could make.

"Oh, God!" she cried, tears filling her eyes. Faith tore across the green, hiking up her skirts to move as quickly as she possibly could. Faith threw herself to the ground beside Cassian, and she cupped his face with her hands.

Cassian's dark eyes were open. They were wide with fear. He was alive, but barely.

"Oh, dear God!" Faith sobbed as she noticed Cassian's wounds. His white shirt was stained red with blood. He was shot. He was going to die.

Cassian was trembling, and he grabbed a hold of Faith's hand. Faith squeezed his hand tightly.

"Doctor Sampson!" she screamed, recalling that the surgeon had been present.

Mr Kelly was by Cassian's side as well, looking just as traumatised and fearful as Faith was. "This man is alive!" he shouted to the doctor. "He needs help!"

Faith looked around to see that the doctor, John, and Ruth were all surrounding George. George had also fallen.

Cassian, in his pain, noticed this too. With his other hand, he weakly grabbed on to Mr Kelly's shirt to gain his attention. "You ... take ... her," he spluttered. His voice was breaking, and his skin was paling. "You ... take ... Faith ... and ... Lucy ... to ... Norwood."

"No!" gasped Faith. "I am not leaving you." She shook her head stubbornly. Faith ripped away Cassian's cravat and tore at the buttons on his shirt. She pulled his clothing apart to expose his chest. Faith felt her stomach flip at the sight. His chest was red. Blood was swiftly pumping out of a puncture wound to the right of his chest. Faith knew she needed to stop the blood flow. She grabbed the cravat and pressed it against the gunshot, which elicited a cry in pain from Cassian.

"I made him a promise, Miss Faith," said Mr Kelly, as he looked down at Cassian regretfully. "He made me promise to make you leave if anything happened to him."

Faith knew that Cassian would have planned for his. But there was no way she was leaving this very spot. Faith had a sudden knack for threats. "You try to pull me from this spot and I will cut you," she threatened.

"I expected nothing less," he replied.

"No!" gasped Cassian. "Leave!"

His skin was becoming paler and paler. The cravat Faith was holding to Cassian's chest was quickly saturating with blood.

"He needs a surgeon!" urged Faith fearfully. And a miracle. Cassian needed a miracle.

CHAPTER 22

"Do you have a strong stomach, ma'am?" asked Mr Kelly.

Faith nodded, not moving her hands from Cassian's chest wound. Her hands and her cuffs were now red with blood as well. It was warm and wet, and utterly vile, but she could handle anything so long as this stupid, brave man survived.

"I need to stop this bleeding long enough to get him to a surgeon. I will need your help." Mr Kelly spoke in a low, calm voice. It was almost startling.

"What do you need me to do?" she asked desperately.

"The swords," he motioned to the set of fencing swords that had been brought down as possible duelling weapons. "Fetch me one, now."

"But I cannot move my hands!" protested Faith. If she moved her hands, blood would flow more freely.

"Now!" urged Mr Kelly forcefully.

Faith regretfully abandoned Cassian's side and raced over to where the servants had assembled the refreshments. The fencing swords were lying in a similarly ornate box.

"Aunt Anne, can I help?" asked Olivia softly. Olivia was nervously standing beside a tray of untouched pastries. Her face was ashen. She was in shock.

But Faith had no time for sympathy, no matter how she would have liked to have comforted the girl. "Stay away from it, Olivia. Stay out of the way." Faith seized one of the swords and ran back over to where Mr Kelly was waiting with Cassian.

When she fell back down onto her knees, she saw that the duelling pistol was now in pieces, and Mr Kelly was holding the flint lock in his hands along with another metallic piece of the weapon. He had created a small pile of cloth from Cassian's clothing, and was attempting to use the flint lock to create a spark.

"As soon as I have a flame, you put the sword into it, do you understand?"

Faith had heard of the technique, but she had never known it being practiced except for in the militia. Mr Kelly was going to burn Cassian's flesh to seal his wound.

Faith tore her eyes from the blood that was still pumping out of Cassian's chest and focussed on watching for a flame. Mr Kelly was working tirelessly, panicking and panting as he continuously struck the flint against the metal to gain a spark.

"Please, please, please," Faith prayed.

After several agonising moments, Mr Kelly cried out as a spark ignited the cloth. Faith did exactly as she was told, and plunged the sword into the flame. She knew the flame would not burn for long as it quickly devoured the cloth. Mr Kelly seemed to have this thought as well as he quickly untied his cravat and added it to the pile.

The tip of the sword soon turned yellow, as if it were molten lava.

"Press it onto his wound," encouraged Mr Kelly. "You burn him until you no longer see any blood flow."

Faith was shaking as she brought the sword towards Cassian's chest. But she did not hesitate. She had a way to save him and she would do it. Faith pressed the molten blade into Cassian's chest, and the sickening crackle and singeing smell was enough to turn one's stomach.

Cassian screamed in agony. Faith had never before heard such a noise, but she did not care, nor did she stop. So long as he kept making noise, he was alive.

The scent of burning flesh permeated the air, and Faith continued to move the thin blade across his wound to ensure that it was properly burned, and not even the tiniest seepage could get through.

"Help me get him up," instructed Mr Kelly.

Faith abandoned the sword but was virtually helpless in lifting Cassian to his feet. Mr Kelly took most of his weight. Faith wrapped her arm around Cassian's waist but she knew she was not aiding in any way.

"There is a carriage waiting through there." Mr Kelly pointed to the wilderness that adjoined the Runthorpe estate. "We need to carry him about a mile. I am not familiar with this county, Miss. Is there a hospital nearby?"

Faith looked back over her shoulder fleetingly, to see that Doctor Sampson was still working on George. Was he dying? She did not know, nor did she care. "No," Faith replied. "There are only town doctors. Doctor Sampson caters to the gentry but there is another doctor in the village who charges farmers' prices."

"Alright," agreed Mr Kelly. "We will need to move quickly."

Faith felt herself take on more of Cassian's weight as they moved through the trees. They were dragging Cassian's body, but

Faith did not struggle. She felt as though there was something flowing through her body, willing her on, and giving her the strength to get Cassian to help.

They trekked for about a mile, but it felt like a thousand before Faith could see a break in the trees and the beginning of a road. She saw Mr Green waiting, leaning against the carriage with a book in hand. He quickly noticed their approaching party.

"Good God!" he exclaimed.

Faith shouted directions at the driver and ordered him atop the carriage, wasting no time on manners.

Faith wrenched open the door to the carriage and helped Mr Kelly to push Cassian inside. Once the door was closed, Faith heard the crack of a whip and the horses took off towards the village.

She carriage jolted and bounced about, so much so that Faith was afraid that they would lose a wheel, but she supported Cassian by holding his head against her chest. In doing that, she kept a hand on his neck, feeling his pulse constantly. His heart was beating weakly. Cassian was slipping in to unconsciousness.

The carriage came to a stop outside Doctor Jeremy Ward's small cottage in the heart of the Runthorpe village. Doctor Ward accepted payments in eggs and mending, and not the coin that that Doctor Sampson demanded. The poor people could afford Doctor Ward's services.

Mr Kelly climbed out of the carriage first, and helped Faith to pull Cassian down. Together, they supported Cassian over to Doctor Ward's door, where Mr Kelly promptly beat it with his fist.

The door was quickly opened by a young doctor who was wiping his hands with a cloth. His astute eyes quickly went to Cassian, and to his large, horrendously burned wound on his chest. "Bring him inside," he instructed.

Doctor Ward's cottage was small, and boasted only a kitchen and sitting room in the downstairs. Doctor Ward led them into the kitchen and quickly moved his breakfast things. He fetched a fresh sheet and laid it on the table for Cassian.

Mr Kelly lifted Cassian onto the table while Doctor Ward collected his medical bag from the other room.

"What happened to this man?" the doctor asked accusingly. He quickly set about in removing what was left of Cassian's shirt and coat. "Who is he?"

"His name is Cassian Kensington. He was shot in a duel," replied Mr Kelly.

"A duel?" repeated back Doctor Ward as he inspected the wound. "It looks as though he was burned with a hot poker."

"Yes, he was. I instructed Faith to seal the wound to stop the bleeding."

Doctor Ward checked Cassian's pulse, and then listening to his breath sounds. "Help me to turn him over," instructed Doctor Ward. Mr Kelly helped the doctor lift Cassian onto his side briefly so that the doctor could see his back. "No exit wound," he said to himself. "The bullet is still in there."

"How do you get it out?" asked Faith breathlessly. Would Cassian survive surgery?

"We don't," replied Doctor Ward. "The wound is high in the right chest. All it would have hit would be muscle. His breath sounds are weak, but equal. The bullet has not hit his lung. The main concern with wounds like these is to stop the bleeding. The cauterisation you did, Faith, may just have saved his life."

"You are going to leave the bullet in his chest?" asked Mr Kelly slowly.

"For now," he replied, nodding. "Surgery is not always necessary. I could do more harm than good if I went into his chest, digging around for a little bullet."

Faith nearly vomited. "Won't it hurt him if you leave it?"

"Bullets are made from lead, which is incredibly harmful to the body. But as the lead is not in its most dangerous form, it takes a much longer time to have any ill effects. I would recommend an extraction in the future, when this man his healthy again, and when he has the ability to decide on the procedure, but I do not recommend it for his immediate survival."

Faith blinked. She knew what she was hearing was logical, but it did not make any sense to have something that could cause lead poisoning to sit idly in Cassian's chest.

"Will he live?" asked Mr Kelly.

"The bleeding has stopped," replied Doctor Ward. "What I must do now is to clean the wound and wrap it to prevent festering. If it festers, it will lead to blood poisoning. I would not cease praying if I were you."

Faith watched as Doctor Ward cleaned Cassian's monstrous burn with alcohol. He then applied clean bandages and wrapped them around Cassian's chest. Doctor Ward and Mr Kelly carried Cassian upstairs to the bedroom, where they set him down gently.

"When will he wake up?" Faith asked softly as she took the chair next to the bed.

"In times of trauma, the body often shuts down to give itself time to repair. Mr Kensington has lost a lot of blood. He will wake up when he is well enough to." Doctor Ward went to the door. "I will send my wife up with some tea in a little while." With that, he left them alone.

Faith immediately grabbed on to one of Cassian's hands and she watched intently as his chest rose and fell with each breath. The doctor was right. His breathing was weak but it was even.

"We have not been properly introduced, ma'am. My name is Finnegan Kelly. You may call me Finn if you like." Finn sat down on the opposite side of the bed.

"Faith," replied Faith. "How do you know Cassian?"

"Oh, we are old friends," replied Finn. He held that position for a moment before confessing, "He woke up in my jail around Christmas."

Faith's eyes widened. "Jail?" she gasped. Near Christmas? That had to have been right around the time that Cassian had been inspecting his northern factories for a time. What on earth had he done to wind up in prison?

"I am sure he will tell you about it," Finn said quietly.

Well, he had better wake up then, because Faith wanted to kill him.

"He was right about you though," Finn continued.

"What?"

"He told me you were an angel."

Faith softened. "He spoke about me?"

"He spoke of little else," Finn told her.

A tear trickled down Faith's cheek as her gaze returned to Cassian. "This is my fault."

"This is not your fault, Faith," promised Finn. "This is your husband's fault, and nothing you could have done would have prevented Cassian from fighting for you. So, I suppose in a way it is your fault for making him love you so much."

Faith was not so sure she was comforted by Finn's words.

"Cassian came to me yesterday and told me what was to happen. I told him, as a magistrate, that it was not lawful, but Cassian did not care. He would do anything for you. That was one of the first things I came to understand about him. I agreed to come today as his second, and in doing so he made me make two promises, one of which I have already broken." Finn sighed. "He made me promise him that if anything happened to him, I would take you and Lucy back to Norwood with me where you would be safe."

Faith had never heard of Norwood, but nothing could have convinced her to leave Cassian's side. Even now, she was half expecting her intrusive in-laws to barge in and take her to George's side, but she would never leave.

Faith was certain that George would be fine. He had the attention of the surgeon immediately.

"And the second?" she prompted.

"I was to add a second name to the deed of purchase on the Norwood Cottage," Finn replied.

Faith had not known that Cassian had purchased a cottage. But whose name could it possibly be? It would not be hers. Women could not own property in their own right. It was not allowed. "Whose name?"

"A Christopher Kensington. Do you know him?"

Faith's heart just about melted as her tears fell more freely. Her eyes were just about cried out. Cassian had planned to take care of everyone, even Kit. How could this be the fate of such a kind man? "Yes," she whispered. "Yes, I know him." Faith lifted Cassian's hand to his lips and she kissed it softly. "Wake up," she willed. "Be alright. Come back to me."

CHAPTER 23

"**O**h, Lucy!" cried Faith.

Later that afternoon, Mr Carne had appeared in Cassian's room, holding a wary looking Lucy. As soon as she saw her mother, though, Lucy beamed and reached out for Faith.

"Mama!"

Mr Carne had not changed much in three and a half years. Perhaps his hair was slightly more silver, and his tummy a little rounder, but he still looked like the kindly old man he had always been.

"Though' you migh' be missin' somethin', milady." Mr Carne smiled as he placed Lucy in Faith's arms.

Lucy wrapped her arms around Faith's neck and nuzzled her. "Thank you, Mr Carne," Faith said gratefully.

"I will always have a soft spot for you, milady. You know that," Mr Carne said kindly. His eyes settled on Cassian and he frowned sadly. "I couldn't believe my eyes when I saw him yesterday. The same skinny, half-dead urchin from all those years ago."

"Cassian has been terribly wonderful to both Lucy and me. He is going to be alright," Faith said, more to herself than to the room.

Cassian had not yet woken up. It had been hours and he was still unconscious. Faith had been meticulous as checking his pulse and his breathing rate, and feeling the skin around his wound, feeling for the heat that indicated an infection. Had Cassian been awake, Faith was certain her actions would have been irritating.

"Forgive me, allow me to introduce Mr Kelly," Faith said, realising that Finn was standing idly by the bed. "Finn, this is Mr Carne. He was the driver while I was at Runthorpe. He helped me to escape," she said, for want of a better word.

Finn extended his hand and shook with Mr Carne. "I am sure I speak on behalf of Cassian when I thank you, sir," he said sincerely.

"Not necessary. Your Mr Kensington took care of the thank you's yesterday. He's a good egg, tha' one, milady."

Faith felt her cheeks redden as she placed the back of her hand against Cassian's forehead, feeling once again for fever. "I know. Mr Carne, I am so awfully sorry at the treatment you received from George. He told me he sacked you. That was not right." Faith would make sure that she found work for Mr Carne elsewhere. Cassian already had a driver, but perhaps an overseeing position in one of his factories?

"Milady, I do not regret for a second what I did to help you get out of tha' house. 'Twas worth it."

"I will help you find work elsewhere," Faith promised.

"Mama, why is Cassian sleeping?" asked Lucy inquisitively as she peered at Cassian.

"Because he is very tired," replied Faith coolly, "so we must be sure to take very good care of him." Faith noticed Mr Carne watching her and Lucy. Faith suddenly felt quite awful about Mr Carne and his family having to take in a supposed bastard child, and one that had caused such conflict within their community.

"I am aware this may have been an awkward situation for you. Everyone thinks that Lucy is Cassian's child."

"Oh, I soon set them all straigh'," replied Mr Carne. "Tis amazing how fast gossip spreads, but I assured all who approached me that Miss here ain't no bastard child. She's a lady, ain't she?" He grinned at Lucy.

Faith nearly dropped Lucy. "You ... you told people ... you said that she was not a bastard?"

"Of course," Mr Carne said gruffly. "Tis a nasty thin' to say abou' an innocent girl when she has legitimate parentage."

Faith could see that Mr Carne's heart was in the right place, but what he had just done was advertise to gossips that the Earl and Countess of Runthorpe had a child. Lady Lucy Pendleton was legitimate, and the property of the Pendleton leeches.

Faith looked down at Lucy, who met Faith's eyes with her curious, innocent brown orbs. Which was worse? Growing up legitimate and attached to the poisonous Pendletons, or to grow up as a supposed bastard, shunned by some, but loved by those closest to her.

Faith knew what she wanted to choose, but was that selfish? Faith was not the one whose future was in jeopardy. If Faith raised Lucy illegitimate, then she would be excluded from all sorts of social avenues, gentlemen would not come calling, and Lucy would be alone, all because of a decision that Faith had made for her.

But if Lucy was raised legitimate, all sorts of doors would be opened for her. Lucy would be welcomed by society firstly, and she would have a dowry from the Runthorpe estate to ensure a good marriage. But then she would be associated with the Pendletons. She would be expected to dine with them, to attend balls with them, and by extension, Faith. But worst of all, what if the Pendletons expected Lucy to be raised at Runthorpe. What if George demanded that Lucy live there?

Faith did not know what to do, and the one person that she would have talked to about it was lying unconscious before her. What would Cassian tell her to do? What was best for Lucy?

"Did I do wrong, milady?" asked Mr Carne, concerned.

"No, no!" exclaimed Faith. "No, you were only trying to protect Lucy. I appreciate that."

Mr Carne relaxed.

At that moment, they were interrupted by a knock on the door. Doctor Ward entered, followed by a servant in Runthorpe livery.

"A letter has arrived for you, Your Ladyship," announced Doctor Ward. That was the first time Doctor Ward had addressed Faith as the Countess. He must have realised or been informed of who she was. "And I thought I would check in on the patient."

The Runthorpe servant stepped forward and held out a letter to Faith, bowing his head as he did so.

Faith took the letter from him and broke the seal, immediately unfolding the letter. It was very brief.

You are summoned to your husband's deathbed.

Bring the child.

Yours, &c.

There was so much information in such few words.

Deathbed. George was on his deathbed. Faith needed to sit down. She fell back into her chair and sat Lucy on her lap. She was immediately joined by Finn and Mr Carne, who asked after her wellbeing.

"What is it?" asked Finn.

"Are you alrigh'?" pressed Mr Carne.

Faith nodded, not knowing what to say. She had seen George on the ground, but she had not contemplated the thought that he might be dying. George had the benefit of the surgeon on hand.

And to Faith, George had always seemed like a mighty being to her. Not in the holy way, but in the way that it meant that nothing could stop him. He was rich and powerful. Nothing could prevent him from getting his way.

Well, all except a swift kick to the groin.

George was dying. George was going to die. Faith would be a widow for real this time. She would no longer be George's wife, nor his property. Faith would be free from him.

Lucy, on the other hand, was still attached if Faith made that decision.

"George is on his deathbed," Faith said quietly, still not quite believing the words that were coming out of her mouth.

The room was silent. No one quite knew what to say. Was it sinful to be happy?

Then a sudden thought occurred to Faith. George was going to die from a wound inflicted by Cassian. "What does this mean for Cassian?" she asked Finn. "You said it was murder." Faith knew it was murder as well. Cassian was technically a commoner, despite his wealth, and George was an aristocrat. Were there other rules that she was unaware of?

"There will not be any consequences, Faith," promised Finn. "It is murder, yes, but nobody is ever charged over a duel. The law is quite lax. The court understand the honour in duels, and each man enters knowing that death is a possibility."

Faith breathed a sigh of relief. George was going to die. Cassian, God willing, was going to survive, and Lucy would never know her blood father. Faith had been summoned but there was no way she would be bringing Lucy.

Faith had made her decision, and it was one she knew Cassian would approve of. Cassian would not want Lucy associated with the Pendletons any more than he would want Faith associated with them.

After today, Faith never wanted to hear that name again. She wanted nothing more to do with that family. She wanted to forget that they had ever permeated her existence.

Faith would raise Lucy illegitimate, though she knew Cassian would look after her. Perhaps ... perhaps she was tempting fate to even ponder the thought, but with George dead, Faith could marry again. Cassian could give Lucy his name, and perhaps that would protect her from some social stigma. Faith only prayed that Lucy would forgive her.

"Tell John and Ruth that I want nothing from them, nor anything to do with them from this day," Faith told the servant. "I want no pension. I have no possessions in that house that I wish to collect. I have no wish to ever hear their names again." It was healing almost to say those words. Perhaps it was the closure that she needed to say farewell to the past.

"Mrs Pendleton thought you would say that, milady," replied the servant regretfully. "I was told to tell you that it is the legal right of the father to appoint a guardian for the child upon his death, and that His Lordship chooses Mr and Mrs John Pendleton."

Faith felt all the blood drain from her face as she heard the servant's words. It was the legal right of the father to take a child away from her mother? There was no chance that the Pendletons would take another one of her children away from her.

This was it. Faith was about to give Lucy a future that she did not deserve. "Well, he would have the right to do that if Lucy were his child. I had an extramarital affair with a soldier, and so Lucy is illegitimate," Faith lied smoothly.

The servant believed her. He gulped as he received the information. Faith wagered he had never before heard such candid words from a woman. "I ... I will relay your message, milady." He bowed awkwardly and retreated from the room.

It was only then that Faith realised that Finn, Mr Carne, and Doctor Ward were all staring at her with wide eyes and open mouths. Doctor Ward quickly finished his examination before excusing himself.

"Why did you say that, milady?" asked Mr Carne.

"Did you not hear, Mr Carne? That man has already taken my son from me. He will not have my daughter, too," Faith said fiercely. Faith tightened her grip around Lucy and cuddled her into her chest. "Please forgive me when you are older, Lucy. I am doing this because I love you." She pressed her lips to Lucy's forehead.

Lucy could not comprehend a word. All she said was, "I love you, Mama."

Faith prayed that she remained feeling this way.

The room soon became dark and the lamps were lit. Mr Carne had long gone home. Finn was dosing in his chair and Lucy was very tired, but not yet asleep. Faith was still staring at Cassian's chest, watching the rise and fall intently.

"Story, Mama?" requested Lucy.

Faith did not have any story books, but then, neither did Cassian when he imagined up such fantastic in his study for Lucy. Faith had enjoyed the ones that she had heard.

"Once upon a time," Faith began, "there lived a young princess who had very horrid parents." What story did Faith know better by heart than her own? "Her parents cared only about their piles and piles of gold, and wanted the young princess to marry a prince who had his own piles of gold."

Lucy, instead of drifting off to sleep, had forced herself awake to listen to the story. Finn's eyes had also fluttered open.

"The young princess was not very brave," Faith continued. "She did as she was told. She married the rich prince, and lived in his beautiful castle, and was surrounded by his piles of gold. But she was sad."

"Why?" Lucy yawned.

"She was sad because the prince," beat her within an inch of her life, and killed her unborn son, "loved his piles of gold and not the princess. The princess wanted much more than to be sad in the castle. She wanted to escape and explore the kingdom. So when she learned that she had a tiny princess in her tummy, she decided it was time to go out into the kingdom and see every-thing." Faith stared into her daughter's eyes and remembered the exact moment she had learned Lucy existed. She was half filled with terror and half with hope. But it had been a day that had changed her life forever. "The princess explored, and eventually she made a friend named," Cassian, "Caspian. They became the best of friends, and they helped each other, as only best friends can. The princess helped Caspian to make something of himself, and Caspian helped the princess to be brave." And so much, much more. "Now that the princess was brave, she was able to go back to the prince and tell him that she did not want to be married anymore. And in that kingdom, the princess' word was enough." There was no need to apply to parliament for a divorce because it was a magical kingdom where the women had the right to ... or had rights in general. "Now that the princess was free, she and Caspian were free to live happily ever after. They got married and raised three children. The princess' own little princess, a kindly orphan boy, and one of their own, too." Faith laughed to herself. She was entirely embarrassed that Finn was listening to this story, but at least Cassian could not hear her. "The end." Faith kissed Lucy on the tip of her nose.

Lucy's eyelids were heavy and they fluttered closed. "That was a nice story, Mama," Lucy said lethargically.

"Thank you, Lucy."

"Very imaginative," added Finn sheepishly.

"Thank you, Finn." Faith could not help but grin.

"I liked that ending," Cassian croaked.

"Thank you, Cassian." Faith suddenly tensed. "Cassian!" she cried.

CHAPTER 24

B oth Faith and Finn leapt to their feet, with Faith barely managing to place Lucy on the end of Cassian's bed before she was inches away from his face.

Faith pushed Cassian's hair back out of his eyes. "How do you feel?"

"Like I have been shot," he replied honestly, his voice still thick and gruff.

Faith supposed that was a stupid question.

"You have been shot, my friend," said Finn. "You are bloody lucky to be alive."

Cassian sucked in a tight breath as he attempted to sit up.

"Oh, no!" cried Faith. "No, you stay put. You need to stay lying down and resting." She did not know whether sitting up would burst his wound or not.

Pain was written all over Cassian's face as he attempted to move. He quickly gave up and laid back down. "What happened?" he asked.

"Do you not remember?" Faith wondered. She hoped he did not remember the pain. She was certain that she would hear Cassian's screams in her nightmares for years to come.

"No ... I remember the duel. I remember us both missing, and that is it."

Cassian did not know that he had shot George, too. And fatally. How would Faith tell him?

"George's second shot hit your chest," Faith said carefully. "There was a lot of blood."

"Faith was incredible," interjected Finn. "I never saw a woman so level-headed in such a situation?"

Level-headed? Faith had been a wreck. Perhaps she ought to start gambling if she could hide a bluff so well.

"We needed to stop the bleeding and get you to a doctor seeing as the surgeon present was otherwise engaged. So Faith, here, cauterised your wound with a smouldering sword. She saved your life."

Finn was being awfully kind. If he had not known what to do then where would they be? Faith had merely followed instructions.

Cassian lethargically smiled. "That is twice now. Twice you have saved my life."

"There is no need to keep count when you consider all that you have done for me." Faith would not tell him about the bullet yet. He needed to rest. They would discuss plans for its removal at a later time. Faith had to stop herself momentarily. She was already planning for them as a couple. It was almost like tempting fate.

Cassian suddenly frowned before looking back at Finn. "What do you mean the surgeon was otherwise engaged? What was he doing?"

Faith could tell that Cassian already knew the answer to that.

"Your shot was true as well."

Cassian's tired eyes widened in shock. He stared at Finn in disbelief. "What are you saying?" he asked fearfully.

"A messenger visited us, Cassian," Faith said softly, bringing Cassian's attention back to her. Faith felt as though she could be gentler with the news. "He informed us that George, like you, had been shot. While the good Doctor Ward was able to ensure your survival," or rather promise that Faith's butchering of Cassian's chest with a smouldering sword was the right thing to do, "George's wound was fatal." Faith could hardly believe her own words but they were true.

Cassian was shocked, and then there was guilt. Faith could see it in his eyes. "Oh, good Lord," he gasped. "What have I done?"

"No," snapped Finn aggressively. "There will be no guilt here. There will be no responsibility. He challenged you. He knew exactly what he was getting into and you both made the decision to risk your lives. That is why the law still respects the honour of duels." Faith smiled at Finn gratefully. "Besides, look at what you were fighting for. Look at your prize." Finn gestured to Faith.

Faith was unsure of being referred to as a prize but she appreciated the sentiment.

Cassian stared at Faith, the look of apprehension in his eyes. "What do you think of me?" he asked fearfully.

Was he worried that she would think differently of him? "I think," Faith began, "that you are selfless. I think that you are kind and I think that you are brave and true. You protect the people you care about, and I know that you love me." Faith took old of Cassian's hand and squeezed it tightly. "I know that you love all of us." Faith included Kit in that statement.

Faith could tell that Cassian believed her words. He seemed to visibly relax. Faith could not understand what it was like to be responsible for the death of a man, but in a way she was. George had challenged Cassian to a duel over the presumption that Lucy was the bastard child she had conceived with Cassian.

But Faith did not feel guilt. Perhaps it was a sin, and she would be punished for it one day, but she did not feel guilty in this moment. She wanted to enjoy life. She wanted to live without fear.

"Lucy, what do you say to going and hunting down some biscuits? I am sure the good doctor has some sweets hidden somewhere," Finn suggested, clearing his throat.

"It is past Lucy's bedtime," protested Faith.

"You will thank me later," Finn muttered under his breath as he scooped Lucy up and promptly removed her from the room, closing the door behind him.

Faith and Cassian were left alone.

"Your friend seems very nice," murmured Faith.

Cassian chuckled, though restricted the laughter when it affected his chest. He cringed. "Yes, he is a fine character. I met him in —"

"Oh, yes. He told me that you were imprisoned for a time. You have yet to tell me about that." Faith arched a quizzical brow.

"I will tell you everything," he promised. "But first, I have to ask you ..." he trailed off before regaining his nerve. "You need not answer if you would prefer it, but I want to ask, I have to know. Did ... did George touch you?" Cassian asked apprehensively, fearful of the answer. "I was so worried. I wanted to get you out of that house as soon as I possibly could."

"He tried to," replied Faith honestly. Lord, how George tried. "And if I were still the person I was when I was first married to him I probably would have let him. But I meant what I said in the story. You make me brave, Cassian. Brave enough to fight, to stand up for myself and to protect what is only mine to give." Faith felt very proud of herself, and very grateful to Cassian.

Cassian smiled at her proudly. "You are the bravest woman I have ever met," he declared. "I knew it long before you did."

"I have a made a decision that might not be very brave," Faith confessed.

"What are you talking about?"

"Mr Carne and his family were caring for Lucy as per your instructions." Cassian nodded in confirmation. "The news of the duel, and the reason for it," meaning Lucy's illegitimacy, "spread like wildfire. Mr Carne was only trying to be kind when he corrected everybody he came across. He informed them all that Lucy was George's daughter."

"Yes," Cassian said slowly.

Faith realised he was not familiar with that part of the law. "Somehow the news got back to the Pendletons because the servant was sent here with two messages. One: that George was on his deathbed. The other: that it is the legal right of the father to name the guardian for his child upon his death." Faith could still scarce believe that Lucy could have potentially been raised by John and Ruth and not her.

"What?" cried Cassian angrily. His body tensed and he attempted to raise his torso again, once more crying out in pain.

"Hush! No, stay resting. All is well," promised Faith. "George named John and Ruth as Lucy's guardians but I lied and sent back the message that Lucy was illegitimate, and that her father was a soldier I had once met." Faith was still fearful of the future repercussions of this decision, but she would just have to help Lucy however she could.

Cassian appeared quite confused. "Why did you not say that I was her father?"

"Why would I embroil you in scandal?" Faith asked Cassian plainly. She was already harming Lucy's future. How could she harm Cassian's when she did not have to?

"What do I care about scandal? I would rather it be known that Lucy has two parents who love each other than a nameless soldier being attached to the story." Cassian appeared to be quite annoyed with Faith.

Faith suddenly felt very foolish. Of course Cassian would not have minded if she had named him as the father. Faith pulled her hand from Cassian's in an attempt to give him a little space.

Cassian seized Faith's hand and refused to let her go. "Don't you dare," he said fiercely.

Faith nodded helplessly.

"You don't need to protect me, Faith," said Cassian, his tone much more tender. "It is I who should be protecting you."

Faith willed herself not to cry, but when she thought of the repercussions of her actions, she could not help but be upset. "But what about Lucy?" she asked sadly. "What have I done to her? How have I harmed her? I have all but signed away her future. She is illegitimate. She will be whispered about wherever we go. What sort of dowry would she need for a man to take her?" Faith did not like the idea of a man demanding inordinate sums of money to marry Lucy just because he was accepting the fact that she was illegitimate, but that would most likely be the reality. That was what Faith's decision meant for Lucy.

Cassian painfully shuffled over on his little bed, making room for Faith. Faith welcomed the embrace. She laid down next to Cassian, resting her head on his healthy shoulder. What did they look like? An almost widow resting with a shirtless, wounded, gorgeous man. What if they were seen? Faith no longer cared. What did she care about scandal now, anyhow?

But once again, Faith felt that all too intoxicating sensation of safety. Cassian would do whatever he could to fix Faith's monumental failures. He would make it alright.

"You made the decision that any mother would have," Cassian promised. "You made the decision to keep your child safe and away from danger. My mother did the same for me when I was a child."

Cassian did not often speak of his mother. Faith stayed quiet so that he would continue.

"I knew what my mother did," Cassian said hauntingly, as though he was recalling something very specific, "and she did it for me. She did it to feed her son. If my childhood has taught me anything, it is that mothers would do anything for the love of their children, and so I completely understand what you did."

"I am glad you understand," whispered Faith. "But that does not change how Lucy will suffer."

"I have all this money for a reason," Cassian said softly. "I ought to do good with it. If a dowry is what she requires, then a dowry is what I will provide to a good, decent man with kind and loving intentions." Faith felt Cassian's lips in her hair. "I am going to take you and Lucy to a safe place, Faith," he promised. "A place with good people, a place where you will thrive. Lucy will make friends, and she will grow up under my protection, bearing my name. I would not have it any other way."

"You would have her called Lucy Kensington?"

"I will have all three of you called Kensington just as soon as I can."

Faith Kensington. Faith smiled. She enjoyed the sound of that name. "The three of us?" Faith asked knowingly.

"Yes," replied Cassian. "I made a decision about Kit. About what I will do for him."

Faith smiled. "Pray?"

"I have decided to take him in," he declared. "I have decided to be his father, and to give him a surname. He ... he is a good boy, I know it. He is just like I was. A boy who is constantly overlooked because of his station. A boy who has never been given a chance, not ever." He spoke so passionately. Faith admired it dearly. "He is terribly clever, you know. He had great potential and he deserves the right education. Just imagine what he could be. I can give that to him. I can give him a home and a name. I know that is what he craves above all."

"Cassian, you do not need to justify your decision. It is the right thing to do. Kit will have such a loving father in you."

"And mother?" Cassian asked hopefully. "I know I made this decision without you, but it will be the last, I promise."

Faith sighed. She had become very fond of Kit over the last couple of months. She almost felt ashamed for not noticing his good qualities when she had first met the angry young boy. Faith could easily find a place for Kit in her heart, and she knew that Lucy would adore having Kit as her permanent older brother. She already attached herself to him whenever he was present in the house. "I will be the best mother I can be for him," she promised. "But I confess, I did suspect your plans. Finn told me of the deed of purchase."

"That will be the last decision I make without your input," he amended. "It was a two pronged decision, really. Kit cannot inherit my property from me as he is not my blood, but he can retain what is legally his. It was my way of ensuring he had a future. I also planned on having Finn take the three of you to Norwood if anything happened to me. The estate would legally be Kit's, but you would all have a safe home."

Cassian had purchased an estate in Norwood, wherever that was. That was where he was planning on having them all live. That was the place where he believed Faith and Lucy would be safe. It sounded idyllic. But to entertain the thought still felt as though she was tempting fate. They had no confirmation that George was dead. What if he made a miraculous recovery?

Either way, Faith was not going anywhere near that family again. "I will never see my son again," she realised, devastated. If she left the Pendletons behind, she would also be leaving her son behind. She would never be able to visit him again.

Cassian understood immediately. "You will see him again one day," promised Cassian. "While his body will remain here, you can always remember him and treasure him."

That was a sweet thought, but Cassian could not understand the guilt she felt in leaving her son on that estate. Nobody knew he was there. He was all alone. Not even his mother could visit him.

"Do you believe he is in heaven?"

"Yes." Faith nodded her head.

"Then is does not matter where his bones are. He can see you remembering him and loving him from wherever you choose to do so. We will plant the same flowers when we get to Norwood, in the perfect place. That will be Sky's place."

A sob shook Faith's body. She did not know if it would be perfect, or if it would feel wrong. She could only wait and see.

Just as Faith was wiping her eyes with her sleeve, there was a knock on the door. Was it Finn come back with Lucy, or was Doctor Ward coming to check on the now conscious patient.

"Who is it?" asked Faith.

"The Countess of Runthorpe," snapped back Ruth from behind the door.

CHAPTER 25

Faith scrambled off of Cassian's bed, before the door opened and Ruth entered proudly. Even at this late time of night, she was dressed finely, albeit in a black ensemble. Where on earth had she found mourning clothes at such short notice. Did she carry them in hopeful patience?

Faith gasped. Mourning clothes. George was dead. Faith exhaled. She felt as though she was letting go of a breath she had been holding for the last six years.

Six years of marriage. She had been wed to the barbarian for more than a quarter of her life. It was six years that she could never get back, but Faith now had the opportunity to live. And she needed to for her son.

She could not help but smile as she imagined taking off her wedding band and replacing it with one that she wanted to wear.

"Ruth," Faith greeted bluntly.

"That is Countess to you, Anne," retorted Ruth.

Faith could care less. If Ruth was so desperate for the title, she now had it. Faith hoped she enjoyed it. Ruth was a more vicious person than Faith, in the way that she was willing to step on whomever she needed to in order to get where she wanted to.

Faith knew little of Ruth's background. She wondered if that had anything to do with her attitude. Faith, on the other hand, had been born with a silver spoon in her mouth.

"You should know that I am now called Faith," Faith corrected. "I have left the person I was in my past, as I will do you and that family." The minute she spoke the words, Faith's mind went to Olivia.

Olivia was now Lady Olivia Pendleton, the daughter of an earl, and with all the privileges that Lucy might have had. She was also at the mercy of her mother, who did not seem to understand her daughter. But Olivia had the sort of fire that could not be extinguished by one's mother. Olivia was going to change the world; she had told Faith so herself. Faith believed her whole-heartedly. Ruth could not stop Olivia if she tried.

In turning her back on the Pendletons, she was turning her back on Olivia. But Faith knew she had the strength to survive that house, and to go out and do the things she wanted to. Faith had managed it, and Olivia had twice her gumption.

"I thought I would deliver the sad news to you in person, Anne," Ruth began, disregarding Faith's new name. "George passed away a few hours ago, succumbing to his wound inflicted by your sinful lover."

"I am devastated," replied Faith dryly.

"I can see." Ruth pursed her lips, before looking to Cassian, who was attempting to crane his neck to look at their visitor, as he still could not lift his torso. "Well? What do you have to say for yourself?" she demanded to know.

Faith knew that Cassian understood he was blameless for George's death. She could tell that he had understood Finn's explanation earlier. George could have easily ended the duel after the first shot. Both had risked their lives. But George had been the one to insist on continuing. That decision had cost him his life, and it had nearly killed Cassian, too.

"You are a countess now. You are most welcome," was all he said in reply.

But Faith had not been expecting that. Shamefully, a giggle escaped her lips. She clapped a hand over her mouth.

Ruth ignored Cassian's comment. "The Pendleton family are in mourning," she snapped. "You are required to dress as a widow should. A veil, of course, must be worn at the funeral. I do not believe your lie about your child for a second. George was convinced by the gossip, and so am I, considering its source was your original accomplice. However, the Earl and I are unwilling to attach ourselves to a child whose mother claims she is illegitimate. If that is how you wish to treat your child then so be it."

Faith flinched and Cassian seized her hand. That was how she was going to treat her child. Faith only prayed the love that Lucy received was enough to compensate for the stigma that would come with it.

"I will not be dressing as a widow," replied Faith firmly, "and I have no wish to attend the funeral." Faith did not care about the social requirement. She had no desire to engage in society ever again.

Ruth did not seem at all surprised. "The servant informed us of your wish to waive your dower rights." Ruth arced an eyebrow curiously.

Oh, that was why Ruth was here. Money. "Yes," said Faith.

"You are aware of the significance of that sum, yes?" Ruth asked. "As the dowager, you are entitled to one third of the estate's income."

Was she trying to talk Faith in to accepting the money? "I have no wish to receive even a penny of that man's money," snapped Faith.

"I must admit, I am surprised." Ruth shook her head. "No matter. We shall happily put to use the added income. You will need to waive these rights legally, of course. I shall not have my husband's name dragged through the mud if you decide to take your sudden lack of income to the press."

Cassian was tense. Faith could see that he was holding his tongue.

It was clear that Ruth thought very little of Faith. They were evidently very different people. Faith mused that her own parents would have enjoyed having Ruth as a daughter. She was someone who would have strived to achieve the most advantageous match she could. But clearly, Ruth's own connections settled her with a clergyman, and a second son. Fate had simply provided for her.

But to waive her legal dower rights meant engaging with the Pendletons on one more occasion. "When?"

"Forty days," replied Ruth. "After the transition of power. We will be expecting you." With that, Ruth turned around and walked swiftly from the bedroom, leaving the door open.

Cassian and Faith looked to one another, clearly both still recovering from the information they had just received.

"What do you think of all this?" Faith asked him.

As much as Faith did not care for the social ramifications of her actions, it could affect Cassian, and by extension his business. Faith had not seen a newspaper yet, but she was certain the biggest story in years was about to break. Anne Pendleton was alive and George Pendleton was dead.

Not to mention the fact that she would have to journey back to Leicestershire again in forty days.

Cassian let out a breath before saying, "I think you should marry me."

"Because I think that we ought to – what did you say?" Faith's eyes widened. Had she heard him correctly?

Cassian was looking her directly at her, a look of intensity in his dark irises. "You told me once that the only reason you refused me the first time was because you had a living husband. That is no longer the case. You have always been an angel to me, Faith. You will never comprehend just how much I admire you, and how fervently I love you. I promise you I will be a kind husband to you, and a good father to Lucy. What do you say? Will you marry me?"

Faith had always known it would happen, but she had not been expecting it so soon. Had she been expecting it, she would not be sitting there with her mouth wide open. Cassian was asking her to marry him!

So Faith chose to do the first thing that popped into her head. She placed her hands on the sides of Cassian's face and kissed him stupid.

"Ow!" cried Cassian against her lips.

Faith jumped back, realising that she had been leaning against his bandage. She blushed. "Oh, I am sorry," she apologised.

"Is that a yes?" he asked, raising his eyebrows in anticipation.

Faith's blush deepened. "Yes," she replied, nodding. "I will marry you."

A wide smile spread across Cassian's face as he held his good arm out to her. "Then get back here," he beckoned.

"I will hurt you," Faith reminded him.

"I do not care. You're worth it."

Faith had been right. Her return was the biggest news story in years. Probably as big as her death three and a half years ago. The story was in ever newspaper, and her name, at least her previous name, was on the lips of ever gossip monger in every town they travelled through.

But Faith ignored it. Anne Pendleton was forgotten. She was Faith Kensington now. Well, she soon would be, anyway. It was such a surreal thought, but then all Faith had to do was glance beside her to see her fiancé sitting next to her in their carriage. Cassian was sleeping, his head resting against the side of the carriage as it jostled along.

Cassian had stayed in bed for just shy of a fortnight. In those two weeks, Cassian was told about the bullet in his chest, and the potential health risks later on. Cassian decided that he would correspond with Doctor Ward and organise for a suitable time to arrange the surgery. Faith so looked forward to that stressful event.

As soon as Doctor Ward told him he could travel, the carriage was organised to take them home. Home to Norwood, and not London. Home to wherever it was that Cassian had planned for them. Faith was so excited.

Once they reached their Norwood home, Cassian's plan was to collect the deed of purchase from Finn, and then go to London to collect Kit. Cassian knew that it had been a while, but he hoped that Kit was being patient.

Once they were all together, Cassian and Faith planned on getting married in the village church, before making the trip back to Leicestershire to be done with the Pendletons forever.

Then, and only then, could they start their lives together as a family.

Sitting opposite Faith was Finn and Lucy. Finn sat patiently as Lucy lay sleeping, using his leg as a pillow. During Cassian's convalescence, Faith had come to know Finn as a kind and decent, albeit slightly teasing, man. He enjoyed jesting Cassian just as much as he enjoyed looking after his new friend.

Finn was very handsome, and he clearly sat in a position of respect and influence as a magistrate. Faith wondered why he had not found a wife to settle down with.

Perhaps in this new place, Faith would make friends and she could help Finn to find someone nice. Cassian had assured her that she would thrive in Norwood. There were people she could help.

The beginning of March was always a very sad time for Faith. The third being the birthday and death day anniversary of her first son. It was the first of the month, and this time five years ago, she was still pregnant with him, and he was still alive. She wondered if Cassian would remember. It had been Christmastime when she had told him the date. Even if he did not, Faith would share it with him.

"Here it is. The Norwood village," announced Finn.

Faith immediately looked out the window as they travelled through the village. People were out and about in the small village, interacting with each other, smiling, and waving. The little shops were open and selling their goods, and she could hear organ music coming from the church. Faith spotted the magistrate's office, which must be where Finn spent most of his days.

Within a minute, Norwood was gone, but Faith loved it already. It was small and quaint, and the type of place where one could get to know every single person. She prayed her past had not followed her here, but even if it had, Finn promised her that the people were kind and fair.

After travelling for about a mile outside the village, Faith noticed that they were travelling through a set of rather grand looking iron gates.

"Welcome home," murmured Cassian excitedly.

All coherent thought left Faith as she stared at her new home. She gasped as she took in the true beauty of the estate. The first word that came to mind to describe it was alive. The estate was alive with spring blooms and greenery, which only made the white washed stone house, covered so perfectly with ivy, seem all the more idyllic.

"I told you this house would win her over," jested Finn.

Faith only smiled. He was right about that. This house was beautiful.

"Do you like it?" asked Cassian.

"I love it," she replied wistfully. "It is perfect." This would be the house where they would raise their family. Faith could see it already.

As the carriage pulled up outside the door, it opened, and Faith immediately recognised Mr Wade. Cassian had even arranged for his servants to move to Derbyshire. Faith wondered if they all had made the trip.

As soon as Lucy saw her favourite butler, she tore out of the carriage and jumped up into his arms. Mr Wade laughed as he adjusted Lucy's weight so that he could try to assist the rest of the passengers.

Cassian waved him off politely and helped Faith from the carriage. She was followed by Finn. Standing on the ground before the house, Faith craned her neck towards the sky, taking in all three storeys of the beautiful house.

"How are you Lady Lucy?" Mr Wade asked Lucy.

Lady Lucy? Where had Mr Wade got that from? Faith deduced Cassian must have filled him in on her situation.

"Good," chirped Lucy. "This is my house!"

Mr Wade chuckled. "You don't say?" He looked up at Mr Green, who was still sitting in the driver's seat. "You can take the horses around to the stables. Mr Carne is expecting you."

Cassian had taken on Mr Carne in the wake of his dismissal from the Runthorpe estate. He was now the steward, in charge of the estate's horses. Mr Carne's wife, who had been employed as a housemaid in Leicestershire as well, was also employed in the household.

"How are you feeling, sir?" asked Mr Wade of Cassian.

"Healthy," was all Cassian said in reply.

Faith knew that Cassian still was experiencing pain and aches in his wound. She hoped it was from the healing burn, and not because the bullet was floating around anywhere and doing damage.

"Would you girls like a tour?" Cassian asked. "I am sure Lucy would like to see her bedroom."

Lucy cheered and scrambled down from Mr Wade's arms. Mr Wade bowed his head respectfully as Faith walked towards him. Cassian had clearly sent word on ahead of them of what had happened. Would all the servants know of their engagement?

"Mrs ..." he went to greet her but then realised that he did not know what to call her.

"Faith," she insisted.

"Faith," he conceded. "It is good to see you."

"You as well, Mr Wade."

"And after the tour, shall we make those amendments to the deed of purchase?" Cassian asked Finn.

Finn nodded. "The document is in the study upstairs, whenever you are ready."

Just as soon as they crossed the threshold, Faith was greeted by a bombardment of servants, all of whom she knew and had befriended in London, most notably Hattie, who had become one of her closest friends during her time working for Cassian.

Hattie hugged Faith tightly. "Oh, I am so glad you are returned!" she said excitedly. "We were told you eloped but the papers printed the story. We read all about the Earl and the duel and everything! How are you?"

"I am glad to be home," replied Faith. No words had ever been more sincere. Clearly the story had reached Norwood, but her reputation in their eyes did not seem to be tarnished by it.

Hattie looped her arm through Faith's. Just as Hattie went to lead her away, Faith grabbed a hold of Lucy's hand. "So, tell me," she encouraged, "are you engaged to the master?"

Faith nodded bashfully. "Yes, I am."

Hattie beamed. "Oh, I knew it. I knew he always had eyes for you."

"We are going to get married just as soon as Kit is brought here from London. I think Cassian is going to collect him just as soon as his name is added to the deed."

"Kit?" repeated Hattie. "Coming here?" Hattie seemed confused.

"Yes." Faith furrowed her eyebrows. Why was that so perplexing? "It is our plan to take him in, and to give him a family."

"Oh, I just assumed that ..." Hattie trailed off. "Oh, never mind."

"Assumed what?"

"Well, that you had agreed to part ways, that Mr Kensington had ended their lessons."

"Why would you think that?" Faith demanded to know. The raise in her voice alerted Cassian, and he immediately came to her side.

"What is going on?"

"Hattie, why would you think that we would agree to part ways with Kit?"

"What?" gasped Cassian.

"He left your book, sir!" Hattie led them all down a panelled hall before opening a set of double doors. The room was a large library, full of empty shelving. Cassian's very small collection barely took up two shelves. Hattie immediately retrieved Cassian's copy of Utopia. "Kit came to the house for his lesson, but we were in the middle of packing. The next thing we know, this book is on the doorstep with a note inside." Hattie handed the book to Cassian.

Cassian looked incredibly anxious. He opened the book and caught the loose piece of parchment that escaped. On it were two printed words: Good By.

"Goodbye?" Cassian read. "Goodbye? Why would he ...?" He frowned and looked at Faith. "Does he think we left him?"

What else would the poor boy think if he happened upon the house being packed up? And Cassian had been in such a rush to follow Faith and to protect her from George that he had neglected his growing responsibility to a very vulnerable boy.

"You need to go to London," said Faith. "Now."

CHAPTER 26

"I cannot go to London just yet," replied Cassian.

"What? What do you mean?" Faith looked incredibly puzzled.

Cassian appreciated her urgency, and Lord knows Cassian felt it too, but the third of March was a very important date on Faith's calendar, and if Cassian left now, it would go past unnoticed, and Faith would be alone, and once again unable to visit her son.

"Finn, can you ensure that the purchase agreement is amended and correct?" Cassian asked Finn. "I want to take it with me to London."

Finn nodded, albeit looking just as confused as Faith. "Certainly. I will see to it immediately." Finn left the library and headed in the direction of the foyer.

"Hattie, will you please take Lucy downstairs?" Cassian then turned to his housemaid. "I am sure everyone will want to see her."

Hattie obeyed and held her hand out to Lucy, coaxing her to come along. Lucy skipped over to Hattie and placed her small hand into Hattie's waiting one. They, too, left the library.

"What is going on?" asked Faith firmly. "You heard what Hattie said. You need to go to London."

Cassian had only brought the one overcoat with him to Leicestershire, and so he was still wearing the same clothing that he was when he had first happened upon Faith in and amongst the wildflowers visiting with her son. When Faith had been pulled away by her husband, and the duel had been set, Cassian knew that it was highly likely that Faith would never have the opportunity to sit with her son again.

So Cassian had overturned the soil with his hands, selecting an area a few feet from where Faith had been sitting, so as not to disturb the grave, and had collected half a dozen daffodil bulbs. They were still in his pocket. He was no gardener, and it was highly likely his actions had killed the poor flowers, but he hoped the gesture would be enough to make Faith feel like she could remember her son anywhere.

Cassian fished the bulbs out of his pocket and held them in the palm of his hand. "I know it will be the third in two days. I know this year will be another you feel you are not with your son. But I have brought these bulbs for us to make a new place for him here. These are the same flowers you buried him amongst. We will be creating our own family here, but I want you to feel as though you still have a piece of your son with you."

Faith brought her gaze from the bulbs in Cassian's hand up to his eyes. Her eyes were glassy and filled with tears and her bottom lip was trembling. Faith stood up on her toes and pressed her lips against his softly. She then wound her arms around his neck and hugged him tightly. Cassian closed his hand around the bulbs so he would not drop them and returned Faith's embrace.

She said nothing, but he knew his gesture meant the world to Faith.

It was almost frightening the lengths that he would go to in order to make Faith happy. Her happiness was everything to him.

Cassian could not fathom the love he had for the woman, and how she had consumed every inch of his world in so many months.

Faith's pain was his pain, and he would do anything to ease it.

Faith pulled back, and placed her hand on his cheek. "You go to London," she whispered, "and you bring home our son."

Cassian had lost a colossal amount of blood only a mere three weeks ago, and a week long trek to London had not done him any favours. He felt weak and tired, and the site where Faith had burned him still bloody hurt.

But Cassian felt glad when the carriage started to move through the streets of London. The sooner he found Kit, the sooner all could be rectified, and they could be on their way back to Derbyshire to commence their new life.

Cassian managed to pull himself out of the carriage when it came to a stop outside the church. The street, which he had frequented so often during his last month in London, suddenly felt very foreign to him. His house was not a half mile to the right, and yet he felt like he did not belong there anymore.

The country was where they belonged, together as a family. Cassian did not need to be in the city to look after his factories.

Cassian knocked on the door of the church twice, before opening the large oak door. The pews were empty as it was a Friday, but Reverend Atwood was standing at the altar rehearsing his Sunday sermon.

The Reverend seemed to notice and recognise Cassian immediately. "Mr Kensington? My, it has been a while," he remarked.

"Too long," replied Cassian.

Reverend Atwood descended from the altar and met Cassian in the aisle. Cassian really wanted to sit down on one of the pews, but he felt it might be rude.

"I am not one to read anything but the good book, Mr Kensington, but it has been hard to avoid the headlines. Is it all true?"

It was not hard to hazard a guess as to what the reverend was referring to. "It is," confirmed Cassian. "Faith's identity, the duel, everything." Was it not a mortal sin to lie in a church? "But I do not regret any of it, Reverend. I got everything I wanted in the end. Does that make me a bad person?"

"Do not be overcome by evil, but overcome evil with good," quoted Reverend Atwood. "Romans 12:21."

Cassian interpreted the reverend's words not as an exoneration of guilt, but as words of wisdom in how to go on. Overcome evil with good. He would endeavour to. "I am here to see Kit," Cassian explained. "Or rather, I am here to take him with me. Faith and I have decided that Kit belongs with us as our son."

The Reverend's face fell. It was not the expression that Cassian had expected. "Oh, dear. Mr Kensington, I am afraid you are a little late. Why, young Kit left us nearly two months ago."

Cassian's heart stopped. "Kit ... he left?" he repeated, his voice breaking. What had he done to that poor boy? "Why did you not stop him? Where did he go?" Kit had no place to go!

"Nobody could stop him. The boy was determined," replied Reverend Atwood calmly. "Kit decided that he was old enough to leave, and so he did."

Kit might be fourteen years old, but he was not old enough to look after himself in the way that Cassian had. Kit did not know the ways of the world. He was still relatively naïve. Anyone could have taken advantage of a young boy in need of work.

"Do you know where he went?" Cassian asked desperately.

Reverent Atwood nodded once. "The workhouse," he replied. "Until he old enough to be an apprentice."

"The workhouse?" Workhouses were deplorable. Filled with the poorest souls on earth. Cassian had heard such terrible things about workhouses, in particular how the conditions were made worse on purpose to discourage able bodied workers. It was the one place Cassian's mother had forbade him to go, even if he was desperate.

"I directed him to the one on Mersey Street. You should start there," encouraged the reverend. "I know not of what happened, Mr Kensington. All I know is that boy was the happiest I had ever seen him when you were teaching him, and one day he returned from your home broken-hearted. I hope he will forgive any wrong doing."

Cassian hoped for the same. "Thank you, Reverend." The Mersey Street workhouse would be where he would start, and he would search every other workhouse in London if he had to.

Cassian still felt awfully weak as he left the church, but he refused to give in to the thoughts begging him for rest. His child was in a workhouse. That was a far more pressing issue.

"Take me to the workhouse on Mersey Street, please, Green," requested Cassian as he climbed back inside the carriage.

"Yes, sir," replied Mr Green.

The workhouse was a ways away. Out of the way of the rich, where they did not need to see the poor. The select few liked to pretend that these people did not exist. Cassian could attest to that.

The workhouse was a large, red brick building. It was rectangular and severe, and imposing to those who stood before it.

"Shall I come in with you, sir?"

"No, I must go alone," replied Cassian, as he approached the door. No sooner had he rapt on the iron door, a peephole opened and a large, green eye peered at him.

"Who are you?" grunted a harsh voice.

"My name is Cassian Kensington," replied Cassian. "I have come to enquire after one of your workers."

"Who?"

"Kit. He is a boy, fourteen years old. He is quite tall, and he had distinctive curly blond hair," described Cassian.

"Never heard of him," sniffed the man.

With the amount of people working behind this door, Cassian would not be surprised if Kit went unnoticed. "May I come inside and search for him?"

"No."

Cassian fished a coin from inside his purse and held it up to the peep hole. "May I come inside and search for him?" he asked again.

Cassian immediately heard the clicking of the lock as it unlatched. The iron door swung open and a balding, portly man snatched the coin from Cassian and quickly pocketed it. "Be my guest," he said, inviting him in.

Cassian entered the workhouse to find that it was not what he expected. The door opened up into a large, rectangular year. The building cast a shadow over the yard, as it stood three storeys high. From the windows that looked down upon the yard, Cassian could see all sorts of people working away at whatever task was set them. They all seemed to be wearing the same, practical, grey work suits.

The men in the yard wore the same thing, with the addition of a practical grey cap atop their heads. The yard was littered with stones. Some large boulders, others more moveable rocks. Each worker held in his hand a large hammer, a tool that they were using to pound the rocks into small pieces.

The noise once inside was deafening. The constant banging was almost maddening. Each man grunted and puffed as he swung his hammer over his shoulder to pound the boulders over and over.

Their grey clothes were covered in dust and sweat stains. Their faces were blackened and their movements were laboured. These men were exhausted. But was Kit one of them?

Cassian searched the large sea of men, but they all looked the same. Tall, skinny men were all he could see, and that was exactly the build he was searching for. Cassian needed a better view. With what remaining energy he had, Cassian climbed atop one of the boulders and cupped his hands around his mouth.

"Kit!" he shouted into the crowd. Cassian's legs shuddered and his eyes fogged over as he lost his balance. Cassian threw his arm out to brace himself as he hit the ground and fell unconscious.

"You really are a wandought, you know that?"

Cassian blinked his eyes a few times until his vision focussed. He was sitting up against the workhouse outside on the street. Mr Green was waiting nearby, holding the reins of the horses, and Kit was kneeling before him.

Kit must have dragged him outside.

Kit looked stronger, if anything, and that appeared to be his only change. His hair was just as blond and curly, and was poking out from underneath his cap. He was kneeling, but he looked as though his limbs were longer, as if he had grown some. His face was covered in the black rock dust, and his green eyes were hard and stern, reserved almost, as though he was protecting himself.

"You think me weak?" murmured Cassian. He noticed that his wrist was hurting after the fall. He twisted the joint to test the pain. It did not feel broken, merely sprained.

"Anyone who faints at the sight of a little hard work is weak," retorted Kit gruffly.

Kit was hurt. That was clear. But he had come to Cassian's rescue, and so he still had an attachment to Cassian, or so he hoped.

"I am so sorry, Kit," Cassian said sincerely. "What you must think of me."

Kit's eyes narrowed. "What do I think of you?" he seethed. "I don't think of you. Why would I?" he lied.

This boy felt abandoned. How could Cassian make it up to him? How could he get Kit to understand? "Kit," persisted Cassian. "I wasn't there like we agreed. I wasn't there for our lesson. I left."

Kit winced, the hurt in his eyes evident. He stood up and took three steps from Cassian, facing out into the street. Cassian could see how tense he was. Kit's posture was rigid.

"You don't owe me anything," replied Kit. "I didn't expect anything less when I showed up that day."

"That is a lie, Kit," countered Cassian. "You wanted everything from me, and I let you down." Cassian did not think he had ever let anyone down before. He had never really had anyone depend on him before. The responsibility for another person was incredible, and something he did not take lightly. "I failed you," he probed, in an attempt to elicit a response.

That had done it. Kit spun around on his heel with tears in his eyes. "Yes, you did!" he cried. "You left without having the damned courtesy to tell me!" Kit swore. "I get I ain't nothing important to you. I get I ain't family or nothing. But if you're someone like me, who doesn't often get a taste of what one of those feels like, then it hurts to have it all ripped away like that!" Kit pulled the cap from his head and ran his fingers back through his hair. "Nobody's ever done anything for me like what you did, sir. I just ... I just thought you cared is all."

Kit's tone had gone from angry to vulnerable. Cassian could not believe he had been so thoughtless.

"I do care, Kit," promised Cassian. "Have you been reading the newspapers?"

Kit frowned. "What does that matter?"

Cassian presumed not. "Will you let me explain to you what happened? Where I have been?"

Kit reluctantly nodded, and joined Cassian at his side once more.

Cassian explained to Kit just exactly what had happened after they had returned him to the church. He detailed how Ruth had discovered Faith was Anne Pendleton's alias, and used this information to force her back to Leicestershire.

"You mean she's not really Faith?"

"She is to us."

Cassian told Kit how he immediately set off after Faith, with the intention of hiding her and Lucy at the home he had purchased in Derbyshire. That was why he had ordered his home in Kensington packed up. The truth was that Cassian had forgotten about Kit in that moment, and their reading lesson was not on his mind. All he could think about was getting to Leicestershire to save Faith.

Finally, Cassian revealed the climax of the story. The duel. He detailed how the Earl had been killed, and Cassian had been shot, Faith had saved his life, and he had been convalescing for a fortnight.

"That is where Faith and Lucy are now. At our home in Derbyshire."

Kit looked very shocked, and he had reason to be. It was an incredible tale. "Is that what made you faint, sir? Your injury?"

Cassian nodded. "I have yet to regain all my strength."

"Oh. Well, I am sorry for calling you a wandought and a leasing-monger," murmured Kit.

"You never called me a leasing-monger," replied Cassian.

"Oh, well I was thinking it," Kit admitted.

Kit thought Cassian a habitual liar during his absence. His character really had taken a beating.

"I deserve it." Cassian sighed. "Kit, in telling you this, I am not trying to take away the guilt on my side, I am only merely explaining the context for the sin. I forgot about you in the moment, and I will be eternally sorry for that."

"It's alright, sir. Your missus needed you."

"She did." Cassian nodded. "But you needed me as well and I was not there."

"I can take care of myself."

"But you should not have to." Cassian pulled the deed from the inside of his coat. It was now or never. He prayed that this proved to Kit just how serious Cassian was in looking after him. "Have you been practicing your reading?"

Kit shook his head. "No."

"Well, give this a go." Cassian unfolded the deed and handed it to Kit.

Kit studied each work carefully, and he read reasonably fluidly. "Land purchase agreement. This is to certify that the Norwood Cottage land in the parish of Norwood and county of Derbyshire was purchased on the twentieth day of December eighteen hundred and five for the sum of fifteen thousand, one hundred and twelve pounds. Vendor: Finnegan Patrick Kelly, Esq. Purchaser: Cassian Kensington, Christopher Kensington." Kit read over the last part in the same even voice, before suddenly comprehending what he had just read. He brought the deed closer to his face as he studied that last name. "Christopher Kensington ... is ... is that me?"

Kit had once told Cassian that he had no surname because he did not have a father. Kit had spent his life without an identity. "The law would not allow you to inherit my assets because you are not my son by birth. So I have put your name down on this deed to ensure that you will always be protected. You own property, Kit."

Kit shook his head, seeming like he did not care for the legality of the document. "This!" he cried, turning the deed around and pointing to his name. "Is this my name?" Kit was trembling. "Two names? A last name?"

Cassian smiled. "How do you like the name Kensington?"

Kit beamed as he struggled to find words. "I ... I like it."

"How do you like the father that comes with it?"

Kit could not stop shaking as the widest, happiest smile filled his face. "Father?" he stammered.

"I am new to fatherhood, you understand. I cannot promise that I will never make another mistake, but I can promise you that you will always have parents who love you, and who only wants the best for you. You can depend on me, Kit." Cassian was certain he would make many mistakes. He had never been a father before, or a husband. He had only ever had himself to worry about. This was a new, daunting step, but he would not trade this new family for anything.

"I never thought ... never could have imagined ... parents," breathed Kit, still clearly overwhelmed. His eyes returned to Cassian. This time they were filled with joy. "I have a father? I have a name?"

"Yes, you do."

Chapter 27

Faith had been the mistress of Norwood Cottage for near a fortnight since Cassian had left for London. It felt very odd to be in charge of a household that she had once worked for, but then, as Hattie kept reminding her, she was never much of a servant. No housemaid needed to dust a study for as long as she did. It was always clear that Faith and Cassian were meant to be more than servant and master.

The sheer size of Norwood Cottage made the name truly ridiculous. It was not a cottage, but a castle, only without a moat and towers. The enormity of the building made it quite impossible for Cassian's once small staff to keep it in order, and so more servants were sought from the village.

Faith had left that job for Mr Wade. She had not yet ventured into the village. She had not dared to. Not even the quiet little village of Norwood was exempt from the city newspapers. Her story had flown across the country, and surely each and every one of these people knew her dirty little secrets too.

Would they accept her? Faith was not game enough to ask, not while she was still unmarried. Faith knew that she had broken about half a dozen society rules with how she and Cassian had conducted themselves. To an outsider, it would be scandalous. But only they knew the truth.

Faith supposed she was just as wary of another's opinion of her as they next person. Cassian was so determined that Norwood would be the fresh start that they needed. He was so excited for Faith to stretch her legs and get out into the community. Faith was nervous.

So, instead she had busied herself with making this big house her home. By comparison, her home in Leicestershire with George was bigger, but it had always felt like a prison. This house felt so full of opportunity. Lucy would grow up here. Kit, God willing, would grow up here. Any future child she might be blessed with would grow up here.

Faith often found herself wandering into Lucy's new bedroom, which Cassian, or rather Mr Wade, had had filled with gorgeous toys. This would be the bedroom where Faith would one day tuck her into bed for the last time, on the night before her wedding.

Faith had never before had thoughts like these. Her focus had always been on the present. Where would their next meal come from? What would happen if Mrs Berwick could not watch Lucy and she could not work? Faith had never before entertained thoughts of the future because it felt taboo. Things could always go wrong.

Things could still go dreadfully wrong, but Faith had reason to hope.

Shortly after Cassian had departed for London, Faith had taken the bulbs he had collected for her, and a pail of water, and had gone for a walk about the garden. Faith could not comprehend the gratefulness she felt to Cassian for this simple gesture.

Whether or not it would feel the same as before, she did not know, but Faith currently felt as though she had a piece of her son's resting place, and a way to make a place for him in her new home.

The grounds of the Norwood estate were extensive and glorious. They most definitely were well tended to. There was not a lake, as there was on George's estate, but there was a pond deep into the garden, protected by pussy willow trees. The furry catkins were in full bloom, and it looked as though there were small snow balls on the branches.

The pond was shallow and still, and she could hear the noises of the creatures who resided there. It was a very peaceful and natural place. It was the perfect spot. Faith knelt down at the base of the tree nearest to the pond and placed the pail of water and the bulbs aside as she began to shift the grass and dirt with her hands.

Dirt quickly caked underneath her fingernails but she did not mind. Once an adequate hole at formed, Faith placed the bulbs, root down, in the dirt, and then covered them back up again. She poured water over the site slowly, and stood back up again.

"Happy fifth birthday," she whispered.

This would now be Sky's place. Faith would bring Cassian here, and when Lucy was old enough to understand, Faith would bring her here. Faith said a silent prayer before leaving and making her way back up to the house.

For the rest of the time while Cassian was away, Faith got to know Finn Kelly. Because Cassian was not there to tell her, Finn detailed to Faith exactly how he had met Cassian.

"I had to throw his drunk backside in one of my cells. We met formally when he woke up the next morning," Finn had said jokingly, all the while being serious.

Finn told Faith or his childhood in Ireland, and his family's move to England for better opportunity. His father had made his fortune in farming land, and had left the business to Finn upon his retirement. Mr and Mrs Kelly now loved comfortably in the Irish countryside.

Finn had become a magistrate after the last one had retired. Finn presided over Derbyshire as one of its four magistrates, having been deemed by the people as having good sense, mercy, integrity, and an unbiased ability to achieve justice and keep the peace.

Finn was not paid as a magistrate. He was a volunteer, but he enjoyed the office, and the new connections he had made through it.

Finn also got to know Faith, and Faith found herself divulging her tale.

"I think you do yourself a disservice by hiding from the people in Norwood, Faith," Finn declared. "You are not so different. Believe me, I know. I hear everything. It just so happens that your story was aired publically, but you will find likeminded and sympathetic people. Standing up for one's child is nothing to be ashamed of."

Faith smiled. "Why have you not married yet, Finn?" she asked curiously. Finn was very handsome, and he had a very kind and intelligent head on his shoulders. He would make a fine, decent husband.

Finn shrugged his shoulders. "I suppose I have not met the right woman yet. I desire the kind of woman Cassian has been so fortunate as to have found. The kind of woman who always puts others first, so that I may put her first."

Faith's heart melted.

"A fine face and a lovely figure wouldn't hurt, either," he added jokingly.

Faith laughed. "Well, I shall keep an eye out for you."

"In all seriousness, the way I see it, Faith, is that if I am going to marry someone, I want to really love her. Marriage is for life. I have no desire to marry the prettiest girl in the village just because she is pretty. I want a partner, and I do not mind waiting for her."

"She will be a lucky woman," Faith told him honestly. She only prayed that Finn did not have to wait too long for her.

Cassian's carriage arrived back in Norwood two weeks to the day that he had left.

Faith and Lucy both raced out to meet the carriage. Mr Wade and the new footmen he had taken on ventured out as well. When the carriage pulled to a stop, Mr Green climbed down from his seat as the first footmen went to open the door for the passengers. He assembled the steps and Cassian was the first to climb out.

Faith held her tongue to stop a gasp from escaping. Poor Cassian looked dreadful. He was pale, and he had dark shadows underneath his eyes, so dark that he looked as though he had been punched twice. His movements, as well, were slow and careful.

Travelling so soon after such a horrific injury had not done him any good. But the smile on his face just as soon as his companion jumped out of the carriage to help him made it clear that Cassian had no regrets.

Kit! Kit was here! Oh, all had gone well. Faith was relieved.

Kit wrapped his arm around Cassian's waist and supported his weight. Cassian accepted the help and leant on Kit. Faith quickly abandoned her post and went to Cassian's aid, collecting his other arm.

Cassian placed no weight on Faith, much to her chagrin. "What happened? Is it your wound? Is it infected?" Faith asked, concerned. "Sit down," she instructed, as they came to the steps.

Kit helped Cassian to sit down on the steps of the house. Cassian shook his head. "I am fine," he promised. "Just tired."

Faith did not take his word for it. She immediately pressed her palm to his forehead and thanked God when she felt there was no fever.

"Faith," Cassian said firmly, "I promise I am well. It was just a tiring journey and I did not sleep very well."

That would not stop Faith from sending for a doctor just to be sure. She wanted that wound inspected.

"Do you think she missed me?" Kit whispered to Faith, nodding towards Lucy who was standing at the top of the stairs.

Lucy stood with her hands in fists by her sides, with the biggest grin on her face. She was shaking with excitement.

"No," Cassian said, looking to Lucy over his shoulder, "that reaction is for me, of course."

"Are you happy to see me, Goose?" asked Kit.

Lucy squealed and bounded down the steps into Kit's waiting arms. Lucy arms wound tightly around Kit's neck as she wrapped her legs around his waist. Kit returned the hug.

Kit had grown even taller since Faith had last seen him. He was taller and lankier, and he looked like he needed a decent meal. His blond hair was longer; his curls almost reached his shoulders now. But his face was the biggest change Faith noticed, particularly his smile.

Faith had never seen a happier boy.

Faith had no idea how to be a mother to a fourteen year old boy. But she knew she could only start with loving him, and that would not be a hard task at all.

As soon as Kit put Lucy down, she wrapped her little arm around his thigh, as though she was afraid he was going to go away again.

Kit looked to Faith, and Faith could immediately see his nervousness. Kit had nothing to be nervous about. Faith was the one who was nervous.

Kit took a deep breath and placed his hands in his pockets. "What do you think of me?" Kit asked Faith anxiously.

Faith smiled. "I think you belong right here," she said confidently. Kit visibly relaxed. Faith stood up on her toes, but even then she was not tall enough. Sensing what she wanted, Kit leant down so that Faith could place a kiss on his cheek. The nervousness disappeared as they both laughed. "Will you be a good older brother to Lucy?"

Kit tugged on one of Lucy's curls playfully. "The best," he promised.

Faith knew that Lucy would benefit from having a strong older brother. She might need protection in the coming years. People could be cruel, particularly to those who were different from them.

"And I will be the best mother that I can be for you," promised Faith. She suddenly paused. "Oh, do not feel any pressure to call me "Mother" or anything like that. I understand you may find that uncomfortable." Faith did not want to tread on the toes of Kit's natural mother, whoever she may be. She did not yet know of Kit's feelings towards his natural parents. That would be one of the many things Faith looked forward to learning about her new son.

Kit chewed on his bottom lip awkwardly. "Well, I would like to call you that, if you don't mind. I never had a mother before. I would really like one."

While Faith could have said something as equally enchanting, she promptly burst into tears and let out an unladylike sob. Faith wiped her eyes with her sleeve as Kit placed his arm around her shoulders. "Now, now, Mother. There is no need to cry."

Mother. That was Faith. She was hearing it and it was real. She felt a wave of maternal protection flow over the tall boy who was standing next to her. This child was hers, just as her other two children were.

"Wade, can you send for Mr Carne and have the other carriage brought around? And the cart, if the servants would like to go," instructed Cassian.

"Go where?" queried Faith. "Surely you are not going out again. You need to go upstairs to bed."

"I will. Later," replied Cassian. "Right now I have another affair to attend to. Is Finn here? Finn!" Cassian cried over his shoulder.

Kit was grinning sheepishly. He was in the know.

"What is going on?" Faith demanded to know.

Finn appeared at the door and descended the four steps to stand with the party. "Welcome back, Cassian," he greeted. "You must be Kit," he said to Kit. "A pleasure to meet you. I am Finn Kelly." He extended his hand.

"You, as well, Mr Kelly. I am Kit Kensington," he said proudly.

"Fancy attending my wedding this afternoon?" Cassian asked casually.

"A wedding. How grand!" Finn grinned. "Absolutely. I will send for a bottle of my finest champagne."

"A wedding to who?" Faith asked sarcastically. Surely he was not serious. Cassian looked so tired he could faint. Faith was a blubbering mess. Today was not the best day for a wedding.

"To you, of course," replied Cassian. He furrowed his brows. "Why not? We have three Kensingtons in residence. I would like to make it an even four."

"A wedding takes planning!"

"Best man." Cassian pointed at Kit. "Bridesmaid." He pointed at Lucy. "Witness." He pointed at Finn. "And most importantly, the bride and bridegroom."

Faith looked down at her plain blue dress. It was by no means a wedding gown, and not nearly as fancy as the gown she had first been married in. "But I look awful. Nothing like a bride."

"Faith, you are beautiful. I have been in love with you ever since you looked into my eyes and saw me and not the pauper I looked like. I have waited a very long time to marry you. You could be wearing a potato sack and I would not care. I do not want to waste another minute. If the last few months have taught me anything, it is that life is far too precious to deny ourselves happiness."

Faith stared down at Cassian and saw the sincerity in his dark eyes. He loved her. He really did. Faith felt as though she had paid her dues ten times over during her marriage to George. She had struggled and she had suffered, and somehow, through all that darkness, she had found her way to this man. She would love him for the rest of her days.

"Well, at least let me do something with my hair!" Faith cried as she ran up the stairs with the biggest smile on her face. She could hear the men laughing behind her as she excitedly cried, "Hattie, I need you help!"

CHAPTER 28

Kit had never before witnessed such a scene than he had on the day of his parents' wedding.

Parents. That word still seemed foreign to him. Taboo even. It was almost as if he feared waking up from the dream that was now his life.

Kit, the orphan boy from London, had a mother, and a father, a sister, a surname, and a home.

But Kit was certain that he would always remember the crowd of well-wishers that had gathered outside the church to witness the nuptials and to bless the happy couple. Cassian had stopped in the village to organise the ceremony with the vicar and the news had obviously spread.

Faith had been a bit of a recluse apparently, hiding away in the house, avoiding the villagers for fear of judgement. Her story was on the front page of every newspaper and on the lips of every gossip, after all, but these people did not seem to mind. Dozens of people waved and cheered as the carriage drove the family to the church, and the smile that spread across Faith's face was like sunshine.

The only smile bigger than Faith's was Cassian's. He was staring at his bride to be with absolute adoration. It had always been obvious, but Kit could see that Cassian truly loved Faith. He wanted everything for her, and Kit knew that his concern extended to himself and to Lucy. Kit knew he was very privileged to have Cassian as a father.

The wedding was beautiful and the happy couple honeymooned at Finn's estate, situated a mile or so from Norwood Cottage.

It was all over in ten days, at which point Kit found himself sitting in a carriage bound for Leicestershire. Gone was Faith's blissfully happy demeanour. Cassian was no longer smiling. Even Lucy seemed on edge, as though she sensed something was wrong.

Faith looked very anxious. She gazed out the window but her hands were shaking nervously. Cassian placed his hand over hers in an attempt to calm her.

Kit had not been entirely informed as to what Faith had experienced during her first marriage. The newspapers did tell and extraordinary tale, and Kit had not felt it right to ask his new mother about her past, especially if he was uncomfortable doing so.

But they were journeying back to what was once Faith's home, in order for Faith to renounce some sort of right. Kit was not exactly sure. The legal terms went over his head a bit.

Kit did not like that Faith was feeling this way. She was too kind and too loving to be feeling anxious. He wanted to comfort her, but he feared saying the wrong thing, and so he said nothing.

"We are nearly there," murmured Cassian. Clearly he had recognised a landmark.

"I know," muttered Faith in reply. Her voice was so weak and her frame was so tense.

Although Kit was unsure of what had happened to Faith, he knew one thing for certain. These people were not nice people.

Kit caught his father's eye just before the carriage took them through the gates of the Runthorpe estate. Cassian gave Kit a reassuring nod. Just that simple gesture helped Kit to relax a little. No matter what was to happen, everything would turn out alright. Cassian would make sure of it.

The carriage pulled to a stop in front of an even larger manor. Kit would have been in awe had he not seen a shiver flow through Faith. She was feeling ill. Cassian rubbed Faith's back reassuringly as the footmen came to open the carriage door and unload the trunks.

"We will not be staying! Leave the trunks," Cassian called out to them. "I would rather sleep in a pig sty than stay here a moment longer than we are required to. Kit, I need you to look after Lucy," Cassian instructed. "Stay out here. We will not be too long."

Kit nodded and watched as Cassian and Faith left the carriage and ascended up to the front door. Faith appeared as though she was holding on to Cassian's arm for dear life as they crossed the threshold.

Whatever it was they needed to do, Kit hoped it was swift.

Kit and Lucy climbed out of the carriage to stretch their legs once the footmen had left them. Mr Green had released the horses and had gone to water the, and so they were left alone.

"Where has Mama gone?" Lucy asked Kit, her little face frowning with worry.

Kit could not provide her with an answer. "She will be back soon," he promised.

Lucy placed her small hand in Kit's as they walked aimlessly in a circle.

"Psst!"

Kit's head swung around toward the source of the noise. He only saw a flash of red before it disappeared around the side of the great house.

"What was that?" asked Lucy curiously.

"I don't know, Goose. Shall we investigate?" Kit knelt down on the ground and encouraged Lucy to climb on his back. Once she was secure, Kit took off running after that flash of red.

Kit weaved in and out of brush as he jogged with Lucy, looking around his surroundings as he searched for the person he had seen. He slowed down when he noticed a horse and cart waiting idly by the side of the wilderness. How odd. What was it doing there?

Kit gently let Lucy to the ground. Just as he was about to approach the horse, Kit about had a coronary as someone grabbed his arm.

Kit was suddenly met with a pair of the bluest eyes he had ever seen. They reminded him of the sky when it was perfectly clear. Her skin was pale and smooth like porcelain, though her cheeks were flushed from running. The red he had seen was her hair. She had lovely, wavy red hair, and lots of it. She wore it down, and it hung around her waist.

She was beautiful. She most beautiful girl Kit had ever seen.

"You look strong. Are you strong?" She spoke with such determination.

Kit was taken aback by the tenacity in her voice. "I ... uh ..."

"Great!" The red-haired girl beamed and grabbed his hand. Lucy began chasing after them. She dragged him along the side of the house towards a door that was half open. Kit had not noticed that before. The door was adjacent to the horse and cart. They were some twenty feet apart. "I have been moving this crate covertly through the house for the best part of an hour." She opened the door for Kit, revealing a sturdy looking wooden crate that was sitting in the doorway. She placed her hands on her narrow hips as she stared down at the heavy thing. "I know I will not be able to lift it onto the cart. Please can you help me?"

Something in Kit switched, perhaps it was his sense of heroics, or the need to be overly masculine to impress this beauty before him. He nodded, rolling up his sleeves. "You want this on the cart? No problem. Give me thirty seconds," he boasted. Kit approached the crate and positioned himself in front of it, placing one hand on top, and the other underneath the lip. One, two, three. Kit heaved, and let out a noise of almighty exertion.

But the crate did not budge. And Kit fell on his backside.

Both Lucy and the red-haired girl burst into fits of hysterical laughter.

Kit frowned, embarrassed. "What have you got in there? A hundred books?"

"Probably closer to two hundred," wheezed the girl.

Two hundred books? And the expected him to lift them? Was she insane? Why was she moving two hundred books?

Kit climbed to his feet and rubbed his sore behind. "Shush, Lucy," he hushed, but his young sister neglected the instruction. She continued to laugh as she skipped about the open grounds. "Who are you, anyway?"

When she stopped laughing, the red-haired girl replied, "Olivia. Who are you?"

"My name is Kit Kensington," he replied. "That is my sister, Lucy." He pointed to the laughing, dancing three year old.

Olivia extended her hand to Kit. Kit had only ever thought that men were supposed to kiss girls' hands. Nevertheless, Kit shook Olivia's hand. As he did so, she beamed. "That is how the men do it. A shake. Respect. No spit transferring on to hands."

Kit frowned. "What sort of hands are you shaking?"

"Whenever one of Papa's friends arrives they always kiss my hand. It is revolting. Shake my hand like an equal, if you please."

If Olivia lived here, and her father lived here, then that had to mean that she belonged to the family that Faith seemed to dread so much. But Olivia did not seem so unkind.

Olivia pulled the lid off of the crate and discarded it. "Will you help me take them in piles, then, Kit?" she asked. "I need to take these into the village today." Olivia grabbed a pile and began to tread towards the horse and cart.

Kit quickly followed, seizing a stack of books. He quickly appraised the titles. Science. Philosophy. Languages. These were books of learning. He had managed to read the titles, but he was not so sure of how he would go with the content. His reading was still a little weak.

As Olivia walked, her hair swished from side to side. It really was quite mesmerising to watch. Kit would have continued to watch had Olivia not turned around and caught him. She did not seem offended though. In fact, she blushed.

"What are all these books for?" Kit asked, changing the subject. "Where did they come from?"

"I stole them from Papa's library," replied Olivia. "He will not notice. Papa only reads the Bible anyway. He was a clergyman before inheriting Uncle George's title." Olivia placed her pile in the back of the cart before heading back to the crate.

Kit quickly followed.

"There is a school in the village. School is really a loose description of the place. It is the church, and really the lessons are what should be taught during Sunday school. I went to one, you see. To observe. I was not impressed." Olivia grabbed another stack of books. "I had a governess, Kit. I had an excellent education because my father could afford it. And that makes me wonder," Olivia stopped, "how is that right?" She looked at him with a truly bewildered expression. "How is it right that one's means determines one's level of education?" Olivia continued towards the cart.

"It isn't right," Kit agreed. Olivia could not understand how heartily Kit did agree with her statement.

"Education is a right, and not a privilege." Olivia offloaded her second stack. "Or at least it will be if I have anything to do with it."

"You are determined," Kit observed.

Olivia's blue eyes met Kit's. "Oh, I am." She sighed. "I asked my father for thirty pounds in order to hire a teacher for the village. He refused, naturally. And so I convinced him to take the money out of my dowry. I placed an advertisement for a teacher nearly four weeks ago. She will be here to start on Monday. I knew I could not convince my father to purchase books for the school so what he does not know will not hurt him."

Kit had never before seen such gumption or ambition in a girl. He had never before seen this level of determination, or such a sense of justice. Olivia was extraordinary.

"There are children," Olivia puffed, as she offloaded yet another stack of books, "all over this country, who are illiterate purely because their parents are not rich. I feel as though I am the only one aware of it. My parents do not care. Their friends do not care. Nobody cares, and so nothing will ever change. Somebody has to care. Somebody has to change things."

Kit placed a hand on Olivia's shoulder, stopping her as they reached the cart. Kit saw her cheeks redden again. "I am glad you care," he said sincerely. "I ..." Kit willed himself to not be embarrassed. "I could not read until recently," he confessed. "I am still learning." Olivia's face softened. "I was an orphan, you see. I had the Sunday school kind of education. Real school was not for the likes of me. I honestly hate to imagine where I might have ended up had my father not found me, taken me in, and taught me to read." Kit knew that he would have stayed at the workhouse, stayed and worked, or died from exhaustion or injury.

"I am glad for you," Olivia said softly. "That is truly wonderful. I hope there can be many more like you that benefit from education."

"Please do not take offense, but I find you very odd," Kit remarked. He meant that as a sincere compliment.

Olivia grinned. "Why? Because I concern myself with things more meaningful than dress fabrics and perfumes?"

"Yes," replied Kit honestly.

Olivia shrugged her shoulders. "I read a book a while ago. It was right about the time I learned that everything my father had would go to a distant cousin upon his death. My sole purpose in life is to marry well." Olivia rolled her eyes. "But I read a book written by a French woman, on the rights of women, or at least how it should be. It inspired a sense of justice in me, I feel. Not just for women, but for all people who are seen as less than because of their sex or their income. I will do it, you know."

"Do what?"

"I will change the world. I know I am only one person, and a girl at that, but I want to leave the world in a better state than what it was when I entered it."

Just listening to her conviction told Kit that Olivia would indeed change the world. She would do great things. Kit had begun to feel a sense of justice within himself. He considered himself fortunate. Did he owe it to the people now less fortunate than him to help? Yes, he believed he did.

"I think you are extraordinary," stated Kit.

Just as Kit spoke the words, he heard his name being called from around the front of the house. It was Cassian. They were leaving. Lucy heard Cassian's voice as well. She had been playing in the grass, and was now climbing to her feet.

"That's my father. I have to go," Kit said regretfully.

Olivia, who was standing up on the wheel of the cart after unloading yet another stack of books, did something that Kit did not expect. Using her free hand, she seized his collar and pulled Kit towards her. Olivia then closed her eyes and pressed her lips to Kit's.

Kit was so surprised that he was certain the kiss was awful for Olivia. He could barely comprehend the fact that he was sharing his first kiss with the prettiest girl he had ever seen, or the fact that she had been the one to initiate it.

Just as Kit started to feel confident in moving his lips with Olivia's, she pulled away. Her cheeks were crimson, and he adored it. Kit had meant to say something along the lines of, "Thank you" but instead he mumbled something like, "Girls should not go around kissing boys."

Olivia jumped off of the wheel and placed her hands on her hips. "Well, Kit, I am not in the habit of doing what people expect me to do."

Kit could only smile. He was certain he had the biggest, dopiest grin on his face. Olivia was one of a kind. He could see her as someone that could become very special to him one day. "Can I write to you?" he asked just as he heard his name being called again.

Olivia nodded. "I would like that."

Kit beamed as he ran over and scooped Lucy up. "Goodbye!" he called over his shoulder. "Good luck!"

"Thank you!" Olivia shouted back. "I look forward to your letter!"

Kit ran back along the side of the house and came out into the driveway where his parents were waiting for them both. The horses were harnessed and ready to go. Kit could already see that Faith was inside the carriage and Cassian looked none too pleased.

Kit attempted to wipe the gleeful grin off of his face. He felt guilty for displeasing Cassian. He did not want to disappoint him.

"Where were you?" Cassian demanded to know. "I told you to wait here."

"Lucy and I were stretching our legs," Kit brushed over to the truth. He helped Lucy into the carriage before climbing in himself, followed by Cassian. The door closed and Kit heard Mr Green move the horses on.

"Well," Cassian announced. "It is all over. Faith, we no longer have to have anything to do with that family again. We will never meet them, speak of them, or think of them. Our lives start afresh."

Kit's felt his heart fall in his chest as he heard Cassian all but forbid him from contacting Olivia.

"Good," replied Faith softly. She rested her head on Cassian's shoulder. "I want to forget this part of my life. The Pendletons are forgotten."

Kit watched out the window as he saw that flash of red at the side of the house. Olivia was watching them drive away.

There was something about Olivia that was just so inviting. She was unlike any person Kit had ever met. She was good and kind. She cared for people. She was brave and she was selfless. She reminded him a lot of Cassian, actually.

Not to mention that Kit would be dreaming about that kiss from the prettiest girl in the world for the next year.

But Kit could see the relief that was now etched all over Faith's face. She wanted to leave them behind her. Cassian wanted that for Faith. To bring any one of the Pendletons back into their lives would hurt his new mother and Kit did not want to do that.

Kit needed to choose, and his loyalty would always remain with his family. Kit needed to forget Olivia, too.

EPILOGUE

N orwood, Derbyshire
July 25, 1809

Cassian had had a dream on the night his daughter was born, just over two years ago. It was more of a memory, really. He had remembered being hungry. Hunger had never been a foreign feeling to him, but he could remember being hungry.

And so his mother, Emma, had left him alone for an hour, and had returned with a loaf of bread. At the time, he had not known what she had left to do, but as an adult, Cassian knew exactly what she had done.

She had sacrificed. His mother made sacrifices to feed him. His mother made sacrifices to keep him alive. That was what being a parent meant. Putting one's child before oneself.

And so it was only right that when his newborn daughter was placed into his arms, that she be named Emma Faith Kensington, after the two women Cassian loved, and had loved, most in his life.

"What are you thinking about, Papa?"

Cassian looked down to see that Lucy had joined him in the drawing room. Lucy was dressed beautifully in her blue summer dress with a matching ribbon in her dark curly hair. She was dressed especially for the occasion.

"I was actually thinking about the day Emma was born," Cassian replied honestly.

Lucy frowned. "It is not Emma's birthday, Papa. It is Kit's!" she scolded, and turned towards the small pile of gifts that Faith had assembled on the little table between the settees.

Cassian had no idea what was inside the packages but one. Faith was the expert in that respect. She always knew what to give people to make them happy.

Lucy adjusted one of the packages so it was sitting perfectly straight. She seemed very pleased with herself. Cassian smiled as he watched Lucy feel the top parcel. She had a terrible habit of trying to guess the contents of gifts that were not hers to open.

Cassian caught Lucy unaware, and scooped her up into his arms as he laid a sloppy kiss on her cheek, causing her to squeal in disgust. Cassian laughed. "I think about all of you, all the time."

It was the honest truth. Cassian had never known such a joy, and yet such a responsibility, than that of being a father. Cassian thought about his children all the time. He wondered about them, and worried about them. Lucy more than the others.

Kit was thriving.

Upon returning to Norwood from their last trip to Leicestershire, Faith had established the village school, and had even taught there awhile until Emma's arrival made it impossible.

Kit had been the one to volunteer for the teaching position after Faith had left it vacant. Cassian had not been too keen on the idea. He had big plans for Kit's own education, plans that included Eton for starters.

But Kit wanted to teach, and Faith had persuaded Cassian to allow it. And for the last two years, Kit had been teaching the children of Norwood how to read, write, and calculate arithmetic. Cassian could see that Kit felt as though he was helping other children like him.

It was one of the qualities that Cassian both loved and disliked about his only son. Kit was forever grateful. Cassian knew that when Kit was a father, himself, that he would understand that repayment was not necessary for the love of a father.

One would have to search far and wide for a father who was more proud of their son than Cassian was of Kit.

His youngest child, little Emma, had just turned two years old, and was the perfect, energetic addition to the Kensington family. Emma was spirited, funny, and very adorable. She would grow up to be enchanting and beautiful, and Cassian was certain that whatever Emma desired would come to her quite easily.

It was the sort of life that Lucy would never have, and that broke Cassian's heart. What broke his heart even more was the constant guilt that Faith felt, and would continue to feel when Emma received opportunities that Lucy would not.

Lucy was only six years old, and yet her status as an illegitimate child was well-known unfortunately. Lucy was not yet aware of her own social limitations as of yet. In Lucy's eyes, she was a normal child, just like the others in her school. Lucy loved going to school, and she loved boasting to the others about her teacher, Mr Kensington, who was also her older brother.

Lucy had a little friend, Violet Barry, who was frequently a guest at Norwood Cottage. The girls loved to play pretend in the garden, or upstairs in Lucy's bedroom with her dolls.

But Violet came from a wealthy family, and her mother had forbade Lucy from ever entering her house. Lucy did not understand why she was not allowed to go to Violet's house to play, but she had quickly forgotten and adjusted.

It was Faith that retained the guilt. Lucy's exclusion would only worsen. Cassian knew that there would be hard times ahead for his beloved little girl.

Cassian placed Lucy back down on the ground and looked out the window. The drawing room window looked out onto the driveway. They were expecting Kit home any moment.

It was his eighteenth birthday, and they were going to celebrate. Cassian had closed the door on his study for the entire day. Family dinners would be few and far between in a month.

Cassian had hired two controllers for his factories, one to oversee the north, and one in the south, so that he did not have to travel. While their presence had reduced his workload, the paperwork did still seem to pile up.

"I hope you have not been feeling Kit's birthday parcels, Lucy," Faith said in a warning tone.

Lucy had a terribly guilty look on her face. "No, Mama," she lied.

Faith entered the drawing room carrying a large white cake, covered in gorgeous frosted decoration. Faith was followed into the drawing room by Emma, who was toddling along behind her.

"Those who lie forfeit cake," Faith warned.

"It was only the top parcel, honest!" cried Lucy, as she watched Faith place the cake down onto the table next to the parcels.

"There," Faith said, satisfied.

Cassian smiled at his wife. He enjoyed the immensely proud expression she wore as she admired her work. She had been working ever so hard to make a beautiful cake for Kit's birthday.

It had been the right decision to move his family to Norwood. Cassian had been correct in thinking that Faith would thrive, and she had.

Faith was beloved by the community, which was what made the prejudice regarding Lucy so difficult. How could they love the mother, and yet punish the child?

Nevertheless, Faith had endeavoured to involve herself in the community. Of course, she had established the school, but she also formed friendships with the villagers, and she doted on those less fortunate. She always found work for those who needed it, and always took baskets of food to those who were struggling.

Faith's kindness knew no end. Though Cassian was not at all surprised. He had been a recipient of her kindness all those years ago. He was still convinced that Faith was an angel.

Faith caught Cassian's eye and gestured proudly to her cake. Her face made him laugh. He loved that woman. He loved her fiercely.

"Am I late?" Finn asked as he entered the drawing room, removing his hat.

"No. Kit is not back yet. I sent him to fetch a book from the school, though I know he knows what we are up to. He is a good boy to play along." Faith smiled as she greeted Finn.

Finn Kelly had almost become a permanent resident at Norwood Cottage. He dined at least five times a week, spent the night most nights, and was known to Lucy and Emma as "Uncle Finn". Finn was Cassian's closest friend, and so Cassian knew part of Finn's partial residence was loneliness. Finn's family lived in Ireland, and he lived alone in his big, empty house.

Cassian kept encouraging him to get married but Finn wanted his elusive perfect woman, whoever she may be.

Emma trotted over to Cassian and reached up. Cassian smiled as he lifted Emma up into his arms. Emma's hair was just like his, unfortunately, though Faith looked after it so her curls were not as wild and messy as Cassian's. Emma's hair was nearly black, and her neat curls fell to her shoulders. In her hair was a pink bow that matched the flush over her cheeks and then hue of her little lips. Her eyes were the same as Cassian's as well. Charcoal black, though wide and childlike, filled with wonder and excitement.

Cassian kissed Emma's little nose and held her tightly to his side, though Emma quickly wanted to be released when Cat ran into the drawing room.

Cat was the girls' Christmas present. Cat was a small, impossibly sweet King Charles spaniel dog, with large floppy ears and a dark coat. Emma had cried "cat!" when she had seen him on Christmas Day, and so the name had stuck.

It was always an interesting conversation piece whenever anyone asked why they owned a dog named Cat.

Lucy and Emma stroked Cat affectionately as Cassian came to put an arm around Faith. His wife leaned in to him.

"How are you both feeling?" asked Finn. "It is a month now, is it not?"

"Yes," sighed Faith. "A month until Cambridge. I don't want him to go, but I do."

Cassian felt much the same. Cambridge University was such a wonderful opportunity for Kit, but Cassian would miss him dearly. "I want Kit to have everything that I did not, and that includes an excellent education."

"I wonder why Mother needed this book so urgently?" Kit asked loudly from outside the drawing room.

Cassian chuckled as he saw Kit enter the drawing room with his eyes shut, Faith's book request in hand. Kit was a good sport, and an even better young man. He was good natured, even tempered, and kind hearted. He loved his family and they all loved him in return.

Kit was still a very tall young man, but he was no longer so skinny. Years of proper meals had ensured that his weight was now proportionate to his height. He was a good looking boy, as well, with curly blond hair, a strong jaw, and bright green eyes. Cassian knew his handsome son would attract all sorts of women while away at university ... come to think of it, he needed to speak with Kit about that.

"Surprise!" they all cried. Cat barked.

Kit abandoned the book as Lucy and Emma raced over to grab Kit's hands. Kit needed to bend down to reach Emma as she was so much smaller than him.

As he was hunched over, Faith was able to reach Kit's cheek. She kissed him and said, "Happy birthday, darling."

"Thank you, Mother," he said gratefully.

"Sit, sit!" encouraged Lucy excitedly as she pushed Kit to sit down next to his pile of gifts.

Kit sat down, as did they all, as he looked at his pile guiltily. "You know you don't need to buy me anything."

"A young man only turns eighteen once. It is a very important age!" declared Faith. "Besides, we wanted to. They are all little things you can take away to university with you."

Kit obliged Faith as he gratefully unwrapped stationery, new quills, inks, a hair comb, and a straight razor.

"Just in case a beard should ever decide to grow," Finn teased.

"Oh, shush," scolded Faith as she collected the last gift and gave it to Kit. "This is from your father especially."

Cassian smiled as he saw the excitement in Kit's eyes as he unwrapped the parcel.

Cassian's gold pocket watch fell into Kit's lap. Kit frowned as he opened the watch, and no doubt saw he engraved letters: C. Kensington.

"But, Father, this is yours," said Kit.

"And now it belongs to you. You are a man now, and I wanted you to have something important to take away with you," Cassian said sincerely. "We are fortunate to share initials. Saved me the hassle of getting it engraved again," he added.

Kit smiled as he attached the watch to his waist coat and tucked it into his pocket. "Thank you. I will treasure it, Father," he promised.

Cassian knew that he would. "It will be a big undertaking, Cambridge," Cassian remarked. "And we are really proud of you for accepting the privilege."

"I am well aware such an education is a privilege," replied Kit, "and I do not take it for granted."

Cassian furrowed his eyebrows at Kit's emphasis on the word, but quickly brushed it aside. The cake was being served and they were celebrating. Perhaps it would be the last time that they would all be together until Christmastime.

They ate copious amounts of cake until the entire pudding was gone. Dinner had been served and Lucy and Emma had been put to bed. Finn had retired to his unofficial bedroom, and Kit had gone up not long after.

Cassian and Faith sat downstairs in the drawing room on their own in the dark, their faces only illuminated by candlelight. Well, Cassian sat, and Faith slept. She had fallen asleep against his shoulder.

"My angel," he whispered as he watched her breathe evenly.

Cassian had lived very happily in Norwood with his family these last three years. Things were about to change. Kit was about to go away. The girls were growing up in an uncertain society. But Cassian knew that so long as he had Faith by his side, he could handle anything.